The Cheaters
The MISTRESS
Her Story

Verona J. Knight

AuthorHouse™ LLC
1663 Liberty Drive
Bloomington, IN 47403
www.authorhouse.com
Phone: 1-800-839-8640

© 2014 Verona J. Knight. All rights reserved.

No part of this book may be reproduced, stored in a retrieval system, or transmitted by any means without the written permission of the author.

Published by AuthorHouse 06/11/2014

ISBN: 978-1-4969-1420-0 (sc)
ISBN: 978-1-4969-1419-4 (hc)
ISBN: 978-1-4969-1418-7 (e)

Library of Congress Control Number: 2014909223

Any people depicted in stock imagery provided by Thinkstock are models, and such images are being used for illustrative purposes only.
Certain stock imagery © Thinkstock.

This book is printed on acid-free paper.

Because of the dynamic nature of the Internet, any web addresses or links contained in this book may have changed since publication and may no longer be valid. The views expressed in this work are solely those of the author and do not necessarily reflect the views of the publisher, and the publisher hereby disclaims any responsibility for them.

The characters in this book are fictitious and their stories are fabricated.

OTHER WORKS BY AUTHOR

Adult Romance:
The Cheaters The Wife The Revenge

Books of Poetry:
A Mind Not Lost: Book 1
A Mind Not Lost: Book 2

Cover concept by: VIIXV by MirrorImages Photography

About the Author

Verona J. Knight is mother and wife. She put aside many of her ambitions because of a lack of confidence along with taking care of her family. From her experiences of heartbreak and others, she learned from all sides of the emotional train wreck.

The painful experiences inspired her to put her thoughts to paper in hopes that she'll be voicing others' thoughts as well as hers.
She started with writing poetry A MIND NOT LOST Poetry Series. After, going on to writing novels to get her points across using characters. Finishing the first book The Cheaters The Wife The Revenge, which expressed the wife's feelings and her ability to cope with betrayal, she still had more to say. She went ahead to telling the mistress's side in The Cheaters The Mistress Her Story. Written, from the imaginary conception of what a mistress might do and say, all through the eyes of the wife's mind.

As the saying goes 'there are three sides to any story', she'll continue with The Cheaters The Husband The Payback. Her way of telling all sides.

Contact on: Facebook, Twitter, Instagram
Facebook: Verona J. Knight Cole-Ford

Why I Write

    I remember going to church one morning and kept hearing the pastor saying 'hold up your hand'. At the time my body was in church but my mind wasn't. I didn't hear the full question but I heard 'hold up your hand' repeated. My attention came back to church and I saw that the pastor was looking directly at me since my hand was the only one in the air. Apparently, the question was 'if you think that the Lord has failed you, hold up your hand.'

I left church that day in humiliation. I sometimes did think that the Lord failed me though I did nothing to warrant it but I didn't really mean to hold my hand up. We often take simple actions lightly. For me that simple 'hand raised' moment got me to think about my life instead of feeling sorry for me.

Apart from having my children and a husband, I wanted more to show for my life on this earth so I wanted to be more. My husband went out to work every day and I ran the business from home but because it was from home, it wasn't recognized as working.

When I found out about my husband's affair I felt unwanted. I went from hurt and depression then to the revenge stage. I had no idea how revenge would come but I knew, it would. I started writing things down so I won't forget then they turned into poems to myself; just my thoughts in writing. I had so many feelings flowing and had no vessel to use, a way of expressing them or no one to express them to.

During that time an episode of The Oprah Show on cheating men, reminded me that I'm not alone. I started to write everything I wanted to say and decided to use characters to do it. And the more I kept writing the more I found to say. Then I thought I should have a lover of my own and if he cannot be real then he'll be fiction and I'll make him my own, my idea of my perfect lover. It got to the point where my imaginary lover became real when I talked. My imaginary life became a book where I can do and say anything with no consequences.

It took me a couple of years to get my answer about my hand raising incident at church. Had I not gone through the painful experiences along with the embarrassment, I would not have achieved my accomplishments, and came out so much stronger than I ever was. My adversity became the rock on which I stood to search for my worth.

My advice to anyone who might have had the same or similar experience is to keep going. Take a rest from searching and look around because sometimes your worth is looking back at you. From my situation I've gotten stronger. I've learnt that I come first in my life. I also know that the Lord did not fail me. I want these books to tell people that our pain was given to teach us strength.

Special Acknowledgements

CHRISTOPHER, BODENE, MALCOLM, AND AKEEM
My greatest blessings. There's only one like you and you are special

MY HUSBAND
Thank you.

MY MOTHER and AUNT
I love you.

"He saw my faults. He's still providing all my needs."

Dedicated to all mistakes/lessons.

Because I also judge me by the 'friends' I keep, some people's actions will force me to turn them into 'just people I know'.

Foreword

The Cheaters The Mistress Her Story, shows the depth to which one might go to try and take a man from his marriage. When the one we place our trust in betrays our love, it opens the door to a painful world. A mistress cares nothing about the pain their cheating lover creates at home. While on the other hand, also unknowingly creates a painful world of their own waiting in the future; even though they convince themselves otherwise.

The wife might doubt herself, questioning her role in causing it all but the last thing on the mistress's mind, is blame. Sandy is Dwayne's mistress and is caught up in the middle of his and his wife lives.

The Cheaters The Mistress Her Story, will let you walk with Sandy and her relationship with Dwayne. It will also take you inside her family and friends lives. Sandy's ability to release Dwayne's sexual fantasies overtakes her life since she believes it's her way of keeping him happy.

Listen to Sandy tell her side of this threesome in *The Cheaters The Mistress Her Story.*

Chapter One

The first time I saw his face I knew that I was looking at a special man. There was something different about him, but whatever it was I couldn't identify at the time. I remember looking up and seeing his handsome, muscular, clean and though casually dressed, his chiselled body very well put together peaking beneath his muscle hugging clothes. My heart skipped a beat or two when I saw his glance heading in my direction.

It looked like he was just hanging with his friend and dropped in at the party. Even though we didn't actually meet each other then, from what I saw that night, that glimpse said something. Told me I would love having a man like him to go home to every day.

The more I watched him that night the more I needed to get to know him. By the end of the night my mind and body decided that he would be a part of my life; whether he wanted to be or not.

I got anxious about making it happen. That night I was thinking ahead of myself and made a promise to myself that I would find out everything about him and everything that was important to him.

I watched him that night walking across the room with such assurance, with his confidence spilling from his body. He needed nobody to tell him how or when to do whatever he wanted to. Along with everything a part of his exposed personality was tagging along beside him; that demanding personality I thought would be useful if I needed a hand later.

All that I saw excited me enough and I thought of how much a man like him could bring to my life after all the dead beats I've been through; including my kids' fathers. My mission to find out all there was to know about him intensified. His stay wasn't too long but enough for me to asked friends about him and my friend Beverly did.

The first thing I found out was his name, Dwayne, and that he was married, but that wasn't enough to change my mind in anyway. Of course I was disappointed but not disinterested. I wasn't going to change my mind about wanting him. In the back of my mind I also already figured that a man like him must have someone in his life. I was thinking along the marriage lines but I was hoping he wasn't.

One important thing I found out was about his hung-out places which one of them was a bar in the evenings. I thought why not make some stop-by visits there in the future. Even heard about few other places I might run into him using mutual friends. Even thought he didn't notice me much that night, I think I did enough noticing for both of us.

* * *

It took a few stop-bys at the different places before I ended up seeing him. I did whatever I could and when the right moment came, naturally, I created a friendly introduction. By the time he and I met, I already knew quite a lot about him. (I still haven't told him I saw him back then.)

It was the work on my part why we met back then and are together now. I started stopping by the bar, with and without my other friends. Whenever I did I made sure he noticed that I was noticing him. Every time he looked in my direction he saw me looking back at him. After a few times, we started to play the look to see if the other is looking game. I knew he had to look to see if I was still watching him while I did the same.

After awhile, my smiles greeted his eyes and he returned one to me. It didn't take long after that for him to start talking to me, having real conversations. After that started I didn't feel out of place anymore so I felt fine dropping by the bar on my own.

After going to the bar a few times, he started keeping me company until I left to go home. He also walked me to my car to make sure I was safe; such a gentleman. He watched out for me and it felt damn good since I couldn't remember the last time anyone gave me so much attention without wanting something back for it.

Before I met Dwayne, the men who showed me kindness did it because they believed there was sex waiting for them down the road. And if they gave attention for any length of time without the sex their attention quickly turned the other way.

With all that I tried to find some mutual friends to use to make sure that we kept running into each other. He probably thought I was following him, which I was but from my end he didn't seemed to mind.

After several months we became closer friends, seeing each other all the time, but like I said definitely with hard work on my part. Spending that time together finally gave me a closer look inside his life. We became sort of close friends.

We started with small talks and jokes before we started confiding a few personal things to each other, even though he stayed away from talking too in depth about his family. Most of our talks were casual but friendly. After a while, I found myself looking for problems so I would have something for him to advise me on.

We were both enjoying the closeness of our friendship after, and even though he tried to keep it at just a friendship, in the back of my mind I never gave up on having him as more than that. With each thought, I saw him and my body pleasuring each other. And with every thought I got more excited than the thought before, giving strength to my reasons why I should continue on my pursuit to please myself. I gave myself some restrictions with hopes that I wouldn't make a fool of myself, and hoping I wouldn't lose control, going out of my way too much.

The last thing I wanted to do was scare him off before having him and I welcomed every thought each time his face invaded my mind. My hope was that a man like him should be easily convinced that he needs a woman like me in his life to make him happier. His wife can make him happy and adding me to the mix will make him even happier.

I could see that his attraction to me was getting stronger and I enjoyed watching his body react to mine when we were around each other. Screaming, on the inside, whenever he was close; putting fire between my legs. With that I tried to find as many reasons to pass him close as possible. Feeling both our energy, even if just brushing up against him, sent my vagina crazy. That feeling being returned gave me a sense of satisfaction and it was enough for a little while but after several months it wasn't enough anymore.

It got to the point where I had no idea how to react anymore to what was happening to my body. Whenever he came around, my body barely could contain itself. After months of trying to control myself, I began experiencing a feeling of being too restrained. I just wanted to touch his body in so many ways; to bring us both pleasure. His gorgeous body taunted me with each glimpse and drove me crazy with every single touch.

I later realized that he figured out what he was doing to me and thought he would have some fun doing it. Sometimes all I got was a gaze indicating his interest, and if that gaze seemed too long, my hunger felt satisfied enough to help ease my aches for him. I swear I even surprised my panties a few times.

Many times my mind got cloudy and all I wanted was to leave this reality with him, and just for a while, pretend that he belonged to me. Every thought of him had my body reacting. I watched the smirks his facial muscles created whenever he noticed my body's reaction. It gave his demanding personality a great sense of championship knowing his ability to make me go quietly crazy.

* * *

Our relationship took a turn for better the night I decided to go with friends and have a drink at the bar for my birthday. It was the weekend and I knew Dwayne and his friends would be there so we could share some part of the evening together for sure. I wanted to see him. After the long hours at work I needed some relaxation time to enjoy my special day, and the bar was it.

The people there were nice enough, so I felt comfortable around them, after going there for several months. Most of the faces became familiar and I hardly saw strange faces which felt safer than any other place I could have gone to celebrate. After that night things took a turn towards better for sure.

Dwayne and I became as close as being each other's confidant after my birthday celebration. I found it refreshing to have a man like him taking time to make me feel that I'm good company, making me feel special. To spend hours talking and finding things to talk about with so little effort was refreshing. There were times we went on for hours without noticing the time and none of us thought it was strange. I ended up not minding my week at work because I had something to look forward to on my weekends.

Every conversation with Dwayne felt like I was talking to an old friend, one that I had known forever. The fact that I could talk to him about anything without him judging me in anyway, felt safe. He would also give me advice from a man's point of view about things that would affect my future. I even talked to him about my past relationships and all the problems I had and was having with my kids' fathers. Sometimes he even gave me advice or suggestions about career decisions.

At times I found myself wanting to throw myself at him without him asking just to see what he would do. All I kept imagining was how it would feel having him inside me. I thought it was insane that I was so hungry for him even though he never tried anything, away from casual touching that I think he purposely used to taunt me with. He was flaunting his body like a piece of meat to a starving animal, heightening my curiosity even more and that made me want him more than ever. I went crazy with every single thought.

I also provided a female ear for Dwayne whenever he needed one. He had his stressful times that I tried my best to help get him through, whatever it was at the time. I confess that I wanted to hear his problems to bring us closer. Hearing his troubles gave me a feeling of partnership instead of just a friend.

The comfort he brought to me by then, had me thinking about how much he changed my life since that first night I saw him. (Do I ever need to feel him.) Becoming his friend and confidant was a bonus bringing me a closeness I never felt before. I kept thinking I needed more. Even though he didn't know he was the main reason I continued going to the bar, he seemed happy to see me when I showed up there.

I knew he was God sent for me and I was falling in love with the idea of falling in love with him. Actually, by then I was in love with him and it felt good, especially because of the awful men I was used to having in my life.

The strong attraction I had for him evolved into something else all because of my past. And the time I was spending with him proved my first impression was correct, he was different. The comfortable cozy feeling I got when we're together gave me more reason why I needed him.

The way my body felt and reacted said it all, I was right about what he could bring me if I was more to him. I called my time of getting to know him foreplay and there were times I went as far as testing him. I would say something sexual just to see his reaction.

I concentrated more on reading his body language even though sometimes it was harder to do than other times, but I still tried.

* * *

One day Beverly and her husband had a business meeting with Dwayne at his house so she and I pretended we had some shopping to do. We told him we would drive him there and take the car and pick him up after. We only said that so we could go with him. When we got there we told him since the meeting was a short one we would stay and do our shopping later. She told him if he's planning to work with Dwayne then it would be good for her to get to know Jenny better and he agreed.

We stayed until they were finished then we left but didn't do any shopping. My visit was different than I thought. Jenny seemed alright but I wasn't all that impressed by her. There was nothing special about her and she didn't give any indication that there were any problems in her marriage.

From my conversations with Dwayne I knew that they weren't a perfect couple even though he never came out and said anything about it. My thought was that if his marriage was perfect he wouldn't have any reason to stay away from his house so much.

If he was as in-love as everyone thinks, he would've been running home to her every night but he wasn't doing that. Anyway, when I visited Dwayne's house with Bev she got an invitation from Jenny to a surprise party she was having for him a few weeks later and she asked me to come along with her and Felix. I thought it would be nice so I told her I'd go with her.

Beverly already knew about my interest in Dwayne so having me tag along with them got her a bit excited; she likes gossip. I thought it was a great idea since I was still curious about Jenny and wanted to find out whatever more I could. I was glad that Beverly was with me when I met her the first time.

I'm even more so now since it'll give me some comfort knowing I won't be alone, even though it'll be just another casual meeting. I thought she can help my nerves; hanging with both Dwayne and his wife in the same room.

The invite came at the perfect time to help my body concentrate on the information I would find out. My curiosity was getting the better of me. I wanted to find out as much about his home life as possible. I needed more details and to see where it could take me. I had also planned to see much more of him after that but I had no thoughts about the consequences of going to his house. I knew that I shouldn't be friendly with his wife. I guess I was afraid I was being too harsh on her and might end up liking her, but the thought of not going only lasted a minute.

Evelyn Once Said:

"Sometimes the ones we look to for strength are the same ones draining it the most."

Chapter Two

I saw Dwayne after I got the invitation from Bev and in one of our conversations I told him that he was the only special man in my life and that he meant a lot to me. I think he took it that I was speaking as a friend. He knew that I wasn't seeing anyone special so I wanted to plant the seed to make him know that I wasn't having sex with anyone; making him know that I'm sex starved.

I hoped then that he'd take notice and get curious about my sex life. My thought was that if I got him thinking about it, it might have given him the reason I needed to make him want to spend much more time with me. There were times I even wondered, and asked, if his wife didn't mind him staying out as often as he did but he took it as nothing. I knew when I wasn't at the bar, he was. Sometimes I kept it from my good sense and I secretly hoped he was disappointed when I didn't show up there.

I decided to go to Dwayne's birthday party with Beverly without a date. The last thing I wanted was for him to think I changed my mind about having someone in my life and went out and found someone to be. I couldn't handle him thinking I didn't need his company any more. Going alone was a statement that I was still alone, maybe even lonely. Also, going by myself might make him think that I look good but couldn't find anyone and that he might be the cause.

I wanted to be with him and nobody else. It could make him see that I treasured his company when he's there for me. He was the only person I could see myself with and finding ways to get and keep his attention became my obsession.

I did everything for that attention to help him see my importance in his life; more as the days passed. In our conversations I'd help him visualize me fulfilling all the fantasies the man in my life would have to live through, in every way he needed me to. In my mind, I had no intension of any other man ruining my plans.

I had several men in and out of my life before I met him but I wasn't about to give him reasons to think I was the type to have men coming and going on a regular basis. Like I said, I couldn't afford for him to have any doubts where I was concerned. I knew what I wanted and that was his wife's life with him. I got to the point where he had to understand how serious my feelings for him were and that I want him.

I knew I had to step-up and must find a way to come out. My thoughts then were if I said the words 'I want you' to him I might have given him a heart attack. But, I couldn't let him forget everything and not think about being that special person I was looking for.

* * *

The party night is finally here and when we came, there were already several people here. When I came in I carefully surveyed my surroundings noticing how Jenny seem so comfortable with her life and her family. I never showed any interest to Dwayne about wanting to meet his wife so he isn't curious about why I'm here, away from wanting to have some fun. I also thought maybe he doesn't mind showing me his real life. He probably believes it's his chance to impress me.

From what I see, I have an idea now of how he treats the people in his life; people that he cares about. He never gave me any solid reasons to think he might have interest in our intimate relationship, but he gave me so much attention in the time we've been friends; ignoring his friends at the bar to spend time keeping me company. Now a year after, he also seems to still find time to spend talking to me about my problems. We became the ear each other needs whenever either of us need one.

The party is nice and I even brought Jenny a house warming present. I need to make a good impression on both her and Dwayne. I also want to make sure Dwayne notices that I would have no problems sharing him with his wife if our friendship gets to where I plan.

Throughout the night, we had a couple of very short chats where I told him how nice his house is and how lucky his wife must feel having a family like his. Now checking the list in my head, I already made sure he knew how much I would make a man like him feel special every day, if I got the chance to have one in my life. I had told him if I found one like him, I would never let him forget how good of a man he is and how much he's appreciated. I also told him that I know a man like him needs to know that and I was sure his wife tells him that every day.

In my mind I had doubts that his wife did that but I said it to make him think. I knew he needed someone like me to boost whatever needs boosting as often as possible. Wives get comfortable in their marriage and give their men reason to stray. When women like me appreciate their men and they fall in love with us who even enjoy fucking, they turn it all on us. Jenny looks like one of the comfortable ones.

In my mind, I'm sure his wife sees him as a husband and a father who provides for his family but maybe not much beyond that. Over his and my friendship, I made sure he understood that someone special needed someone like me who would acknowledge all that and more. I see in him the man that needs something else to appreciate also. I make sure that every time we see each other, I leave an impression in his mind that will control his thoughts. Make his mind work overtime thinking about me, just enough to comfort him without stressing him.

I do everything for him so he'll want me to give him everything he doesn't get at home, and whatever else he desires if given the chance. In almost every sentence, I mention how lucky Jenny is to have a man like him. But always in question form so he can also wonder if she appreciates him the way he thinks that he should be.

I did everything I could in the short time so Dwayne would be thinking about me even when I'm not with him. It's not every day he gets an offer to have someone who will do anything he wants and for so little. He must think about me.

During the party I'm making sure he sees me even when he's not looking for me. Making sure he sees me enough so when I'm not here he'll notice and give some thought into finding me. I'll stay for as long as I think I need to then I'll leave without saying good night to anyone. I think if he notices me gone and can't find me, then I'll know he enjoy having me here and misses me. If that's the case then I know he'll ask me about leaving next time we're together. I'm almost sure of it.

* * *

I waited until Dwayne was busy with his friends, after the crowd got heavy, before I left the party last night. I'm sure there were more than fifty people there so if he noticed me gone, it means he was looking for me. I'm hoping that tomorrow my phone will be ringing like crazy and he'll be asking me why I left.

Last night I was anxious for today to come and now it's almost dark and I still haven't heard from him. Maybe he's tired and hasn't had a change to leave his house or he's spending some time with Jenny since she gave him such a great party. I wasn't there at the beginning of the party to see how surprise he was, but I'm sure he was.

*   *   *

Day two now since the party and I still haven't heard a word from Dwayne. I'm not going to wait all day and not talk to him again so I sent him a message earlier. I just told him I had a great time and that his wife gave him a great party. I told him that I enjoyed my time with him and that I also might have a present for him if he let me. I'm sure he probably thinks I'm joking but again he might think I'm serious and follow-up on my offer. I'll just have to wait and see.

*   *   *

I thought Dwayne would have called me right after the text but I didn't hear from him until now. Finally, the call I've been waiting for comes and even though it's been a week I'm still happy. It's Friday night but I have no plans to do anything so when he called and told me he was planning to stop by the bar with his friend I told him I could join him there. I have no intention to stay home after hoping all week to hear from him. In my mind, he wouldn't have called to tell me his plans if he doesn't want to see me also.

I came and his friends are already here with him. They all know me now and also knows that Dwayne and I are friends, so it isn't strange to them seeing me show up to talk to him. I walk over closer to where they're sitting and even though I didn't think it would be strange, they were a bit puzzled, but paying little attention to it.

I think what's causing their reaction is how please Dwayne is to see me and even more so, how strange it is seeing him get up and walk away from them to me. I only waved "hello" to them before he moved. We walk to a different table and I didn't have to ask him to sit with me.

"Hi babe. How are you doing?"

"Great. What's up with you Ms. Sandy?"

"Work. What else. I was planning to stay in tonight but after we talked, I thought I might feel better getting out of the house after all. Get some fresh air without thinking work." I look at him with a soft smile and he smiles back at me but with a little curiosity.

"What happened with you last week? You just disappeared from the party without saying anything. Not even a good night."

I ease back in my seat and put my hands together on my lap. "I didn't want to interrupt you and your wife just to say bye. I just called a cab then left. I was there with Beverly and Felix and I didn't want them to have to leave because of me neither."

"Why'd you leave? Weren't you having fun at the party?"

I want him to know I was having fun but also that there was more at the party that I wanted but couldn't have. "Sure it was nice but sometimes it's better to move away when you see something you can't have."

"Why? Was there someone you saw that you thought you couldn't have?"

I got his attention now and it seems like I've heighted his curiosity more than before. "Oh yah. I felt too restrained and I couldn't handle it any more so instead of putting myself through all that pain, I decided to leave."

"I'm pretty sure this person would've been happy to have you if he knew that you were attracted to him. You were looking pretty hot."

"I think he probably already knows but I don't think he's ready to take me yet."

He's acting like he needs to approve the person I'm talking about. "Is this person someone I know?"

"You know him better than anyone else does."

"Maybe I could talk to him for you."

"There's one problem though."

"What's that?"

"He's married."

I know he figured out that the conversation was all about him. I think he's enjoying the conversation and willing to play my game. "I guess that would be a problem. I couldn't tell a married man you're interested in him. I couldn't help you break up a marriage, now could I?"

Dwayne eases back in his chair listening to me go on and on about this man and I think he's beginning to see how safe it would be for this man. "Now that's the thing, I don't think he knows. I want him so badly that I would be willing to have him however I can. Even with knowing about his married life."

"He must be some special man. You're willing to have him with no expectations in return."

Somehow a look of flattery covered his face. I even think he's enjoying watching me go on about the man. He definitely looks interested in hearing about my feelings for the man. And the questions he asks say that he also has been thinking about our previous conversations. I know he's trying to figure out if it really would be safe for the man.

"Yes, he's a very special man to me."

"Damn. I think I might be getting jealous of him."

I want to make sure that after I leave he'll have no doubt understanding how badly the man is wanted. "The better I get to know him the more I want to be his. No strings attached."

"I think I'll have to have a talk with this man since he might be losing out."

"Please do. I'd show you how grateful I can be."

"He's a very lucky man in my eyes. I'll make sure to tell him that also."

The rest of our conversation seems like foreplay as we relax the sexual tension while staring at each other and doing it for a couple of hours. I can't do this any longer. I have to come out with it.

"Right now all I can think about Dwayne is you. All I want to feel is you inside me. If I keep looking at you, they'll have to start mopping up behind me when I'm leaving here." He gives me a smile, accompanied with a look of relief.

"I'm a very lucky man and I'll make sure to remind myself of it. I'm sure one day soon we'll take care of everything else too."

* * *

When I left Dwayne last night it was still early but I decided to leave him with his friends to think about what I told him. Before I left I made sure I was satisfied with our conversation. I was also satisfied with the answers I was searching for as he reacted to my sexual suggestion. A part of our conversation also touched on the reason he didn't call me back after he got my text.

He told me he had planned on calling me in the week but he got so busy at work and didn't get the chance to. It was good to hear because to me it said I was right. It says that he was looking for me after I left the party without saying bye to him.

I know that I have him now and our conversation confirms that all I need to do is wait and he'll come to me. I didn't plan to rush anything but I couldn't let him sit back while I hide my feelings from him or wait any longer for him to make the first move. If I continue waiting without doing something, he might think that I don't want him anymore and my work might fade with any excitement that's peeking in him.

I did use my body to remind or taunt him to pressure his wants. Using my body seemed to be the best way since he's been giving it a lot of attention. He thinks I'm not noticing, and I'll keep taunting until he can't help but give in. His love for his wife isn't hidden and I have no plans to do anything to suggest I'd want to harm that. On the other hand, I must make sure that sometimes she's reminded that someone else can be interested in him. I plan to bring her some discomfort, just a little misery at home.

Doing things to make him uncomfortable at home should make him want to come see me before going home to her and then her complaints or whatever else the wife does will make it even worse. Since I've never been married, I'll use my imagination and whatever information I get will help make my plan successful. I'll do whatever I have to, to make him want me, with or without his problems at home. I just want him to want me, so badly.

* * *

For the following weeks my body haunted me like crazy. Waiting for him feels like sitting in the emergency room waiting to be looked after. These feelings aching my senses, feels like they're screaming out so loud. I hope that he can feel my wants even when he isn't with me. Yes, I'm scared but I know the time I spend with him at the bar can't satisfy me anymore. I know I can make better use of that time. I know he wants me but I'll have to give a little harder push to make him move faster. I also know he isn't sure how to handle things after we talked.

He might even been unsure because of fears about getting caught, since I know his wife now. A talk on the weekends isn't satisfying and I just refuse to settle for that. Realizing that, I decide that I'll still make random stop-by at the bar sometimes, just to surprise him and the pleasant look hugging his face when he sees me.

* * *

I stopped at the bar a few times in the past few weeks. Some nights I stopped by and he noticed my tiredness and commented, telling me I need to take time for myself and enjoy life some. I told him I would if I had the right company to do it with. For me it isn't the comments that give me hope, but the fact that he knows me well enough to notice how I'm feeling. He must be noticing me closer than he lets on and even caring more than he had before.

He asked me once why I visit the bar after work and I told him it was because I had no man to go home to so I stopped to see him. If he wasn't taking me seriously before then that answer would've left an impression.

* * *

For the weeks following, I made sure he saw me as often as possible. I made sure he heard all the right things he needed to hear. We're at the point in our friendship now were we hug when I leave the bar.

Earlier tonight I dropped in at the bar and now he's walking me back to my car. We hug as I stand and I feel his hand travel down to my ass and cop a feel. I ease back and let go of him just to make sure he's doing what I think he is. He holds my hand and pulls me back towards his face and slides his hand up, stroking my body like he doesn't want to let me go.

"Girl you make it hard for me not to want you."

"Dwayne I've been waiting for this for too long now, and there were times I even thought you wanted me to give up."

"Are you sure you can handle this? I have a family that means the world to me so I don't have much to give you."

At this moment the last thing I want to think about, is his family. It's unbearable. I can feel the moistness creeping in between my legs and feeling him holding on to my face isn't helping.

Without giving it much thought my hand takes his and rest it on my pants zipper. He slowly unzip before I ease his hand into my pants, allowing him to slide it as far as possible. The eagerness to feel his touch down there forces me to tell him to "feel me". His fingers probe around going inside, forcing its way to my panties. I unbutton the waist to help his travel.

Touching, feeling every part, going between my vagina lips, all while it spits more juices from between. I'm so wet that his fingers can't grip on to any part of me, just sliding between and touching my clit. I feel like I'm going crazy having him touch me like this, and in the parking lot of all places. His finger's searching, finding a way inside and my pant's acting as a strap holding it in place as it goes up further.

I feel my body firing up and with no complaints but I can't hold back too much longer. I'm willing to take whatever I can get right now. And I'm enjoying his touch however little it might be. I feel like we're fading from this world into another one and I know he's only thinking about us in there.

Our kiss comes while his finger stays in place and my body's experiencing a nervous shake passing though. One kiss, but one to make minutes brings such satisfaction. My wants, my desires, are about to come through and my heart can't stop racing.

I want to lie down on this hard tar surface right here in the parking lot and open my legs as far as possible for him to drive in. Just to feel him penetrate deep inside while his lips are holding mine with his tongue massaging mine. (O gosh.)

He's slipping his finger in and around my opening and my mind, my mind is going wild. (Holy fuck I feel I'm in heaven.) Heaven surrounds us. His friends are in the bar and can come out at any time but it doesn't matter to any of us the way we're feeling.

We have no fear of getting caught and no fear anymore to show our emotions. Leaning up against my car with his finger in me, along with the danger of anyone passing and seeing us, makes the excitement worth it. (Holy shit, I'm gonna come.) I feel an overwhelming feeling passing through me and my whole body hiccups over and over.

My inside is convulsing (I need to lie down) and my lips are gripping on to his finger. (Oh shit, I'm coming.) My inside walls are pulsating and feels like it's pulling his finger deeper in. (I need to touch more of him.) I can feel his raising hardness pushing to get free and I can't help myself.

I can't hold it any longer, have to let it go. My body is collapsing, falling forward and my head falls to his chest leaving my legs weak. (Holy shit, I really had an orgasm.) Before I can say anything to him, we hear someone coming. It's his friends getting ready to leave.

"Dwayne, I'm at a loss for words. This has never happened to me before and I don't know what's going through your mind right now. What are you thinking of me."

The smile on his face says he's not thinking anything bad and that he also enjoyed it, even without his orgasm. He slightly turns as he carefully takes his hand away from my pants so that no one can see what he's doing. Without drawing attention he slowly withdraws his finger and back away from me. This is one time I appreciate darkness.

He opens my car door so I can sit down, with my pants still unzipped. He leans forward, closer to me and quietly said good night as he whispers. "We'll finish this another time." I recognize the pleasing sign of relief on his face also. Without another word said, I reluctantly drive away since I don't want his friends to get close enough to see any strange movements from either of us. I know his thoughts of me will have him smiling and when he gets home he can let his wife finish what I started.

On my way home all I can think about is if he'll have his wife finish him off. Though I might never know, I know he'll be thinking about me while he's with her. I plan to make certain to relieve him of any stress she might cause as I assume my role in this part of his life. I guarantee that he knows he'll also be taking some of my stress away. We certainly plan to be there for each other.

I already told him I'd be there whenever he wants me to and I'll do whatever he needs me to do with no strings attached. Tonight confirms that he believed me or what happened wouldn't have. It also reassured him that I still feel the same after all these months so I'm not just a 'one-nighter'.

* * *

After what happened between Dwayne and me in the parking lot a couple of weeks ago he's finally ready to take things seriously. I know I got him, but we still haven't spent any sexual time together apart from what happened that night. Now he's finally ready to take us all the way. He isn't the timid type so I can only believe he's careful with me out of concern about my feelings. We actually talked about us getting together but something always changed our plans.

He keeps telling me that he thinks about how much I'd been through and he doesn't want to add to any of it. I tell him whatever I'll be getting from us will still be better than whatever I've had in my past, so I'm fine with it.

Even though I tried convincing Dwayne that I'm fine with us, he still worries about hurting me more if things, for whatever reason, don't work out between us. Without him knowing, for me to hear him say he worries about me, makes me love him even more.

His need to protect my feelings shows that it might not just be sex with us and it tells me that I can give my all. I look forward to feeling him opening my inside so badly. I feel a sense of accomplishment that I managed to pull it off. All my lonely nights are about to be ending. All my work will be worth it. Yes he does that to me.

Lying at nights thinking about him had me squeezing my legs together. My thighs squeeze together so much trying to stop my inner walls from jumping so hard. That's what he does to me. Since our night in the parking lot, I crave him even more.

Dwayne and I made arrangements to go to a barbeque this weekend at one of his friends' house and he wants me to meet up with him there. Of course I agreed. As soon as I got the invitation, my mind started making plans. I plan to make sure that we end up back at my house so we can be alone afterwards.

The week passed by slowly but now weekend is finally here. I had my shower and got dressed and left. On my drive over, all I kept thinking is how I must get Dwayne back to my house and what we'll be doing later.

I'm here waiting but I guess he's running late since he isn't here yet. Even though he's not I don't feel uncomfortable and I see some of his friends walking around. Anthony asked me earlier if I'm friends with the people having the barbeque but I told him Dwayne invited me and I was waiting on him to get here. I figure he knows something is going on between Dwayne and me but I don't think he has the full story. He eased off. They cover for each other all the time so he seemed fine with it.

Not too long ago Dwayne showed up and is talking and socializing a little. I'm getting antsy and told him I want to have him to myself so we said bye to his friends. I walked away and came to the front where my car is parked on the street, waiting for Dwayne to come out.

He walks over to my car pretending to be saying good night just in case anyone was seeing us. He walks up to the driver's side where I'm sitting and as soon as he got close I told him to reach in and he does. The summer dress I'm wearing is long and I knew before I left home that nobody could see anything beneath it if I lean over.

Since I'm not wearing any panties I must be careful. I lead his hand directly between my legs for him to touch what's happening down there. I hold on to his middle finger and he smiles; I guess from memory.

"Reach in and touch me, please. I can't wait." He reaches in where he can slightly slide his finger a little further up my legs so I can feel him touch my lips. "Baby, that's what happens every time I see you."

Of course by now my juices are heading to the seat of my car by way of my ass. He feels my moistness between my lips and with a smile on his face, I slowly pull his hand back out but not before he purposely touch my clit on its way out with my wetness covering his finger. His face showing his delight and lit my eagerness to leave. I can't wait to feel more of him there.

His smile continues while he reaches in to kiss me. "Dwayne I'm not happy with doing anything you might be sorry for later so let's just go where nobody can see."

I want to protect us from his friend and others before we end up shits creek, and before we really get anything started. I suggest that he follow me to my house and he agrees. He reaches in my window and kisses me anyway without even thinking. I can tell that he wants me just as badly as I do him.

"If that's what I do to you I can't wait to see what I'll be doing to you later."

I looked up at him with an intense sense of eagerness on my face. "Let's go find that out."

"Okay. You lead and I'll certainly follow."

"Dwayne I want you so badly right now that my body is starting to hurt."

"I want you too baby. Let's go."

He said I'm to drive out and he'll follow but as soon as he pulls his head out my car window, there she is. Jenny is standing there looking at us. Both of us so surprise that Dwayne seems lost for words.

I could tell it was over for me with him tonight so I just told him I'd call him later then drove away; so disappointed. Now, I'm home and all I can think about is how close I came to having him and just like that it all changed. I left there feeling disappointment almost to the point of tears and with my body hurting so badly.

I've to be here in my bed with my hands between my legs; again as if I'm protecting it from the pain until I can finally fall asleep. And again, the night will be rough on me. And again, more so on my vagina.

Last night I left Dwayne standing in the middle of the street with his wife. I wasn't curious enough to care what she wanted; I was in shock. I left as soon as I saw her and I had no idea what happened between them after. My body was hurting so badly that I couldn't think about anyone else but my pain so I have to wait to satisfy my curiosity. I have to wait to hear from Dwayne to find out what happened.

This morning I woke up thinking about everything that happened and after waiting all morning, I finally heard from him. He told me Jenny was pissed about what she saw. He said he told her the reason he was so close to my car was because he needed to get something.

Told her when she saw him reaching in my car, he was only picking up something that fell but it wasn't what she was thinking. Apparently she thought he was kissing me. Even though he was, he got away with it since she said she believed his story.

* * *

It's been a couple of weeks now since that incident at the barbeque and it did cross my mind that he might get cold feet after that. I can't give him a chance to change his mind about us because of what happened so I gave him a call.

Dwayne gave me an updated synopsis of what happened since Jenny saw us. I told him ever since that night in the parking lot my body won't let me get a comfortable night sleep and the night beside my car hasn't made it any better.

I made sure he knows that I can't stop thinking about him. I pushed the fact to make sure he heard how much my body hurts to feel him. I must let him know how badly I still want to see him. He needs to know my body is crying for him but that I can settle with just seeing him.

I'm thinking that I must find ways to make sure he doesn't forget me and my offer and that I'm his for the taking. After talking for a while he said he'll come over so I directed him to my house.

A little while later he shows up and we sat and talk. I had a shower and put my robe on, only my robe, before he got here. When he look and see that I'm not dressed, I let him know that I didn't get a chance to put something on since the door bell rang as soon as I stepped out of the shower.

"Dwayne, I think I'm comfortable enough with you so I don't have to worry if I'm dress properly or not." (Lie.)

I must make sure he feels my need for his friendship and to make him aware that he's the only one I feel comfortable talking to, also that I want him around to do it with more often. No pressure. At lease no visible pressure. He must want me without thinking I'm putting any pressure on him.

*   *   *

For the past few weeks now, Dwayne stopped by several nights on his requests. I make sure I keep telling him that I'm here for him. We joke around a lot whenever we talk and I use every chance to drop my hints. Saying the right things helps to remind him what we started and that he's the only one stopping it from finishing. I know he wants to spend time with me. I believe that.

Evelyn Once Said:

"It's a choice to 'not be capable of doing' something we're not doing but want to. Anything we want badly enough, we'll learn or investigate so to be capable of doing."

Chapter Three

Since that night beside my car when Jenny rudely interrupted me with Dwayne, he's been to my house several times but all we've done is talked. Since then, our time together assured him that I can handle anything that might come along, and with it all he knows how much I still want him. Even though at times I got a little worried that he might lose interest, I wasn't afraid. I've already helped his interest to develop beyond the 'walking away point' and with as much intensity to bring him to the point where he aches for me.

Now I want him to think about me and my ability and not be able to go without feeling me. To remember our talks and what he wanted from me before we were stopped by his wife that night. The memory of the wetness he felt between my legs. I want him to take me on impulse, knowing that there would be no resistance on my part.

My plan for us that night was to finally make love for the first time so I could introduce him to a life that he would not be able to back away from later. Now, I know he thinks about me often and I have no intention of letting him forget what I am to him and how much more I want to be, so I have to still introduce many different ways to let him know that he's the only one for me. By the time I'm finished he must also figure out that I'm the right one for him.

* * *

Tonight I barely stepped out of the shower before the door bell rang. Dwayne is a little early since it's only about six o'clock and we made arrangements a few nights ago for him to come over at seven. I don't mind him coming early since it'll give me more time with him, about five hours or so.

I've already sent my kids to my parents, after I talked to Dwayne. I threw on my robe and ran down to open the door and there, looking like the best thing I've seen in years, greeting me with that smile. I'm so happy to see him.

Neither of us can play this game any longer. I need to be satisfied. I feel like I've been waiting forever for him to make his move. I know he wants me as much as I do him. (I can't wait any longer.)

I stand staring at him welcoming that look from his eyes telling me he's ready to enjoy me without thinking. As soon as his feet touched my floor, I open my robe to expose my wrapped body. All game playing stops along with any self control. My greeting gives none of us a chance to say much. I feel the pain from my face fading as the anticipation on his face almost glowing, says yes.

Neither of us needs to fight to control ourselves any longer. "I can't wait any longer Dwayne. I'm going crazy, and for too long now. You have to take me now."

Even with all the anticipation on both our part he eases back and stares at my body for a few minutes. Like a piece of sculptor on display, he looks me over. This, his first real sight of my naked body, anticipating his touch as he slightly turns my body around. (Thank you tummy-tuck.)

With a loving smile on his face saying, telling me that he's pleased with what he sees, his voice slowly creeps to my ear, "I can't wait to enjoy you either". He steps closer to me and our faces meet for our lips first savoured kiss.

Without using up too much of our time at my door we came up stairs to my bedroom. My body already shaking knowing the pleasures he's about to bring to it. He looks into my eyes and draws me closer in his arms and my footsteps obey.

"Let me see how happy you are to see me." He takes his hand and slowly slide down my stomach going to my curious spot, testing my moistness. His kisses coming as his finger opens my lips where it was already too moist, and not from my shower. "Mmmm." Hearing the sound of how pleased it makes him, makes between my legs even happier.

I slowly unbuckle his belt and his finger continues its survey for a few minutes. My tongue craves his taste. His pants bulging while I'm unzipping and as it falls to his feet his boxers goes to the floor with it. I'm greeted with hardness trying to rest itself on his leg, but looking like a fish out of water, on the sand flopping out of control. Holding on, I'm pleasantly pleased. My first touch and I've wondered several times before what it would feel like. I'm so happy. The feel, the touch even the smell pleases the pallet.

"Touch me Dwayne. I need you to continue to touch me. Baby, please." I've been waiting too long for this perfect moment. My inside is pulsating and my vagina is hurting and my heart is racing then (oh my god) his finger, there, again. (Oh my God! I'm almost, have mercy, my inside is screaming.)

I want his first entrance to be engraved in his mind forever. But I can't wait and neither can he. With his pants at his feet, he lifts my body off the floor and placed me against the wall, neither of our minds remembering that the bed is right there. One leg steps out of the pants and the other with his leg dragging behind, follows along with us from the bedroom door.

I found my back up firmly against the wall and his lips on my neck as he eases me up, with my feet off the floor a little. His wetness touches the entrance of my flooding vagina, and there (Oh my god. Oh my god! Oh my god!) I feel him. (Finally.) He's through my entrance, going deeper, touching my walls.

My heart is going faster and my body's bouncing as I grip his neck too tight. He's going in deep then back out to the entrance and deeper again. Going back and forth, back and forth, while he scratches the itch I've been feeling in there for far too long now. (Oh my god. He feels good.)

I need some comfort, "release me baby, release me, and lay me down, baby." I've imagined his entry so many times. I'm so damn happy right now my senses are floating. Damn, is it ever worth it! He feels like I imagined so many times.

He eased from my body and laid me on the floor before I kissed his lips; his face still looking as if he's still not sure what's happening. He kiss my nipples while my body gets comfortable and my hand travels down searching as he continue to kiss my every part almost into collapsing. Withdrawing from my body gives me a chance to bring him some of my pleasures so I tell him to lay himself down and let me work on him.

We switch places and I climb over his body; sitting on his stomach with my back to his face. I slide my wet river like vagina on his stomach as if skiing on his belly going to his chest then using it to kiss its way down to his pelvic area.

I ease off to allow my other lips a chance to taste. My tongue separates his unknown while watching it palpitates along with hearing his moans. He's almost crying along with my body and then, that feel, his finger going between us, touching my arm pit, sliding around, over my nipples.

Feeling the life travelling through him brings several different feelings running through my body. (I just need to feel him in me again.) Easing up off his body I lie down and allow him to mount mine. He lifts my legs as I lay on my back; resting them on his shoulders. Again his entry welcomed.

Taking our time and enjoying the pleasures each of us are bringing to the other, making sure we both reach the point of our satisfaction. The slow motions in and out, gliding through me sends my legs tingling. His penis pushing, stretching his inner skin with every push and pull has my inside gripping tightly to his throbs. His hands holding my thighs with every push as my toes tingle out of control.

I feel all the sensations travelling up my legs while my nipples sit between my fingers. His face tightens as each muscle goes firm, and here, the explosion crawling inside me. Every push comes slower and every grip holds tighter until my legs turn into the post that his hands find to hold on to. With his inability to let my legs go they stay in place to feel the splash against my inner walls as if marking its territory.

That's it for me as feeling him splashing turn into the flicker to ignite my orgasm. My legs tried coming together while my body slowly twist side to side. My body, legs, arms and my every part weaken while my inner muscles stop thinking about anything but squeezing the life from his muscle, but my fingers squeeze my nipples instead. Then, slowly, my body goes limp.

Slowly, he collapsed down covering mine on the floor; still inside. The sweat sitting on his face starts rolling down and drops on mine. With every move, after-shocks travel through.

As both our bodies settles, still sensitive, exhaustion creeps in as his hovers down over mine and both lay lifeless looking at the other. My body is still so sensitive. It's still twitching; now savouring it all. My thoughts are now controlling the moment; my moment. (I want him to remember this night forever.) After we got some of our strength back, we moved up to my bed and relaxed there.

We talk about what just happened and also joke about our night in the parking lot. I explain that it was the first time anything like that ever happened to me. Telling him that nobody has ever made me felt like that before so I don't want him to think it was anything simple, he caused that to happen. He seems flattered and I think I got some more of his attention waiting in my future. I want him to look forward to seeing me whenever I ask him to.

After talking for an hour or so, I was back where we started, me wanting him more. I ease my head up from his arms and kiss his chest. "Stay there and relax your body so I can please you some more."

After talking my body is ready for him again and the last thing I want is to relax. I kiss his body, from his neck to his chest. "Tonight is mine." I kiss one nipple while my hand travels ahead of my lips going down between his legs. "I want to enjoy you all night if possible."

My words help him firm up quickly in my hand and ready for me again. I move down to enjoy it. Slowly kissing his stomach then mounting; easing down. Claiming what I want to be mine. His entry controls my thoughts. (Damn. Again!) He's so deep that his facial expression shows that he himself forget he belongs to someone else.

Sitting on top, watching him beneath me enjoying the feel of everything sliding between us fulfils my dreams. (Yes) He open his eyes and reach up to hold me. He eases up and slowly turns our bodies so we can switch places, without him fully withdrawing from me.

My legs hold on going around his body, allowing him in deeper inside. My parts cries as happy touch my walls again and my finger found my clitoris. The pulsating shock waves of sweetness invading my body, sending my brain into a frenzy, making my body lose control. Him coming down closer to my face, kissing wherever he can, makes each push hits bottom. My inside tickles and jumps while my body's shivering as if it's cold. My nipples tingle causes my body to convulse.

My inner muscles grab on, directing him to the deep itch and holds it in place as I release, bringing both of us to our orgasm, releasing together. My muscles tightening inside and his heavy muscle relax in my opening; again I'm lying savouring the aftershock effects crawling through my body, creating a sensitive zone from the top of my head going down to my toes.

Each touch mimicking each shiver that comes before it. As we both hold on to each other we enjoy the feelings that surrounds us, while we both gasp as to say this was long overdue; both our bodies collapsing from exhaustion.

My body finally released Dwayne from its tight grip after having him lying on top for a few minutes; again lying motionless allowing the shock waves to pass through. My heart is palpitating slower with each breath. My body, now weaken unable to take any more.

I finally relax in his arms almost wanting to fall asleep and my thought jumps ahead to our next time together. I must make sure he'll have no regrets and help him know that I was worth it. It's important that he knows that this is just the beginning and better things are in our future. I need him to believe in me and what I told him before; that I'll be here for his taking anytime he wish to have me.

    Dwayne left after we made love some hours ago and I feel a sense of relief that I once thought would never come. I have to make sure whatever his experiences with me are, it'll be like nothing I think he might get at home or maybe not experienced in a long time at home. From my understanding, wives seem to forget about those little things after a while.

After he and I made love like that, with several orgasms on both our parts, he just laid there as if his muscles couldn't lift him even if he wanted them to. By the time we finished we were both lifeless and I loved it.

I wanted to get as much of him as possible in the time I had since I had no idea how long it would be before we spend more time together like that again. I remember asking myself if that's what his wife was getting at nights. After we made love it confirmed that there'll be no doubt in my mind that I made a good decision about wanting him as a big part of my life. And I know there must be a way to make him mine.

Today I'm calling Dwayne to make sure he's enjoying the memory of our night together and to let him know how much I enjoyed him also. I'm making sure he's looking forward to all the times we'll be spending together. I'd love to hear the words coming from his lips that he enjoyed me as much as I did him. His phone is ringing and my heart is racing; hearing his voice.

"Hi Dwayne, how're you feeling?"

"I'm feeling good"

"I'm feeling great right now after last night. You made me experience something I haven't before, and I'm already looking forward to our next time together."

"Are you now?"

"Dwayne I don't think you know how much you mean to me, and have for a long time."

I think he's flattered that I've gone through so much to be with him. I tried to keep our conversation casual while I take the chance to search his voice and see how comfortable he is with me after our night of intense love making. I took the chance to invite him to come see me again. I also wanted to hear how anxious he is to be with me again.

"Sorry Sandy. I can't come to see you right now. I'm planning to finish some stuff at home and I need to be there but I'll call you later in the week and we'll talk then."

"OK, we'll talk then."

I wasn't really calling expecting him to come running over but if he did I wouldn't have been disappointed to see him.

* * *

The following week I called Dwayne several times and we talked about nothing, just talk. I didn't want to show him how desperate I was, even though I was. I keep reminding him how special he makes me feel and how much I enjoy having his company whether it's just to talk or to make love. I want him to know I treasure his company even if it's just on the phone.

I like the fact that he enjoyed hearing my voice. It felt good. The memory of our night together keeps bringing my thoughts back to when I saw him for the first time. And the months we spent together relaxes my body to a point where I can handle my stress and calm down; just by him talking to me. He gave me back the hopes I thought would be impossible to find. The place before I had no stress, before kids and their fathers. He still calms my mind even to this day.

* * *

Several months passed now since Dwayne and I had our night of passion. And even though it wasn't an all night full with passion, it was a 'beyond good one'. I tried to understand his feelings and I was patiently waiting to have him on a regular in my bed but since that night it hasn't happened again. For the time being, I have to do whatever I can for myself until he comes back.

I don't want anyone or anything else to put a strain or provoke distance between us. Since the night we were together he has decided to do more to make his life at home better. He feels he's pulling away from his family and wasn't doing his share for their relationship.

He tried to make me understand how much his family means and that we have to stop sleeping with each other. At first I was heartbroken but I struggled with the reality and eventually had to accept it. In the back of my mind I know he'll come to me again. When he gets to the point where he has no one around to tell him how much he's appreciated, he'll remember me.

Since we talk regularly, I always make sure he hears how much a man like him should be appreciated. Right now those are the little things that have him calling me when I least expect it. I do use those times to remind him that a woman like me is here to show him how appreciative I can be and in so many ways. I also remind him that his wife takes everything for granted because her lifestyle seems normal to her. I always have to play on that.

Nothing I could've said would've stopped him from trying to make a happy life at home so I told him that I support him in whatever way he wants me to. In my mind what better way to show how much I care? I have to help him save his marriage that I don't want saved, then, I'll show him that I'm trying and can ease up about sex and go hard on compliments.

*   *   *

My sister Sharon came over a few night ago. Sometimes it's hard for me to admit that we're related. I don't think we have much in common anymore. She makes one bad decision after the other and she doesn't learn anything from the ones before. Her latest is her obsession with a man she thinks she's in love with and been seeing for a while now.

She has seven kids and thinks that he'll leave his wife just to be with her. I have no idea where she got that from especially since she already does whatever he wants her to. I've to admit that he does a lot for her whenever she needs him to though. The only thing he won't do is sleep at her house overnight and that I can understand since it's the same with Dwayne.

I worry about her sometimes though. The last thing I want to hear is that after her sitting waiting for him he decides she's not for him anymore. Even worse, would be to hear that she's pregnant again.

After the first or second kid I told her to use birth control but she didn't and now all these kids later, I hope she takes my advice. Thinking about her pregnant again does scare the hell out of me.

She came over just to get away from the kids and have some time for herself. Whenever she needs a break from them or if she has a fight with whichever man she's with at the time, she comes to me complaining. I usually sit and listen to her until she leaves without taking my advice so I stopped giving them. Now I just listen and agree with everything she says and make her happy. I don't think she really wants advice she just needs to vent so I let her. After she left all I could think about was how much I missed Dwayne.

My body was missing him so much and I couldn't take it any longer, so I called him. I told him I support his decision about him working on his marriage but I just want to spend some time with him, nothing more. He said we can but he couldn't come right away and that it will happen after the holidays. That I understand since the holidays is a part of the fixing. I have no problem waiting until then.

I know his wife might not even recognize his efforts and pay little attention to them. I've learned from my parents that many wives wait too long before they respond and show appreciation. Not letting their husbands know that they're appreciated for trying. While on the other hand, we need to do the wife's job for her.

We can't afford not to give their men our attention, to show them how their efforts should be appreciated. I've known for a while that every time Jenny complains about his late nights or whatever else, he acts crazy and disappears for a while, all because he doesn't want to upset her.

* * *

The holidays had me feeling lonely and not seeing Dwayne didn't help. I planned it all in my head and I want to leave another impression on him, one that would last forever. Every thought in his head of me should be one bringing him some pleasure.

Even though I told him no sex, I want to make it hard for him to resist me when he sees me. I want to give him the kind of pleasures his body will be aching for and I must make him hungry for me with his every thought.

With all that in mind I start my plan and put a lot of thought into it since I must make it special for both of us. The everyday kind of love making won't do for us and nothing that his wife can give him is satisfying enough either. It must be special enough to make his body react to my name, especially after he leaves me each time. Women like her make my job easy. I don't have to look hard to find something different for us to enjoy.

Now that the holidays are over, he called and we plan to get together tomorrow night. Today I went to a special store and picked up some oils and other pleasurable items for our night. I got the oil recommended to me by the sales person who said it's guaranteed for satisfaction.

I got everything ready for my evening with Dwayne and my hope is to create another memorable night. I can't wait to spend some quality time with him and I told him no sex but I didn't mean it and I'm hoping for lots more. He has no idea how much quality I plan to put in his time with me.

I can't wait and my body feels as if it won the lottery and just waiting to collect. Even though we spent time on the phone it wasn't sexual but a few times our chats drifted off to the night we had together. In those talks the pressure in his voice was obvious along with his feelings about us. I felt his emotions and our next time together will sure be making up for lost time.

After my shower I prepared my bedroom and myself then left. Earlier in the day I told Dwayne I'm going to my girl friend's birthday party but it's just a small bunch of friends getting together at a restaurant close by. We agreed to meet here.

I got here and Dwayne isn't here yet so I had a couple of drink. It's taking him a little while to get here but that's alright since it gives me a chance to spend some more time with my friends.

About an hour later he showed up and sat at the bar while I said good night to my friends. After allowing my friends to drool a little, we left for my place.

By the time we got to the parking lot I knew that I won't have much problems getting what I want from him. I think our past parking lot episode popped in his head and got him going. The drive over was a bit anxious and by the time we started walking up my driveway, I notice his curiosity getting more intense. And as we enter through the front door he sees the surprise I have for him from the hints I left lying before I left the house; the first being the dimmed lights.

As soon as we stepped in from outside, his hand ends up in mine for me to lead him up to my bedroom, without resistance, all so he can see his surprise. I knew ahead that once he got here he couldn't resist me and I think he also knew that we'd be doing more than talking tonight. I got no resistance from him in any way.

Now here I am admiring this fabulous piece standing in front of me in the middle of my bedroom, with his eyes closed as I requested.

Standing in the middle of the room and obediently, he agrees not to move while I go into the bathroom. I need a few minutes to undress and freshen myself. I got my oils and other things ready before I left the house earlier so it would make things easier for me now.

I take what I need and then step back in the bedroom, after spending a little more time in the bathroom than I needed to. That's my way to give him time to get anxious from not knowing what's about to happen next. I walk in and he's still standing with his eyes closed as he promised.

While I was in the bathroom I sprayed a scarf with some nice smelling scents that I picked up at the bed-and-bath store before. Standing on tippy toes I slowly wrap the scarf around his head blindfolding his eyes. The intensity along with the eagerness spilling from his body has my body responding with every heard breath. His racing heart I can hear through his heavy breathing.

I slowly peel off his shirt without him seeing and I kiss his chest. Going between his nipples then using his hand to touch my body, without allowing him to hold on to me, is making both of us anxious. I kiss his chest while unbuckling his pants at the same time. Then, I turn his belt into a handcuff for his hands in front of him, allowing him no control over anything that's about to happen.

His pants fall to his ankles and that muscle of his jumps as if seeking and feeling its way to what is coming next. Bending to my knees I lean forward, going close enough to make it seem like I'm about to, but not kissing it. Breathing, close enough though, for him to feel the warmth flowing from my mouth to his tip; playing with his senses. I want him confused.

After, I slowly stand to touch his chest and nibble. His body wants to go rigid, while his senses are expecting me below. Shivering, reacting as if it's out of control, just the way I hope. Watching his body trembling from the unknown of what pleasures are about to be creeping through, excites mine. Needing to have my next move unpredictable, sends me back to my knees, kissing his legs, while again not touching anything else.

"Don't worry about the blindfold baby, just let me enjoy you. You just enjoy me also."

My body's going wild watching how curious his is. His hands still buckled with his belt allows him no choice in whatever happens next. His inability to see what I have on or if I have anything on is sending his imagination wild. Kissing his legs going down his inner thigh while slowly helping each leg from his pants and boxers sitting at his ankles, also giving way to anything that wants to jump and touch my face.

Using the oils, I covered my body before I came in from the bathroom. I slide my body against his, nibbling on his nipples every chance. Sliding my breast down his body and using them to make a tunnel for his penis to travel between, puts pressure on his breathing. Holding the belt to lead him closer to the bed, I physically help his body get comfortable.

With his back against the sheets and his blindfold to the ceiling, I buckle his hands to the bed post allowing me to mount his body and slide him between my oiled legs; going along his legs, one at a time. His hands fighting to hold me but not allowed. My body heads back up to his pelvis, allowing mine to slightly touch his forcing his imagination to work even harder.

My juices flow as I make donations along the path, moving smoothly over his hardened, thick muscle. I see the pain of being restricted and not allow entry inside as I move to sit on his chest and his muscles tries harder. Moving up, his lip hitting my sensitive parts, sending me crazy and the pain from no entry express torture on my face, copying his.

Easing back and forth, I watch his body absorbs the heat mine is sending. Keeping the blindfold and the belt in place on the post, he stays on his back. He's standing hard while I'm also dripping hard. Our bodies react; waiting for relief yet, not anticipating, him only succumbing to the unknown of what's coming next.

While trying to control my body's reaction, I drizzle some of the 'guaranteed pleasure' oil on his body, before using my tongue to spread. The warmth of the oil and the moisture of my lips touching him control my body quivers. His legs shaking, his body twitching sends my juices flowing even more than before. My body responding to his, a cycle of counter reacting, bring me to an almost orgasmic elevation. I scream out loud in silence as I fail to keep control much longer.

His face saying he's experiencing the same. (I can't wait any longer.) Taking off his blindfold then releasing his hands, he slides my body under his and then (oh god) he kisses my nipples. The pressure escapes to my head and my body isn't able to process so many sensations coming from different places at the same time. My body cries and my vocals moan. Right now my sanity is failing me as (oh my god) his penetration isn't.

The fulfilment that accompanies the relief, allows my welcome to the marvellous fireworks exploding through me, crawling, from my toes, to every parts of my body. My inside tightens and grips as if saying, thank you, thank you, thank you. My vagina says wink-wink and my thought controls me again. (Oh gosh I feel weak. Let me see his wife match that.)

Lying in my bed after what seems like a phenomenon, I have only good thoughts. (Oh Lord. Thank you. This is the way to start a New Year off.). And a little while after, Dwayne's body gives in and he dozes off. Right now I don't want to be reminding myself that this man belongs to someone else, but the reality is that I can't change it yet.

I want him to see that I can handle anything and do what's good for us. Watching him sleep I feel like nibbling on his body, assaulting his muscles that took my vagina and lifted it to taste heaven. In this moment I now relish how much pleasure he brings me and will in the future. His enjoyment I'll make sure is always here for me to give. But, I want to be the good girlfriend so I wake him so he can go home.

I'm not going to be complaining about his wife or anything else. I can't sound like his wife to make him find some-place else away from home or from here with me. He has enough complaints at home so I must be his refuge.

Unpredictable is what I'm planning to be. Dwayne should never know what's next when he thinks about me and should always have a smile on his face with every one of those thought. I'm sure when he thinks about his wife he knows what she will or won't do. I just can't be that predicable and end up causing him to lose interest in me.

* * *

For the following months after our blindfold session, Dwayne and I spent more time together than even I expected. Now almost a year after our parking lot experience we've spent time as a couple also. I spend time making plans then we do it together. Yes, when we started it was with no strings. I have no one else so he knows he has to make sure my needs are taken care of.

I think I gave him enough time to fix his marriage and whatever else he felt he needed to. In the time we've being seeing each other there's been several times where we had to back off. Every time his wife thinks she knows something, his paranoia flares up.

I always play the good girlfriend and show him how understanding I am even when I feel restrained. Sometimes my patience wears down though. Again, no strings, but that was then. Now I need him more.

I'm still and will always be a mystery in the bedroom to make sure I keep him interested but there's more to us now. Sometimes, yes, I know that my memories will get the better of me and now I intend to repeat some of our good times and so far he's enjoying everyone. I too will enjoy being his treat every chance I get.

Evelyn Once Said:

"Never 'lend' what you can't afford to lose and never 'borrow' what you can't afford to give back."

Chapter Four

Dwayne and I are in our second year together as a couple and have made several decisions about our relationship so far. After all this time we still crave each other as much as in the beginning. I remember that first time I tried spending some time with him and it didn't happen the way I had planned, seems so long ago. But since then, I made sure all the times we spend together are memorable ones.

My job is to make sure he doesn't forget us. I must always have a plan in the works. So far I think I'm doing great where that's concerned. We've been seeing each other on a regular basis since our blindfold night, with the exception of some paranoid visiting times. The top of the list is to make sure we're both very careful, which means not talking to anyone about our relationship.

If anyone suspects something, just leave them to wonder but not confirm or deny anything. We also agreed to stay away from each other as long as necessary if the situation calls for it. We'll do whatever we must do to make us work, as long as it doesn't interfere with his marriage. We agreed that if the break up time comes, I must understand that his family comes first.

After that crucial talk, everything has been good. Going through our summer I had nothing worth complaining about since he was there enjoying it with me. I honestly didn't expect so much of his time but I was happy, he wanted to be here with me. I wouldn't change it for anything and I love him more than ever.

The next coming holiday will be Thanksgiving and he won't be with me but I always try to do my best through those times. Because he returns my feelings, I know I have a lot to be thankful for this year. It'll be my time to be thankful for everything that came into my life and Dwayne is one of them.

* * *

Thanksgiving passed a few days ago and Dwayne didn't get a chance to come over to see me. I spent the day with my family but most of the day my mind kept drifting off; thinking about him. Before I fell in so deep we knew holidays would come and I also accepted it for what it is.

I know his relationship with his family comes first, so I can't complain. I just make the best of it as long as I must. I guess that's just how it happens for the 'other woman' on holidays. My lonely Thanksgiving tells me Christmas will be just as lonely, but I'll have to manage.

Each holiday is only for a day and he'll make it up to me afterwards, as usual. That make-up time I do, brings rewards for my patience. And that's why I'm feeling so good about now. Today is the make-up time and he's here ready to give me my time. He even brought me some flowers.

We've been lounging and making love, making love and lounging. I did miss him but like I said, I knew what I was in for when we started. And the way my body's feeling right now, I've no time to worry about what already passed. His family gets him on holidays and I have him for the other days. So far, he comes to me almost every time I call.

I've always wondered why the 'other woman' gets blamed by the wife for problems in her marriage. Why can't the wife look at herself and think before laying blame? If her husband doesn't let others know he's ready for the taking then another woman can't get him.

These wives sit on their asses and get comfortable with their lives. They do nothing to keep it interesting in the bedroom and leave a hole for us to creep in through. When a woman like me comes along and provide some excitement for their husbands, they look at us as trouble makers.

I'll do whatever Dwayne wants me to do and it's no trouble, no bother. I can keep him happy and with no interest in what anyone has to say as long as I'm happy. My only goal is to keep him and make myself happy in the long run also.

* * *

I spent so much time with Dwayne since Thanksgiving that his wife should be wondering what's going on with him. We spend at least a couple of hours together each day and I know if I was the wife I'd be missing him, but some wives like to say they need the brake. I have no problem with that since I can accelerate and snack on him during those times.

I can only imagine how intense and uncomfortable things might be in their house the past year. He's trying to spend as much time with me as possible since Christmas is just around the corner; that means less time for her now and less for me then. Since we won't be able to see each other as we would like to, we're spending time making up for that now before the 'after holiday' make-up times comes. He's making sure my needs are satisfied enough until after the New Year.

Even thought we don't go out together our indoor times are always fun. After the holidays we'll start going on dates a little further away from home and even though we won't be able to spend a full night together, we'll go to dinner or even a movie or do something else. I know he feels badly not being able to take me anywhere I want to and I think that's why he plans to fix that.

Even with that, we'll still have to meet up where our date is because we still can't take any chances. I'm fine with it as long as we end up together. If anyone happens to see us, we can say it's a coincidental meeting. Like I said, I'll do whatever it takes, at least for now.

The Christmas holidays are only weeks away and I need it to be a special one for my family. It'll be a good time for me to think about something other than Dwayne. He's been like my life since our relationship got so intense over almost two years ago. Apart from my kids, my siblings and parents hasn't seen too much of me. My friends cuss me all the time for not having a life lately and I tell them I'm doing great.

I'm starting to sound like he's all that's going good in my life these days but at times that's how I feel. It's not every day I meet a man like him so I do think he's good for me, but he really isn't the only thing. (Damn! Am I ever confused.)

Even though I know how he feels about me, I still hope he feels some guilt because I don't have anyone to hold and hug me on Christmas morning. I still go the extra mile to make him happy and there's nothing wrong if I want him to love me enough, to feel guilt if I don't get the attention I think I deserve.

In the beginning I was just 'a piece of ass' to him but now I'm his woman. I always worry though that with all the religion going on around him at Christmas, he might have a change of heart. But I think he would've had a change of heart before so I'm almost positive I'm safe now. I'm sure he'll still feel some guilt about having me but not enough to not want me. He doesn't seem like he's been fighting hard to try to suppress his feelings.

Whenever enough guilt attacks him, he holds out as long as he can but he comes back with just as much interested and I'm prepared to correct any wrong feelings if it happens. I can never forget my goals. I'm not stupid enough to let him ruin us. I made and still make sure to remind him that he needs what I've been giving him. Again, I'll do whatever it takes and I guarantee that our break-up point won't be coming anytime soon.

* * *

My sister, Sharon, and her kids came over to spend Christmas with me and my kids. I'm so tired of having arguments over her obsession with Luke. I keep telling her that she's setting herself up for another heart break but she refuses to listen. I thought and hoped that we could use this Christmas to give us some together time; to help heal our relationship.

All she keeps going on about is him not spending some of the holidays with her and how it's pissing her off. She actually believes him when he told her she's the biggest part of his life.

Too many times our arguments escalated beyond what it should've and I feel badly about some of my comments to her. Once, I even went as far as telling her that she should've spent as much time and effort holding on to one of her baby daddies as she's spending trying to hold Luke.

I apologised to her afterwards but she told me to mind my own business and judge myself. She said I'm a hypocrite since my time is spent making a married man happy also. She can't see that it's different with me and Dwayne than with her and Luke.

Most of the things I said to her I said without thinking. I didn't mean to say the awful things but she just kept going on and on about him and it drives me crazy listening to her every time. Whenever Luke comes around me for any reason I ignore him. I never have anything to say to him and if I do, it's only to ask him why he's ruining what's left of my sister's life. I'm sure he knows how I feel and that's why he stays away.

It hurts me to know that she's wasting her life on him. She should be trying to make a life for her and her kids and if she's involve with any man it should be someone who's not there only because of the sex.

Her kids need someone stable in their lives that can be like a father to them; since their fathers won't be. She needs to hear the truth from someone and as her sister I'm the only one that's in any position to tell her. If I said anything to hurt her feelings it might take some forgiving but she'll forgive me.

We've moved on since our argument and both of us along with the kids are enjoying a wonderful Christmas. Even without Dwayne. She knows that I'll always be there for her whenever she needs me to be. I know that sooner or later she'll need my shoulders since I can't see Luke leaving his wife. When that time comes I'll feel bad for her but it'll put her back on track with her life, so I won't be sorry.

I do love my sister but her comparing our lives isn't realistic in my eyes. I'll never fool myself and plan my every move around the idea that Dwayne will leave his wife for me, unless he gives me a reason to believe so. I'll only enjoy him as my man for as long as I have him. (Yah right. Try to believe that.) If he decides to leave Jenny for me I wouldn't complain but I don't think I'm planning my life around it happening.

* * *

I managed through the holidays and it turned out great. I even had a better one than I normally do because I got a call from Dwayne on Christmas day. He called to tell me he was thinking about me and because we couldn't see each other, he didn't want me thinking I'm not in my heart.

He also wanted to check up on me to make sure I wasn't having a hard time since he couldn't be with me. Yes, he can be a little overconfident but that's a part of what makes him different; he's sure of himself and with rights to. He was right about how I was feeling so his call did make me feel better.

The days after Christmas, we didn't physically spend time together but we spent a lot of time talking on the phone. He did drop by a few times but just in passing while going somewhere else. Those visits weren't long enough for sex time since our love making isn't usually just a few minutes. We spend a lot of that time pleasuring our bodies before anything else but we take love making beyond the norm. We even use our phone conversations as foreplay now.

Coming to my house to slide in and out of my body before going home to his wife isn't what I have in mind. I leave sliding in and out between him and her. If that's how they get it done at home, I'm making sure that's not what it's like with me.

Having an affair with a married man is the next best thing to being married to the man. He needs you to save him from his wife and he has you so he won't need to go searching for another woman to take care of his needs. In every way, the mistress is needed.

It's New Years Eve and I intend to have the best one ever. A friend is having a party and I told Dwayne I'd love to see him there. He said he'll try to come over and meet me so that way we could spend some time together. I feel anxious about getting our sex life back on track. I know the more I get the less the wife gets and I have no complaints about that. That's really not my problem.

After the party my plan is to come back to my house so we can be alone. Since it's New Year's Eve, he might not be able to make it but I'm hoping. Even if we don't ring in the New Year together though, I know I'll see him on New Year's Day.

I got here and enough people are here for me to socialize while I keep looking out for Dwayne to come. Every minute searching the room with my eyes until I realize I must try to relax my brain for a little. A little bit after midnight he finally shows up. He looks at me as soon as he entered and walks over to where I'm standing. I'm just happy that he's here, better late than never.

It's my crowd and I have him to myself all night, well until he has to go home. He can touch me as much as he wants with anyone looking and without him feeling afraid to. Holding him while Luther is playing in the background and feeling his breath on my skin as he whispers in my ear, is like heaven. Doesn't matter what he says just the fact that he can.

"Sorry I took so long baby. I didn't want to leave Jenny by herself at midnight."

I don't want to hear his bitch wife's name so I quickly change the subject to let him feel that it's alright. "Don't apologise Dwayne. Right now you feel so good and I wish we could do this more often."

"I do too and things will change. Let's just enjoy ourselves right now. I've missed you."

Everyone's still having fun but I want to leave. I want some alone time at my house. I told him my surprise is waiting for him and he has to come with me before he could know what it is. He has no problem leaving with me. Even though it's my territory we still must always be careful.

Always on the lookout, so I don't mind when I've to leave and we meet a few blocks away. Before I left for the party I put everything I'll need to use for the surprise in my bedroom. We got here and I didn't wait long to show him his surprise; as soon as we stepped through my front door to my house.

"I just need you to follow me upstairs."

He has no idea but my plan is to repeat the blindfold session we had a year ago. I want us to start our year off with another memory of that night. Maybe we could make it our annual year opener every year. I hold his hand and tell him to close his eyes so I can lead him to the top of the stairs for his surprise and he does.

As soon as I open the door and step inside my bedroom he opens his eyes and smile. He takes my hand and tells me to close my eyes instead. He leads me to the middle of my bedroom then he takes the lead, helping me take my clothes off. Then, he blindfolds me with the scarf I left sitting on the bed before I left earlier. I guess he figured it out when he saw the scarf sitting on the bed. Now here I am, standing where he wants me to; in the middle of the room.

I can hear him in the bathroom telling me to make sure my eyes are still closed. I have no idea what he's doing but I'm keeping them closed. I don't want to start guessing so I'm waiting for him to come back in the room. So far I imagine it'll be exactly what I did to him before. He can see me standing naked as soon as he comes back in the room, the same way I remember when I did it to him.

The few candles I left in position earlier I assume he lit to leave a soft glow. Lit just enough so I can now see the flicker coming through the scarf he blindfolded me with, without an image coming through.

The stuff I left in the right placing in the room will give him all the ideas I had, so in my mind I know what to expect. With my eyes blindfolded my imagination tells I'm in for a treat but my body says don't be too sure. He might not be going off my plans but off what he thinks will feel good to me.

I can hear his footsteps in the room and I'm sure he's admiring my stripped to the bare skin body just as he left me before he went into the bathroom, anxious. I feel his touch on my nipples, I think, his lips. His teeth holding it in place while his tongue massage the tip. (Damn, surprise me). My breast wasn't expecting to feel his first touch so the sensation is travelling down to the rest of me real fast. I don't know where his touch is coming to next.

I'm expecting to feel him touch maybe my belly button since he's already touching my nipples (holy shit!) I feel him tasting my back instead. Before I can get comfortable with his tongue there an unknown coldness touch my same nipple.

The tip of that nipple's getting hard, then, the moisture from his lips glides over. The sensation shoots to my back and around to my other nipple, feeling like someone trying to surprise me from behind and grab both my breasts instead; gently. But the other one's just getting jealous for some attention that it's also getting hard.

Sensations shooting from my back through my body, coming to my nipples, each touch coming to my body from his lips and not his hands. I feel restrained. I must touch him. As I lift my hand feeling for his face he lets me but he also has a scarf waiting to use on my hands. I think he thinks that I won't be able to keep my eyes closed for too much longer and might pull the scarf off my eyes.

My head leans towards him but he kisses my shoulder instead. He backs away from me and my back tingles again, leading down to my legs. His kisses on my legs, going to my inner thighs are sending me wild. My body's shaking. Quivering. Chills.

He holds me from behind and leads me over to the bed and lay me down. Feeling his lips kiss between my thighs weakens my knees. Before my mind can process the sensations flowing through me, I want to take the blindfold off. (I need to see.) I feel his head nudging my legs to open.

(I need to move . . . my legs.) "Baby please. I need to see you." He's not ready for that yet. He wants my legs to go weak and with his head between my legs. (Oh God . . . I can't take this . . . I need to hold him.) My body has pleasure shooting from my clit, going through to weaken my everywhere going up to my breast (Shit.)

My nipples are so hard they burn. (Damn. Let me see you.) "Baby please, release me. I need to touch you." He slowly kisses coming up my stomach, to my breast, then my lips. He holds my hand and releases the tie. I can feel the moisture sliding and my body's confusion. I lie down with my body tingling.

I didn't wait long for his touch again but still with my blindfold on. He slowly manoeuvres his way to kiss me again and I feel his moistness touch my leg as it dangles. He wants me to wonder where each touch will come, to keep the mystery of it all. With every touch my body responds in a different way, but each time feeling more sensitive than before.

The scented oil he spills on my body is now cloaking the room with the sweet smelling fragrance, while the tingling sensation hugs my body as it drizzles. I stay with my unknown, with my blindfold.

Lying on my back, the oil runs off my body to the side while he spreads it over my breast. His fingers purposely gliding over the tip of my nipples, enhances the tingling sensations. Making my senses scream as I slowly and uncontrollably twist from side to side.

Using one hand to spread the oil, the other creates warmth inside as I feel his finger slowly slides around the opening urging my legs to go apart, but without any entry. My heart feels like it's about to give in and I feel anxious. My teeth, holding my lips, want to bite through. My body's twitching too badly.

The lips of my opening are almost begging to be opened and be violated. The hunger along with the inability to control anything has my juices slowly travelling down the slit below, making my cheeks slide.

Almost in a teasing way it's running between the cracks heading for the sheets. My body's going crazy and I enjoy the warmth of the oils between his fingers on my breast; his tongue circling my navel with his other hand teasing my clit.

My brain's going wild. (Hoooly shit!) My nipples between his oily fingers, the slight pinches he's sending them, shooting, shots of sensations going to my feet and my head at the same time. (O . . . my . . . god . . . I'm weak) The sensations shooting through my body sends pressure to my head; all without entry.

His face travels, heading up towards mine, giving me some relief from his hands. The eagerness of my hands to touch him goes all over, attacking him but with such tenderness brings relief. The heat from his body hovering over my sensitive skin pulls my kisses to his chest going from one nipple to the other.

His touch extracting the sensitivity from my body into his sends us even crazier. My body still feeling tortured almost going weak, getting eager makes my vagina craven. He enjoys draining the energy from my body using the unknown but my eyes needs to see as my hands needed to feel.

He says the word to make me want to hold him even more. "Baby just free your mind. Bring only the best memories from your happiest moments to mind. Just enjoy your man with the memories flowing through." My man is making love to me and it feels too damn good.

My confused senses speeds my heart and the blood races through me. My body feels weightless as it suddenly peaks almost to an orgasm. Unable to take it any longer, my eyes now open and hands unbound, I grab him. I need to see and feel his face on mine. I need to see him watching me tremble uncontrollably from his touch. And I need to give him some on my pleasures also.

"Let me feel you now baby . . . I need to feel you inside me now."

Easing up and turning to my knees seemed almost a challenge but tucking my back in his body allows his hands to travel where they want. His hands coming up to massage my breast as he lean forward, covering my back, he enters with our every senses building between our bodies.

Mine is ready. It's at the convulsing stage while his hands are travelling, reaching below my stomach and heading down. The feeling of anticipation controls my senses through my torturing unfair moment of greed. Before I finish one orgasm I feel another one coming through and he's still going.

The gluttony of being pleasured with such intensity could lead to an explosive moment without warning. The moisture from him creates a gliding affect for him between our bodies, enabling his convulsion that his body's now unable to control. My body opens as if it's the welcoming committee getting ready for the sperm invasion. (This is the taste of pleasure that was worth waiting for.)

Our bodies attached between our legs. The throbbing inside my opening is working with my river between there; giving his, easy access. My knees weaken and his body collapses on mine as we both moan and scream at the same time, another one for me. The grip from his arms is holding me so tight. My hips vibrates to the enjoyment of every ounce of everything it demands and commands. His body attached to mine while he throbs on my inside and clamp on to his.

The creeping sensation slowly crawling through encourages my inside to hold on tighter. While my inner muscles clamps, he pulls my hips into his pelvis closer, in a one-two-three rhythm; each time going in more intensely and holding on tighter, trembling.

After minutes my curled toes straightened, our bodies ease down on to the sheets, timing our exit from our rigid state. The built up hunger finally escapes, bringing us back from the other world.

My body is tingling as I'm twitching uncontrollably with every touch. The after-shocks crawl through me with no sense of direction and reacts with every slight touch. It feels good. Again, I'll say it's a happy New Year to me. And again I have to let him go home to his wife. But I'm fine doing it.

Evelyn Once Said:

"If we let someone treat us like crap, taking our joy, that means we put their worth above ours. Doing that, tells them it's fine to treat us how we treat yourself; with less value than them."

Chapter Five

I know that Dwayne's thinking about me every day now and for the past few months, I've given him way more than what I think he was expecting. He's probably thinking about me even when he's having sex with his wife, well maybe not every time but a few I'm sure. Maybe he's even comparing her and me to see who is better.

I want him to keep tasting our future every time he comes to me. It'll only get better for us and I'll enjoy knowing he looks forward to all our times we'll be spending together, even more so, than the time he'll spend with his wife.

I'll never forget all those painful nights that I only survived because of his help. The nights I spent with him in the beginning, having a few drinks at the bar were helpful. The smoking and all the little bad habits I had, he told me to stop since that's not how he likes 'his woman'; doing things he doesn't like me to. I stopped doing them all and that changed my life in a big way; for the good.

*   *   *

Beverly is the only one who knows how strong my feelings are for Dwayne. After my fulfilled night with him a few months ago she decided to help me with my plans. I've been having a great time with him but now I need more. The past year we've spent as much time as possible together and with as much sex as we could get in. Now spring is here and I talked her into driving by Dwayne's house and if we see him outside we could stop by for a surprise visit.

We drove by several times in the past few weeks and we didn't see either Dwayne or Jenny, but yesterday my luck changed as we saw Jenny outside. We parked the car in front of their house and stopped for a visit.

We told her we were passing by and saw her so we thought we'd stop just to say hello, since she was so nice to us before. She thought it was nice of us and said she wants to know her husband's friends better. That was perfect to hear since I'd love to know her better myself, so we stayed and spent a little time sitting outside talking with her.

Jenny remembered me from the birthday party. She mentioned that she doesn't know many of his newer friends and it was nice of us to stop by. She said away from his old friend like Anthony,

Mark and James, and some other names I don't recognize, she doesn't see any. After hanging with her for a little while we told her we enjoyed our visit but we had to leave. Dwayne came home a few minutes before we left and I could see that he didn't like that we were there.

After Bev and I left he called to tell me not to do anything like that behind his back again. I told him we didn't mean any harm and we really stopped hoping to see him. Told him I waited because I really wanted to see him and if I was doing it behind his back I would've left before he got home.

Flattery will get me everywhere where Dwayne's concerned, so he believed me. I really did want to see him since now I only see him when he comes to my house, so a move like that also tells him that I'm gonna be seen. I do have confidence in how my body work when it comes to his needs so I know that it's getting harder for him now to say no to me.

I didn't mention that I wanted to know more about her or that I was investigating how to deal with him when he can't be around. I won't make any of the mistakes she does and it's always good to know how the wife thinks.

I made sure he also understands that by me going to his house around his wife, it should show how I can handle him with his wife at home and me outside his home. I told him it also prepares me for that moment if I run into her; he knows now that he doesn't have to worry about me.

Beverly is my best friend and she'll do almost anything I asked of her. I ask her to find a way to tell Jenny that I'm interested in Dwayne without telling her it's him, just someone. To find a way of doing it without letting Dwayne knowing what's happening. Now I intend to see how far I can take this relationship.

Beverly's husband and Dwayne are planning a meeting at Dwayne's house and she thought that would give her the opportunity she needs to talk to Jenny while the husbands talk business. I didn't think it was a good idea to use that time since Dwayne might notice something. She thought who would think she's up to anything with Dwayne there but after thinking about it I figured it was a great idea.

* * *

Several days passed since Beverly went to Dwayne's house for the meeting. He and I talked on the phone many times after that but he didn't seem upset about anything so it leads me to assume that Jenny didn't take the bait.

Bev told me she mentioned my name a few times and Jenny thought I seemed nice. Beverly then told her that I'm not as nice as I seem since all I have on my mind is finding ways to take away some woman's husband. She told me Jenny reacted the way she was hoping. Said she could see the change on Jenny's face and with that she knew she got her attention.

* * *

It's been months now since Beverly's little attention grabber and Dwayne still spend a lot of time with me. We usually spend time at my house in bed or just laying in the living room relaxing together watching TV. I make sure he knows he'll be welcome at my home anytime and that I'll have no one else as long as we're together.

I know I've falling in love with him and I don't want him to ever feel the need to be unsure of me. He even fell asleep here in my bed a few nights and even though I was tempted to leave him sleeping, I woke him up to go home.

I wanted him to stay but I thought it would be a good way to show him how much I'm looking out for his best interest; to gain his trust. If I didn't wake him he would have to come up with some excuse for his wife about where he was so waking him to go home means less stress.

I want him to be a model husband so when she starts to complain he'll think he's giving her no reason for her raised suspicions. That way she'll be a nag instead of a lonely wife. This way I won't have to go for long periods without seeing him since he won't have to stay home and play the good husband.

Jenny wouldn't know when he's with me and doing all I do will show him that I'd never go out of my way to help her find out about us; if she does it's on her own. When I tell him to leave and he's a little bit slow in doing so it's because he thinks Jenny won't know where to find him even if she tries. I think she knows where

I live though, from the information dropped during Beverly's visit but I don't know if she remembers.

If Jenny mentions anything to Dwayne about me it must look to him like she found out about him and me all on her own. All he'll see is how much trouble I go through to prevent it and I can't get any blame. It'll all be blamed on her snooping around.

I want him to leave her but it must be her attitude and accusations that drives him away while I'll be waiting to comfort and pamper him. If Dwayne thinks I'm intentionally causing them problems then that would be the end of his relationship with me. He said Jenny asked him about me once and he told her I'm just a single mother who hung with them on occasions at the bar.

She probably thinks that I'm a regular there even though I only continued going when I got interested in Dwayne. I guess no one knows that's why I started going there so often. I'd seen Dwayne several times before I caught his attention. Before he did, I watched and learned a lot about him that's useful to me now.

Even though I was seeing someone at the time it was just that, seeing someone. It wasn't enough to prevent me from finding out about him. Asking questions but not showing that I'm physically interested and I said nothing to anyone, not even Beverly at first. All my questions were just included in our 'girls talking'. I thought he was the best thing I'd ever seen.

That night when Beverly said she knows him, my thought was that someone must want me to go after him by making it so easy for me to find out everything I wanted. Everything's for a reason and I thought at the time it was to bring him to me.

Now I'm in love with him as much as a woman can be with a man and I really didn't plan to take it this far. I only wanted someone to be there for me when I needed but now it's more.

None of my kid's fathers were worth my time but I found that out after it was too late. Dwayne is different from the kind of men I've had in my live and because of that I was willing to have him even though I can't have him. The way I feel, I won't let even Jenny stop me and jeopardize my relationship with him. Yes, she's the wife but I intend to get some of the wifely benefits for myself.

I know we're about at the point in our relationship where he aches for me when I'm not around; the same way I ache for him when he's not with me. All I think about when he isn't here is what's going on at his house between him and her.

I'd like to know everything she does; even when she touches him. Anything that can put a strain on us being together I want to know ahead so I can have the remedy ahead of time. The way I feel lately I'm willing to go on like this for as long as he wants me. That's how badly I need him in my life.

I've passed the 'I want him' stage and I'm at the 'I need him' point in this relationship. Now all of Dwayne's friends knows about me and I can see some of them don't like that he's being seeing me for so long. His ignoring them tells them to back off and they seem to be doing that even though I know what they're thinking isn't good.

They're all friends with Jenny and I think they'll still pressure him but so what. As long as he doesn't allow himself to listen to them I won't lose time caring about what they say. Some of them are still nice to me but the others I stay away from. And since many of them are doing the same things, they can't say too much about him sleeping with me.

I'm just planning to enjoy our love as much as I can and right now, I can deal with their shit. If plans go the way I hope, he might decide he's not happy living the married life for too much longer and they'll be sorry they were assholes to me.

Evelyn Once Said:

.

"There's one problem it's best to deal with sooner rather than later since we can never run away from it; our self."

Chapter Six

Away from a few questions, Dwayne still hasn't said anything to make me believe Jenny has given me much thought even though the hint Bev gave, was to make her worry about Dwayne's and my friendship. It was to make her start keeping track of his comings and goings since I plan to be seen in there somehow.

* * *

Because it took so long for me to see something happen I thought it wasn't working, that's until today. Dwayne told me she asked him a few questions about me so I guess it's working but slower than I'm expecting it to. Since he won't leave her my thought is that I can help her torment him so he'll want to stay away from her or frustrate her into wanting to leave him instead.

If I can do everything to help her stop trusting him, then I can cause enough problems to make them unhappy around each other. He'll never admit to her that he and I are sleeping with each other but I can show her evidence that he lies about me. The only thing I haven't figured out yet is how to help her find out what I want her to without Dwayne getting suspicious. After using Bev to drop the hint I did it hoping that 'her type' wouldn't let a statement like that go.

The way Dwayne talks about her, she seems to be the type who would want to know what's going on with me while watching his every move. Now, I want her to want to satisfy her curiosity so that all my work will finally pay off but I still need to move progress faster. Now how to do that, is the next thing I have to figure out.

Last night I went to a party with my friends and it was great. I haven't done much socializing with them since Dwayne and I started so they don't know that I'm as involved with him as I am. They think that I need to get out and meet other people. I sometimes think they're right.

Those who know about Dwayne asked me several times how I think I'll meet a man of my own if I stopped meeting people. Like I said I know they might be right but I can't walk away from Dwayne now.

I've put in too much time to walk away when I'm in love with him. Even if I meet someone else I know I wouldn't be happy with that person since I'd be thinking about him all the time.

I didn't tell Dwayne I was going to the party and he ended up coming to my house to see me. I wasn't there so he called my cell looking for me. When I told him where I was he went crazy and we ended up fighting.

We've never had a fight before and at first I was pissed that he was trying to tell me where I can or can't go. I didn't see how he had the right telling me anything since he has his wife to do things with and I have to wait for him to get permission to leave her alone before I can see him.

I shouldn't have to sit and wait until he finds time instead of making free time for me. His whole anger stemmed from me going to the party where I'd be dancing with someone who might touch me.

It's been so long since I've had a long term sexual relationship with anyone other than Dwayne that I'd probably have to ask them to do what he does so I can be satisfied. I'm convinced that I depend on him too much for companionship and at this point I probably wouldn't know how to enjoy someone else's company. I know that I need to mingle with friends again to feel like I still control my life though.

It doesn't mean that I'm going to have sex or be touch sexually by anyone else so why he thinks I would allow that to happen, is beyond me. I made my choice not to have sex with anyone else and I haven't. I still don't see why he's telling me I can't go out and have some fun with other people though.

I don't need to go to the bar to see him anymore and now that he comes to my house when I want to see him, it's not necessary. I used to feel bad going there so often before and that's why it was the best thing for me when he started coming here instead. He tells his wife he's going there then ends up at my house.

His friends get mad when he uses them as an excuse to leave his house now, but it doesn't stop him from doing it. But, if I'm to be honest, sometimes I worry because I don't know if I'm eluding myself thinking that I don't need to get some better balancing over my life right now, instead of balancing my life with his.

After our fight I thought about everything that we said to each other and chalked it up as being a good thing. If he wasn't in love with me he wouldn't care where I go and with whom and he wouldn't get jealous.

At first I didn't stop to think that he was acting crazy because of his feelings for me. Why else would he have gotten so angry? But now I see that he went crazy because he loves me too. After thinking about the whole thing my anger is fading. Because of that, I gave him a call to say sorry for worrying him.

He was jealous and that could only mean his feelings for me are much stronger than he lets on. Maybe he himself doesn't even realize how strong his feelings are. I've never given him any reasons to be jealous before and now he might be as surprise as I am about what he's feeling. (Yes, he's finally mine in every way.)

He's coming over later tonight and we plan to go see a movie. We've talked about going out and leaving the house together, instead of one of us leaving after the other. He's still not about to do anything at all to wilfully hurt his wife, but I need to feel like I'm an important part of his life also. Even though he agreed, he insists on us still taking precautions to keep it safe.

He still has no intension on giving up his wife and their marriage but he can't let go of me in the mean time either. He thinks if we spent some time as a couple I'll be happier and that will make him happier also, so he's working on that.

Since we started going out like a couple, it's usually in the city and not local. We go to the clubs if we feel like doing some dancing and if any of my friends are having a party we do that also. Whether it's the movies or anything else that I need to show up for, he goes with me if he can.

My girlfriends are getting to know him and they seem to like him. Sometimes they even feel sorry for him; being separated from his wife and in love with me but trapped in his marriage. I told them that they're separated so that I didn't have to go into details. They speculate and believe that the only reason he stays in the house and not move out for me, must be because of financial reasons.

He works hard and if they divorce he can't afford to give it all to her to enjoy with somebody else. His business is striving and he wants to keep it that way with no turmoil along the way. He never told me directly but I think he's sometimes confused about his relationships; both with her and also with me. For me, his confusion is good news since that only means he can't let me walk out of his life either.

*   *   *

Summer is here and spending so much time with Dwayne left me with not much time to made any plans for my kids holidays. I wanted to take them away but I might have to rethink that now.

Dwayne kids are much older and they do their own thing; he doesn't have to put much time in planning vacations. If they have to plan for family trips it would be Jenny doing the planning for them. I wouldn't be able to know ahead what their plans are so that I can plan around it and be away at the same time. I already accept that he wouldn't be a part of my plans so I on the other hand must do something with my kids on my own.

More than likely I'll stick to doing something locally and plan for them to do different things every day. If I vacation here instead of going away, maybe I can even include Dwayne in some of my plans. Now I have to let him know I'm hoping he can spend some time with me and my kids during this summer.

Dwayne and I talked today about my summer plans and he isn't interested in doing anything with me and my kids right now. He said I should take them somewhere special so that they can enjoy their summer. His thought is that I should take them on a trip someplace where they want to go and he wants me to enjoy it with them. I love my kids and I want them to have fun this summer also. Even though I don't want to leave him, I'm fine doing that.

I've never felt like going or have never gone anywhere far away since we've been together so that's why I was reluctant. Even now that I'm thinking about it, I still have to wonder how much fun I'll have without him. Even though I'm hesitant I'll plan to go away for a couple of weeks.

* * *

The kids and I left on our vacation and now we're at a place where we can have some fun and enjoy ourselves. It's also where I have another sister we could spend some quality time with. Since mine and her kids don't get a lot of time to spend together, it's also a chance to do that. We left the Chicago weather to come to Florida for our visit. I thought since we haven't seen them in a while, they'd give us the out of town visitor's treatment.

My sister and I talk often but unless she comes to Chicago we don't see each other much. I use to visit her before Dwayne and now she gets mad with me because I stopped. She knows about Dwayne since she's one of the few people I trust to not judge me.

She's married and the only thing she's ever said is that it could be her marriage someone was trying to break up. But she also said she won't talk to me about it since I've to figure it out for myself.

She thinks if she comes down on me it might make me feel like everyone wants to tell me how to live. She made sure I know that when I need her she'll be there for me, no matter what.

During our time here, we've done the parks and beaches with the kids and I enjoyed some clubbing with relatives. It's been more fun than I thought it would be even though I've thought about Dwayne constantly. But we're going back home today and even though it was fun, I feel good that I'll be home soon.

I called him several times since I've been here and he sounds happy to hear from me every time. There were some calls that he didn't answer but he apologized for not answering them when I finally got him.

* * *

The kids and I came back a couple of days ago and even though it was only two weeks, we got a lot of fun compacted in there. Everybody was very attentive and helped the kids. At six and eight years old, everything is exciting to them so my family made sure they saw everything. They'll remember this trip for a long time to come.

Seen that I have more vacation time, the only reason I didn't want to extend my visit was because Dwayne wasn't there to enjoy it with me. I gave him a call when I came back and he couldn't come to see me then but he called today and said he'll come over later to welcome me home.

I told him how much I missed him and that I couldn't wait to hold him since two weeks seemed like forever without him. He said he missed me too and he would come over as soon as he gets the chance. It would've been nice to have him here waiting for me when I got home since I left him a key, but I want him so much right now that I just want him here as soon as possible.

I just sent the kids over to my parent's house for a few days since it's the weekend and they haven't seen them since we got back. I also want to have some quality time with Dwayne tonight so I can't worry about them right now. And my body is saying hurry since I haven't had sex for two weeks and I intend to make up for that. I'm actually feeling almost like I did that night Jenny interrupted us by my car.

My body is really aching and I'm anxious. After the kids left I came up to take a shower. I just want to keep standing here and have the water running down my body with my eyes closed; just stand here.

I need to relax my body until Dwayne gets here. I never felt these kinds of feelings for sex before I started having sex with him. Yes I've felt for sex with others before but I mean, I've never ached so badly.

My first thought is to enjoy having him release me of those tensions by making love, but now I'm just scared. I worry sometimes about what will happen to me if he and I break up. How will I handle these feelings? How would I take care of them? Instead of relaxing in the shower now I feel like I'm making myself more stressed with worry.

I'm not getting as stress free as I want to so I just turn the water off and step out of the shower. With water still running down my body, I wrap a towel around myself. Sitting beside my bathtub I towelled try and lotion my body so it'll be soft for his touch, then I put on my robe and walk to my bedroom so I can put something nice on for him to take off.

I step in the room and find the lights turned down low, setting the mood and I know I didn't leave it that way. On the night stand, a bottle of champagne that I didn't leave there, is sitting beside my bed with two classes. At the door to my room I see Dwayne standing at the edge of the jam entering the room with flowers to put beside my window.

He came in and did all that while I was standing in the shower and I didn't hear a thing. Because the water was running I had no idea what was happening out here. He used his keys and came in to surprise me. (Damn he looks good.)

I'm so happy to see him. To have him do this for me makes me feel really special. (Oh my god. Do I ever love you.) There's so much I want to say to him right now about how this makes me feel, but I'll do that later. I forgot about sexy underwear or anything like that I had planned. I feel so special right now.

I just drop my robe and walk over to his arms for him to hold me. I kiss his chest. Holding on to him so tight that if I was stronger

I would probably hurt him. I even feel more special hearing him say that he missed me just as much and I have him. Hearing those words coming from his lips to my ears just makes my day. I love this man so much that I hurt.

With all that I see, I just start undressing him. He kisses my forehead while I unbutton his shirt, all while he's caressing my arms. The lotion on my skin allows his hands to glide and the hunger from my body heightens my sensations before our skin touch each other's.

I step back to allow his clothes to fall. Both of us now standing naked by the door, again my body gravitate to his arms and they embrace me. The warmth of his breath flows to my head and touch my face, sending my emotions overboard and my heart's racing. The warmth from our bodies against each other is comforting.

Between my legs moistens while he leads me over to the bed and my mind brings memories of what I know will come. As I lie down and wait for him to touch my inside, I know I'll be enjoying him with every part of me.

With the foreplay of my mind, I feel his lips on my breast and my inside pulsating beyond control. His lips travel from side to side, giving some attention to my nipples, and my toes curl. My legs want to rise to open and give him access but the kisses got me a little confused.

Now it looks like he developed an even greater taste for me while I was away since he can't get enough of my flavour either. I have him doing things in every way and every part of my body that he probably never thought of doing things to, he's doing those parts tonight. And even pain is pleasurable with him right now. I always plan new ways to keep our sex life interesting but now I think he's also doing the same for me; the time away gave us many ideas.

Having his lips touch and his tongue tasting, I can't help myself. I can't hold my legs down any longer. I can't control myself. I raise them and hold on to his head, holding it in place. I doubt if he can hear my screams from the pleasing sensations collapsing my senses right now. I can't let go before I get to that point, that point where I need to release more of me; but I need to feel him inside also.

Finally I feel my path opening and his muscle digging deeper and deeper towards the itch. Laying over me; I grab his back. With every push, I feel my inside holding on and the throbbing turns blissfully aggressive, going into a whirlpool of pleasure.

My inner thighs has a web of feelings crawling from deep inside going to my feet and out through my other body parts as my hand reach for my nipple. Confused senses sends my inside pulsating, and my breathing turns into gasping.

My head gets heavy and my inner muscles hold and strangle anything that's inside me; leaving him behind waiting for his. My body selfishly enjoys all that's coming and without feeling guilty. I open my eyes to see his facial muscles standing in his forehead, while his body goes out of control, twisting, fighting to follow mine.

My inner walls feel the throbbing beating against it and his release spurting as if bouncing around. The satisfaction on both our faces tells us of the hunger we both felt while we were apart. His body comes down on mine. He rolls off, landing beside me and I roll into his arm; even though he can barely hold me. I feel very welcomed home. We'll just lay and re-coop before we start all over again.

* * *

Dwayne gave me such a nice treat by surprising me last night. We made love almost all night and today I've only a smile when I think about him. His phone kept going off but we were so intense that he didn't stop to answer any calls. He showed no interest that he cared who was on the other end of any calls.

He had me crying for more after every orgasm and after a while my body begged for mercy. I've never had so many orgasms in one night before. Even with my fragile body I made sure he also got some of what he missed while I was away. I made sure he was glad to have me home, to be all over him again showing how much I missed doing it. We were so exhausted afterwards.

My body was feeling so good that thoughts of my next vacation were floating in my head. If this is how much he misses me when I leave for vacation and if this is what I will come back to each time, I want to vacation more.

Lying in his arms I knew he would have to leave because it was late and also because he checked his phone to see who was calling before and it was Jenny. Not even that bothered me. He called her back and told her that the music was too loud and that's why he didn't hear when she called before. He told her he had just checked his phone then and that he already left and would be home soon.

He got up and got dressed then left right after he came off the phone. I didn't have the strength to walk so before he left he gave me a kiss and told me welcome home. My body felt so good I didn't care that he had to leave. I also knew that there was no way he would have enough energy to go home to perform. She's no competition.

* * *

It's been several weeks since my vacation. It was an exciting and fulfilling summer but now it's almost finishing and the kids will be back in school soon. Dwayne usually stop by to see me in the mornings when he's leaving to go out to work but for some reason he hasn't done so all this week. That's not feeling right with me since the last time we spent any quality time together was more than a week ago.

I gave him a call earlier because I didn't want to go any longer without finding out why. He told me he noticed a vehicle that looks like Jenny's passing my house a few times before and the last time he left me, he saw it again. He's almost positive it's her and even though she hasn't said anything to him he doesn't feeling comfortable coming to see me as much as he wants to. He didn't call me because he didn't want to cause a scene.

Apparently his friends also saw her passing the bar a few times without stopping. Since he had no idea if it was her circling the bar, he went home and told her he was with them when he was really with me.

He figured something was going on with her since she hasn't confronted him about anything and he's a bit puzzled why. Because of all that, he thinks we should cool down a little until he feels comfortable with us again. He also wants to find out what she's been up to.

My thought is why is he so obsess about her reasons for not being curious, but yet when she does ask, he gets defensive. But that's a man for you. I guess I can't do anything about it now. I love the fact that she's watching him if she really is doing that. Sooner or later she'll say something and start pressuring him again and I'll be here for him.

* * *

At this point I think it's getting ridiculous since it's been over two months since I've been with Dwayne. I couldn't do much about stopping him for slowing down his and my sex life but two months is beyond what I thought. After such a nice welcome home from my vacation, I shouldn't be able to count how many times we've been together since. He shouldn't expect me to sit here waiting for his ass to surprise me.

He made love to me a few times only to leave me waiting until who the hell knows when again. He must know by now that I'm not going to be his on call relief when he gets the need for me, instead of his wife. Our relationship has gone far beyond that stage now. My thoughts are going to be heard and I plan to do it now and not later.

    I called Dwayne and told him he's a selfish asshole. After we argued a little, he came over and we spent some time talking some more. He understood what I was saying but he also insists that we must slow things down; indefinitely. He knows how much I need him and I know he's using it to his advantage. But I can't help myself. I just can't stay angry enough to walk away.

Now I'm already not looking forward to the holiday which is coming soon. I'll have to make some changes now to help me through the rest of the year again. (Lord, help me.)

Evelyn Once Said:

"Be careful where you put your trust since that's where the greatest pain can come from."

Chapter Seven

Another year is ending, again. My whole summer was great and away from Thanksgiving and Christmas, I can't say I have too many complaints.

Christmas day my kid's fathers came over to spend time with them as usual. This time, I found myself looking at these men wondering if things could've been as good with them as it is with Dwayne if I'd given them a chance. We were much younger and wasn't as experienced and I figured I'd have to take that into consideration before I can pass judgement on them. Whether or not it would've been, it was hard to judge.

I remember when I met my first child's father. He looked so handsome and after I got to know him he was also very kind. We fell in love and made plans for our future. Where we'd live, how many kids we'd have and how we'll be financially comfortable.

We didn't want to aim for wealth, just financially comfortable. Within a year I was pregnant and our dreams, they turned into almost a nightmare.

During my pregnancy and until I had my daughter everything seemed to be going great so we moved in together and made plans to get married the following year. After that, I started seeing someone in him that I didn't know and didn't like. His laid back and satisfied with not having much attitude wasn't giving me much help in life. I wanted more for my future and I wasn't planning for a future with someone with little ambition.

After a while I could see that whatever he used to do to impress me, was done just to get my attention. I think he would've done whatever I asked him to but at the time I wasn't in the frame of mind to be behind him pushing his every move. I didn't want to feel like his parent.

I needed someone who could be my partner and not someone to be another child for me to take care of. That's when I decided to call it quits and I moved on without him as my partner. I had my baby and he kept his relationship as a father but that's where it ends.

After leaving my first child's father, I went on and continued my schooling and stayed on my own. About a year later I met someone, my second child's father, and I thought he was perfect. We ended up going through almost the same scenario as with my first and in the long run with the same results. I seemed to identify with needy men and see them as being perfect.

I needed somebody who could help to bring out the best in me. When I think about it now I must say I do have some regrets. I was young and didn't give enough thought into what I was doing. Now they both have moved on with their lives, with other people, and are doing well.

The irony is that I have my heart trapped in a relationship now with someone else's husband. I'm in a relationship where I'm living on hopes and I'm constantly wondering if it'll ever go beyond what it is now.

I figured I was meant to be a single woman, having two failed relationships. But in the beginning, it's not how I had it planned; doing it with two kids. I've made my children my priority but along the way I've also had some casual relationships; to satisfy my needs. Looking for someone to be with was not on my agenda so I was fine alone, but with two children, it's been hard on relationships.

I made a promise to myself that I would be more careful before I have another child. I told myself if I have one more it would be with someone that can help me further myself and my future; somebody who's capable of helping me grow and better myself, someone that will be a partner and father in every way. All that went out the window when I met Dwayne. He helped me to better myself but also prevented me from seeing what else is out there.

Now if I start looking, I'll be looking for him in that person. But he also made me see that there's better out there for me than what I've had before he came along. And even though I see that special person in him, I just never planned on my special person to be a married one.

I sat there looking at this man, thinking about too many things at the same time and then I found myself thinking about my life before Dwayne. I wasn't the happiest person in my previous relationships but I also wasn't in a hopeless position. Now I know that.

My sister Sharon gets angry at me more now because she thinks I'm being judgemental about her and her lifestyle and not looking at mine. I've asked her before why she dedicated so much time getting a married man to leave his wife, but she didn't seemed to have a good answer to give me. She has so many baby daddies but never found one to keep as her real man.

Her second baby father had his own family when he started with her and she knew about them. Even with that, she got involved with him then got pregnant anyway. I was angry and thought she was stupid and I told her so. If she wanted to be his sex thing, why get pregnant.

I remember her telling him about the baby and he left her, but not before he accused her of trying to ruin his marriage. It's his marriage and he stepped out of it but then wants to blame her for whatever went wrong.

It took years before he got involved in his child's life and only after his wife accepted that the child had nothing to do with any of it. Now he and his daughter have a good relationship but he can't stand my sister. Even with all that she went through, she still did the same thing and ended up with more kids.

I remember her response one day we were arguing about her being with Luke. She looked straight at me and told me that one day I might understand. She said she and I are not so different from each other. Not because we're related but because we have the same ideas. She thought the only difference was that I take a little more time to assess but I still jump in.

I disagreed with her since she became a grandmother already and I'm a year older. That shows that she lost her way long before I took my first jump and started having her kids way before me. I'm not in that space.

I'm not losing my life to anyone. I'll do everything to make Dwayne come back to me after he leaves my house but I can't force him to do so. He comes to me because he needs me. She seems to be having kids to use to try and make that happen and now she has only baby daddies.

I accept that Dwayne isn't ready to leave Jenny for us but I don't have to lose hope. I still go out of my way for him until that day he sees me as his future but I'm not trying to trap him. It does scare me now to see where I've come and what I've done. I've passed up two opportunities with two men that it took me too long to see in a different light.

I tell people that I left them because they were deadbeats but that was my opinion; the reality of my young mind. I judge my sister for her life style when I shouldn't. I'm far from being in the same shoe as her but I'm doing the same in the area of making trouble in another woman's life. The last person I expected to control my heart was Dwayne, but he is, and all while he brings me joy.

I know he loves me and he shows it by doing everything he does to see me, even with all the stress our relationship has brought him. If he wasn't in love with me he would've left me a long time ago to save himself from all the trouble. And after his wife started with her suspicions, instead of him stopping with me, he goes out of his way to make me happy even though it's not convenient for him sometimes. Because of all that he does, I try to understand the bad, while I appreciate the good times also.

     Christmas did come and go and all week I haven't heard much from Dwayne. Even though my house was filled with people, all I kept thinking about was him. We saw each other before Christmas but after such a great summer, along with everything else, his attitude the past few weeks makes me uncomfortable.

He gets leery about us this time every year and develops a conscience. Because we didn't spend time together during the holidays, my days seemed so much longer than they really were and got really lonely. Now, last night he was supposed to come over but he had to change our plans again because Jenny wanted him to do whatever and he always gives in to her. What else is new?

I want to be at the top of his list and I think that will be on the agenda this year. This is getting too hard. I deserve more of that attention and I think it's time he starts to give in to me more. Yes,

I know he's married to her but I do more to please him than she does, so I deserve at least that.

I'm still upset that he changed our plans and I got up this morning and sent him a message to tell he that. I need to see him and I won't take no for an answer today. I can't call him so I send him a text messaging since that's my only alternative.

Conversation between Sandy and Dwayne:

Sandy—How much longer must I wait to see u Dwayne?

Dwayne—Soon. It's the holidays. Soon

Sandy—I'll have champagne glasses. I miss u baby

Dwayne—I'll be making it up to you soon

Sandy—My Christmas was ruin without u. I want u with me all the time

Dwayne—Please don't play with my heart Sandy you know how I feel

Sandy—I can give u at least 100 reasons y I'm in love with u Dwayne

Dwayne—My heart is not made out of stone. I miss everything about you. Your lips and the way you touch me. You affect my life so much that it scares me

Sandy—Same for me baby. I'm writing this to u in tears. I hate it when u r not around me. I'm feeling pain baby

Dwayne—I even miss the way you walk

Sandy—I want to feel the bass of your voice vibrating my body to make my pussy jump

Dwayne—I'll see you soon baby

I know it's the holidays but he should know that it's as important to me as it is to Jenny. I should be able to have some time with him over the holiday. He's with his family and I'm here alone.

I try to understand the problem with him finding the time but coming to see me during the holidays is just like any other day; it's always hard. Knowing that he's there with her and I'm alone this time of year is harder on me now. Who the hell am I gonna be with if not him.

He can come even if it's for a couple of hours. Just tell her he's going to the store or something, I don't give a shit what, but come to me. All the promises I get from him are getting tired and I can't settle for that anymore; a new year is about to start.

Things must change and I must make sure of it. The New Year must bring changes because I can't and refuse to go on like this anymore. (My goodness.) I can't believe this man has the same affect on me after all this time.

Even though I've had several men before, he's the one to take my love, use my love, and jail my love. This kind of love is a first time thing for me. The pleasure I feel when his body touches mine, isn't compatible to any other man I've been with. These feelings I can say without a doubt I've never felt from anyone else before or since. He's the one I love and can't and don't want to forget. With all that said, even when I'm pissed, I'd give him anything he desires, even though he's still married to someone else.

Whether or not he'll leave Jenny isn't a priority for me anymore. That never stopped him and me before and it won't stop me now. I just want more of him. Right now his marriage is just a piece of paper.

My job is to keep him happy and keep his heart on me and with me. Have him so happy that when he leaves to go home it'll be because he has to and not because he wants to. I'll still give him everything I think he's not getting at home. And I'll still tell him everything he wants to hear.

He'll remember why he's with me and has been for all these years. Jenny gets everything she wants and she's still telling him to give her more. I on the other hand have been taking what I get and showed him how much I appreciate him. Even though I want more, he'll think it's his decision to want to give it after he sees how appreciative I am. This way I know will lead to both of us being happier.

It's time to find something to excite us in the bedroom again; our new year's delight. Not to say our bedtime moments aren't exciting.

But sometimes Dwayne needs surprises where he can enjoy me more. He usually does after seeing how much I'm dedicated to him and all the time I put into us. Show him how much I appreciate everything he does for me, even when I don't think that. I know his home life is probably lacking in that department also so it makes it easier for me.

I also know he enjoys me better in bed because he still wants me. Even when he wants to take breaks he's still sometimes jeopardizing his marriage to be with me when I call. That makes me want to do more for him knowing that also. He won't have to guess how important he is and how much happiness he brings me.

This time of year frightens me since I hear myself sounding like what I think Jenny sounds like. Demanding and not appreciating. He's the best thing for me and it's the little things he does that gives assurance of his love. No one can get my love away from him. He knows whenever he's feeling stressed, he can always count on me to take care of him and all his needs. Now I'm feeling stressed and he should know to come without me asking.

Jenny sits on her fucking throne getting anything and I've worked double shifts sometimes just to survive. She gets up and put in a few hours for the day then acts like she's working her fingers to the bone. Why can't I have that also? He tells me that she does nothing all day. Now I don't know if he was boasting or criticizing.

He said she wants to go back to work outside their home, saying she needs her own independence back. It's not important to me if or when she finds a job because she's only doing it because of her needs and not because he told her to. Let her ass go out there and find out what it's like to have a real job. If I do thing right one day I can have that choice too.

She can keep the ring because that won't keep my ass warm at night and I'll take and keep her husband for myself. Let her walk around showing the ring on her finger and I'll walk around showing my man on my arm.

This morning my phone woke me. At first I thought it was Dwayne texting me but I look and see it's from Jenny. I figure something must have happened to have her texting me this early in the morning or even in the first place. Apart from the party and the pass-by at her house before, I've never had a real conversation with her. I read her text and see that she's upset.

"When I interrupted you and Dwayne by your car window last time you told me nothing was going on between you guys. I see now that you can give him 100 reasons why you're in love with him. Things seem to have changed quite a bit since then."

"Jenny I don't know what you're talking about"

"I said I'd leave my husband if what he told me about the two of you wasn't true. Over the years I've put up with some bullshit and I'm just tired now."

"You have to tell me what you're talking about"

"I'm talking about your text to Dwayne about you wanting him to be with you because your Christmas was ruin without him."

"We were just fooling around, it was nothing"

"Don't you think you should find your own man to fool around with instead of using someone else husband or are you waiting for me to leave him for you"

I wish I could confirm that she's talking about our man. He belongs to me even though he's not married to me. I'll play this game for Dwayne's sake. *"Jenny I don't think that you'd do that and I'm really very sorry about this. We can have a talk after the New Year. He never once denied his love for you though."*

"I'll call you when I calm down to hear what you have to say"

"Jenny I'm sorry for causing any problems between the two of you." (Yah, right. Bitch.)

I know she's too intelligent to believe whatever I say but I'm too smart to say anything different. I know more than anybody how good a man Dwayne is and I know she had a hand in making him that way. Now I have no problems reaping the benefits of her work.

After talking and upsetting myself I need someone to talk to. The only one I can really talk to about anything to do with Dwayne is Beverly so I called her.

"Beverly I don't think you'll believe what just happened."

"Why . . . what happened?"

"Finally Ms. Bitch found something out about Dwayne and me that she can take seriously."

"I guess by Ms. Bitch you mean Jenny. What did she find out?" I can just picture Beverly sitting up in her bed ready to hear the juicy gossip.

"All of the text messages between me and Dwayne. I mean the ones we sent to each other over the holidays."

"How do you know she found them? Did he tell you that?"

"No. She text me messages earlier about them. We agree to meet after the holidays to talk about all of it. I think she just wants to find out more to have against Dwayne."

I hear the high pitch in her voice saying that I'm crazy. "Why'd you want to meet with her? What do you think can come from meeting up with her?"

"I've to tell her that I'm sorry and tell her what Dwayne and I talk about. He and I discussed what I should tell her if this day ever happened, if she ever found out about us."

"I don't think that's your job, it's his."

"You know I've to be the good girlfriend and show Dwayne that I'm looking out for his best interest."

"Whatever."

"I can't let him think that I'd do anything to cause trouble between him and her. Not right now."

"What you mean is that you're going to lie to her about you and Dwayne. So when are you meeting her?" Beverly's curiosity and judgemental voice is still talking.

"Well I'm going to see him at the party later so I'll talk to him about it. I want to double check with him about meeting her and talk again about what I should say."

"I can't see why you have to explain."

"I already told her I'll meet with her next week after the holidays but I can always change my mind if he thinks that I shouldn't meet her."

"Just be careful. I can't tell you not to meet her but make sure you know what you're doing."

"I can't say if it's wise but I want to do it."

"Alright we'll talk later. Let me know what happens after you talk to her. Actually call me tomorrow and tell me what he has to say about it. Have fun at the party."

"Okay, I'll call you tomorrow. Happy New Year."

Now I can get dress for the party. I don't want to look too happy to Dwayne when we talk about what I imagine is going on; especially after I tell him about Jenny's and my conversation. He and I talked earlier and he said he's taking her somewhere, then he'll drop her off at home and meet up with me at the party afterwards.

I'm making sure I have everything I know he likes underneath my dress. I've some sexy plans for him later and I plan to enjoy him while we ring in the New Year together. Knowing that she knows about us excites me. (Holy shit, I'm actually moist.) I guess I want to feel him deep while I imagine her going crazy at home wondering if he's with me.

Every push deeper inside will bring me good thoughts along with my pleasure. I just love the thought of driving her ass mad. She can finally feel what I go through when he's home doing whatever with her.

I'm not at the point where I'm number one but I'm not his secret lay anymore. Now that she knows we're both sharing him, I feel so much better. She might plan to put in some extra effort in their marriage now and I'm definitely not going to ease back and get comfortable thinking I've won. I'm sure she knows I'll be putting in some extra time also; lots of sex. I'm not worried about her, cause I know if she was that good he wouldn't have needed me in the first place.

I keep reminding myself that she's the wife but I'm the one who keeps him happy, and for quite a while now. He stays out with me at nights because he wants me. Even though she gets angry it doesn't make much of a difference. He takes all her cussing then comes to me for my love after.

For an intelligent woman, she should've realized by now that she's just a fixture in his life. She should also have realized that his feelings for her aren't as strong as before. Why else would he be out of the house so much. I think if she admits it to herself then she'll also have to admit that his late nights, involves me.

He loves me but right now he's there because of his kids. I don't think he wants them to feel he deserted his family. I also think that when he says his family comes first, he's really thinking about them. One day he'll stop caring and he'll just say to hell with her and move on; of course I'll be waiting here in the background, smiling.

Evelyn Once Said:

"*If we learn from our mistakes then only those on the outside will think of it as a mistake.*"

Chapter Eight

    I didn't want to get here too early because I was sure Dwayne wouldn't be here yet. I figured my get-ready time along with my drive over should put us here about the same time. But, I got here and again I'm standing at a party alone waiting for him to get here. This is just what I didn't want to happen.

I'm looking around and some might think I'm waiting for someone to walk over and talk to me, thinking that I need someone just to keep me company. I don't feel like socializing with anyone but they don't know that. I feel like I should be home.

I'm only here to please Dwayne. He wanted to come because of his friends. I just want some extra time with him before he came to my house so I came here. If I had my way he'd just leave his house straight to mine and forget about everyone and everything else.

I wouldn't mind having the New Year catching us doing what we'll be doing for the rest of the year; making use of every moment we find together. I wished that it would catch us together making use of whatever time we get, doesn't matter what, as long as we're together.

It's not all about sex with us anymore but if that's what he wants then we can do that too. I can't complain though since he did tell me he had to go somewhere else first but I just didn't expect him to be this late.

I see him just walking in now after an hour of waiting. (Finally.) He sees me and he's looking at me but not moving too fast like he's happy to see me. I smile to let him know I see him. I take a step to go towards him but he doesn't look as anxious as I expect him to be. I take another step while I'm watching him, thinking he'll also walk towards me but he stops so I do too. When I look a few steps behind him, I see Jenny walking in also. (What the hell is she doing here?)

When I talked to him earlier he didn't say anything about her coming with him. I can't try to figure it out on my own and I can't do anything about it right now but he'll have to explain later.

I'm sure he can read my lips motion and see the rage in my eyes even with the people between us. (What the fuck.) What happened or what it means, he sure as hell must explain to me later. I'm not happy to see her here and this is not the way I wanted to start my year off; fucked up.

I understand that he can't say anything to me while Jenny's standing beside him watching his every move but I wish he could. I can see he's trying to ignore me but I'm desperate to have him acknowledge me somehow. I'm trying my best to keep my composure and not make him feel uncomfortable and I guess he figured it out when I see a text message from him telling me to relax and he'll explain later.

Even though he sent me the text it's not doing anything to stop me from being angry. I'm assuming he told his friends who're here by themselves to keep me company since a couple of them are very attentive; getting me drinks. I also notice they're talking and passing time with me more than they had in the past. He probably wants his wife to see someone else paying me some attention, that way she'll think the text messages she saw on his phone are us just fooling around as we said.

I'm pissed because she showed up but I'm more upset because this is supposed to be my time with him. She had him all through the holidays. I don't want to be here and I should leave but I just can't. I want to see what he does with her and if he can get any time to talk with me.

It's torture watching them together. Jenny keeps holding on to him as if she's trying to tell me something; that he's hers. (I can't handle this shit anymore. I need to get the hell out of here and go home.) I want to cry but I can't. It's too much for me to handle. I've to leave instead of agonizing myself any longer.

This anger is making my stomach hurt. My heart is racing too much. I'm so disappointed. Now I step outside and must deal with these tears and I can't stop them. I can't control my emotions and I must go home to face my loneliness.

Last night I came home and I barely got any sleep. This morning Dwayne called me bright and early to see if I'm alright after what happened at the party. He explained that Jenny decided at the last minute she was going with him and he couldn't say no after what happened with the text messaging.

He said he wanted to call but didn't get a chance since Jenny was with him everywhere he went. I believe him because I was noticing the way she was acting at the party. I knew then that she was trying to tell me something. Her actions were like a billboard claiming a product.

I guess I'll know more about what's going on in that head of her after she and I meet. I don't really know why I'm meeting with her since I've nothing much to say but I also can't tell myself not to. This will convince Dwayne that I'm okay with this whole shit, even though I'm not. I'll tell him about the meet with her when I see him later today but I still have days before she and I meet.

* * *

Last week when I told Dwayne that Jenny and I plan to meet he wasn't too happy; a bit nervous. I got here and we took a corner table so we could talk without anyone disturbing us, even though the restaurant isn't very busy. She's acting as if she's not in the long conversation mood but just wants to get to the point.

I tell her that the first time I came to her house Dwayne and I were just friends and nothing more. I know he won't leave her for anyone and I must make sure she understands that I know that. I've to also let her know that we're friends and that's all since I have no plans of getting involved in a 'dead end' relationship.

I tell her if there's an attraction that's all there'll ever be to it. I also let her that it's something Dwayne and I talked about and decided if we're going to be friends then it can never go beyond that. Telling her both Dwayne and I agreed. I'm making sure she understands that the night she saw us by my car that there was nothing happening, that we were just fooling around and nothing beyond that.

I'm trying my best to ease her suspicious mind and I think her body language says she believes me. (I hope I'm reading her right.) I'm trying all I can to get us out of this but she's not making it easy. Asking about things that happened that I'm not prepared to talk to her about and she actually cornered me a few times. I decide to try and gain her trust as much as I can so I said I'll truthfully answer any question she asks me, which is a lie.

"Jenny, I know you have no reason to trust me but I'll answer as honestly as I'm able to."

"How long ago did both of you started this relationship?"

"We both cared very much for each other but it's not like you're thinking."

"What do you mean it's not what I'm thinking? How would you know what I'm thinking!" I didn't expect her to raise her voice.

"I fell in love with Dwayne but he never told me he was in love with me."

Even thought I won't let Dwayne know about this part of our conversation, I tell her that we made the mistake once and it never happened again. I tell her that he and I talked about it and decided if we're to stay friends it can never happen again and we kept our promise.

I want her to understand that whatever's happening between Dwayne and me is nothing, we're friends. I tell her that Dwayne was so upset that he could do anything like that to hurt her and he would die if she finds out. I also said that because Dwayne loves her so much he would die if he knew that she knows anything like that.

I'm trying everything possible to convince her that Dwayne's not doing anything to wilfully cause her pain. Let her know that because I don't want to lose his friendship I wouldn't do or try anything to change that. Nothing I say is stopping her anger though, but is calming her enough to continue our conversation. I actually thought she was going to get physical a few times.

"So you're saying that you're in love with my husband?"

"I feel ashamed to admit it but, yes I am. I didn't plan for this to happen but it did."

"Is he in love with you?"

I let her know I can't answer that but from what I see, no he's not. "I doubt he knows how I feel since we stay away from that kind of talk. The messages were just us joking. It's the first time we ever done anything like that though. Because of what happened in the past we were making fun of it all and it was like him teaching me the things to say when I find a man of my own. It was like role playing. Both our heads were in the wrong place in the wrong frame of mind before but we're back where we should be now; just friends." Nothing I say will stop her from questioning me about mine and Dwayne's feelings.

"He never said he was in love with you?"

I'm trying hard to let her know that there's no emotional connection coming to me from Dwayne and she has nothing to worry about where he's concerned.

"Right, I'm sure. Things can't get any worst so you don't have to lie to me."

I can see that she's not comfortable with this. I don't think she's really interested in my feelings but she's trying to find information on Dwayne's.

"Listen Jenny. I had some bad experience with men and relationships in the past. When I met Dwayne the last thing I was thinking is how I'd be hurting anyone."

"I can see that."

"We became friends and I told him about my past relationships. He became very supportive and it went from there."

"That's a big jump from friends to sex partners."

"Jenny, it wasn't like that." The last thing I want is for her to keep thinking of Dwayne and me as sex partners. "I found out that you and Dwayne were having your own problems at home."

"He told you we were having problems?"

"No. He didn't come out and say that but if things were that good at home he wouldn't be out so much."

"Are you a therapist too?"

"No, but it didn't take much to figure that out."

"I see."

"I gave him the attention that he needed and we both started to depend on each other for comfort."

"I see."

"Jenny you can stop saying 'I see' and take me seriously. None of this was planned; we were just venerable and it happened. It's not happening anymore so we'll just leave it at that."

"Excuse me! We'll leave it at that! Excuse me!"

"I didn't mean it that way but I came here out of good faith. To make you see that it's not what you think."

"No. You came here to play and convince Dwayne that you're good. I'm not fooled by your crap. It's taking too much out of me right now not to put this fork through you. You would think that it's because you're sleeping with my husband but you would be wrong."

"I'm not sleeping with your husband."

"Whatever. If I hurt you it would be out of anger because you're trying to take me for a fool. But I'm not going to lower myself just to satisfy my anger."

We didn't talk much longer before she stood up to walk out. At the end of our conversation she said something about some Karma crap then left. I even apologised again before we left to show her how sorry she should think I am.

I know about karma but I'm not thinking about that right now. The only intension I have right now is to live my life the best way I can. To enjoy it with whomever and doing whatever I can when he wants me.

I told her I'm sorry and I am sorry for hurting her, but I can't honestly say that I'm sorry for sleeping with her husband when he's the only enjoyment I have. I did my best to put her mind at ease and it's her problem if it didn't work, but it's also my gain if it doesn't. I don't really care if she wants to make life at home miserable for Dwayne because I know he'll use me for refuge. All I know is this should show Dwayne that I can play the game how he wants me to.

* * *

It's been days since my meeting with Jenny and I expected to hear from Dwayne but I haven't. I called him but he can't talk. Said he'll call me back a little later, as soon as he gets a chance.

I want to talk to him about what Jenny and I said to each other even though I haven't decided how much to tell him yet. The last thing I want is to tell him anything to upset him and I know if I say I admitted to sleeping with him once it will definitely piss him off.

The reality of it all is sinking in and he'll have to face that I've become a true part of his life. She should know that I'm here whether she wants me to be or not. Even thought I told her I'm stepping away from Dwayne, I know I'll be in the back of her mind every time he leaves their house. Whenever she doesn't know where he is, I'll be her first thought; that I've no problem with.

Dwayne and I, we're a couple and even though we're not married it doesn't mean we're not together. It hurts me like hell when he's with her; thinking she's getting what's mine. The more I think about it the more I want to know why my messages were still on his phone for her to see. He's finally calls me back.

"Hi Sandy. Told you I'd call you when I can. So what happened in your meeting with Jenny?"

"First, why'd you leave my messages on your phone for your wife to read them?"

He doesn't sound like he thinks he needs to defend himself. "Jenny never read anything on my phone before so something must have happened for her to do that."

"But you still didn't answer why you left them on your phone."

"Guess it's my way of keeping you close."

Sometimes I can't tell if he's joking or if he's serious. I'm smiling but still I know this time he's saying that to stop me from asking. "Dwayne if we spend more time together then you'd hear everything I've to say in person instead of reading them off your phone all the time."

"Baby let's not go through this again. That's why we've gone this long without Jenny finding out."

"Dwayne when we started I told you it was just sex but things changed and I need you with me baby. I love you so much that I'll do whatever you want me to do so we can be together." I just told him I love him. (Holy shit. Is he going to say it back? Say it the way to make me feel he's in love not just love me.)

All these years he keeps telling me how much he care for me and that he loves me, but never just come out and say it with emotion or without hearing it first. It sometimes makes me feel like it's a response instead of a feeling. Now who knows how he's feeling with everything going on.

"I'm trying too baby. What did Jenny want from you?"

"She told me that she found messages between us that made her believe that we're sleeping together."

"What did you tell her?"

"I told her what we talked about. I told her what you told me to say in case she ever found out. I told her we were just fooling around and that it didn't mean anything."

"What did she say when you told her that? Did she believe you?"

"I think that she did, especially after I told her that I was sorry and that it wouldn't happen again."

It seems like that's the only thing he wants to know. I guess Jenny didn't confront him about what I said; about us sleeping together once. That means I don't have to say anything to him. He's telling me he must go back to work now.

"OK, I'll call you later. I've some work I've to get done now."

"Dwayne wait!" I've to tell him in case she tells him later. "I also told her that I'm in love with you but that you're not with me. (Why won't he tell me he loves me too?)

"Why the hell did you tell her that!"

"I thought that she might believe me more if she thought I wasn't holding back."

With all I've said to him and telling him I love him he only heard the part about me telling Jenny I love him. "Alright, we'll deal with that later. Bye Sandy."

* * *

Dwayne seems like he's staying away from me. Since we talked about my meeting with Jenny he hasn't called me back the way he said he would. I knew he would be pissed but not this pissed. I expected him to come over to see me by now. When I called him last night he was already on his way home and couldn't turn around so he said he would stop by sometime today.

It's likely he'll stop early on his way to work. It's usually easier for him since he needs no excuse for leave the house and in the evenings he's expected at home. I guess he figured that I'm a little upset with him because he hadn't called me in so many days.

In our situation what can I do? I agreed to lay low for awhile to let things blow over with Jenny but he didn't say it would be like this. Not even phone calls. Since this year started I notice that something has changed, it hasn't been as good with him. But that's not the change I was looking for.

I still think it's unfair to me if he expects me to sit by and wait until Jenny decides she's happy before he can make me happy. He should notice how patient I've been with him and how I'm handling the way things are. I've done a good job doing that; and for years now.

I got needs he has to take care of and it's not because I can't find someone else to do it; but because I chose him. Yes I chose to live this way, but not for him to have his way and I don't get to satisfy mine.

I could be with someone else and have him on the side but I won't do that to him or the other person. I'm not like that. He wants me for himself even though I've to share and that's why I should be getting quality time too.

My answer to anyone who thinks that I'm crazy to wait for him is that I'd be crazy if I didn't; even though I complain to myself. I'm not willing to sleep with anyone else or do something to cause me to lose him. I'll continue to remind him that my body needs him more often and he has a job; to take care of it.

By now I'm beyond being disappointed but I'm just going with the flow. I've to tell him about my feelings again. I get tired now when I've to put everything on hold to sit and wait just in case he comes by.

I got up this morning and took my shower after the kids left for school and even with all my complaints I'm here now waiting for him to come see me. I'm in no rush since it's my day off and I've all day. I hear his car in the driveway so I open the door to meet him.

"Hi baby, I can't stay but I wanted to stop by and see you for a minute."

"Dwayne you can't tell me later right now. Look at my body, it needs you right now baby."

"Sandy I know I shouldn't tell you that but I've got a lot to get done today."

"Yes I heard you, but so do I and I'd like to start right now if you let me. I just want to get comfortable."

Before he can say another word I undressed right at the door. He can't say no to me once he sees what's wanting him. I see the smile on his face saying, damn. That smirk tells me I have him.

"Girl do you know what you do to me?"

"I hope so, and I know what I'm going to do to you right now."

"You're gonna be the death of me, you know that."

"I don't want to be the death of you. I just want to be your pleasure."

"Baby I know that you miss me and I miss you too, but right now I'm under a lot of pressure."

"I'm here to relax you Dwayne so let me start. Please baby, relax in me." He can't refuse my baby voice.

I just lean my body up against the wall I open my legs for him to see between them. I want him to see what's missing him. I want him to feel compelled to enter right away. (It's working.)

I take his hand and insert his finger to feel warmth, bringing his smile and my kiss together. I know I don't have too much time before he has to leave and I've to work fast; a quickie. I walk him over to the sofa and I unbuckle his pants. My hand opens and travels in his pant to check if he's feeling the same way I am. My body trembles in anticipation as thoughts about him sliding up invades my mind.

His pants and boxers drops down his legs, stopping at his knees. My body's responding to him and starts to tingles and shake; he can feel my starvation peeking. I use my fingers and slightly tap his chest, telling him to sit so I can mount. (Damn.) I feel my muscles clamping in anticipation even before he enters, my body's attacking like a piranha.

Before he's fully inside, his thrust opens me; slowly taking it's time. I feel the slow motion of the crawl and my greed as usual takes control, forcing me to quickly lift my body and go back down hard. The hungry force is hitting me harder and I feel that touch, him touching, the bottom of my stomach. That familiar touch and my mind take over.

My greed to keep him with me all day is creeping in but my desire to enjoy him in the moment is stronger. My legs are holding on, up and around his hips while I'm enjoying his hold around my body, with every forward and backward movement.

With every thrust he rams my inside and with every stroke my body yells while welcoming the relief that wants to come. My arms grab in confusion trying, reaching to hold on around his neck. His hands holding, securing my hips in place and his face entertains the look of joy my body is now about to bring it, setting the rush in motion, such pleasure. I feel the earthquake while I float. And the ecstasy that surrounds us while I bounced, causing my tilt, my back bow. Arc. Refusing to lift me any more. My inside pulsates.

Such little time, but enough to weaken our bodies while his muscles hold me firmly as I milk him dry. I feel my senses succumbing to blissful gratification crawling to my toes, leading to the rest of my body. His body reacts to mine, releasing with a heavy moan as he tightens his grip; hugging my waist. My arms tightening around his neck, keeping my body in the right place for him as if we're plugged into each other.

Every inner wall in me pulsate while I feel his splatter at the top of my inside splashing. I feel the release seeping around inside trying to come out after we've squeeze the strength from each other.

We both relax on the sofa after my body adjust to coming from its high and I release my grip from his neck after a while. My legs feels well used and need to regain some strength before we carefully ease our bodies to separate them from each other. As I ease up he helps lift my hips off and he slowly exit and his juices follows.

After we cleaned up a little, we take a few more minutes to talk about the past few weeks. I want to remind him about his responsibility to me and satisfying my needs. I remind him that I've no one else in my life and if I can't see him, I get lonely. He needs to remember that he must make time for me, without me having to ask; and not just when his wife's schedule gives him permission.

"I know baby and I won't let it happen again. I'm sorry."

"You know how I feel when I don't see you and it's because I love you. I know how things are but you should also know how things are for me too."

"I know and I love you too but we still have to be careful. It won't happen again, I promise."

After hearing what he just said I don't care that he has to leave. I'm happy to hear those words and I'll be good for the rest of the day. After a few more minute of talking, he left to go to work.

He'll be thinking about me all day and he won't take long to come back for more after this reminder. I think about him every minute of the day so I'd love if he does the same about me. I sometimes wonder if I were one of those married women, would I be as anxious as I am to be with my husband all the time. From what I'm feeling I think the answer is yes.

Verona J. Knight

Evelyn Once Said:

"For some, heartbreak is an addiction. They keep falling for the same kind as the one they left and who they said were no good. Next time you start falling, catch yourself."

Chapter Nine

The past month has been good. Dwayne's trying and I appreciate his efforts. Jenny is still at him about me and the fact that after all this time she still is, shows he's happy with me as much as I am with him. I feel good; he's not giving in to her.

I'm going to my cousin, Monica, for dinner this evening. Bunch of the girls are meeting there to have a lingerie party and we usually make it a girl's night with dinner and drinks. Every other month or so all the girls get together to see new ideas in the sex circle; creams, toys, or anything else new. We all try to keep up-to-date so we can keep things interesting in the bedroom; keeping our men from straying. I took a shower then got dressed and left for Monica's.

I got here and only a few of the girls are already here. Monica and I head to the kitchen to take a few minutes and catch up on each other's goings on. We talk briefly about mine and Dwayne's life and then on to hers. She tells me about her marriage and complains about getting bored with the routine.

She and Dave got married about six or so years ago but Monica was always a spontaneous person. I personally think she got married too soon after meeting Dave but it was her choice. About a year ago Monica ends up meeting someone else and her life changed severely.

I know she loves Dave and have no intention of leaving him but Sean seem to fulfil her sexual needs more than he does. Sean is also married and always tells how much he loves his wife but there's something missing. For now Monica also seems to be what he needs.

All these married men are having fun finding something away from home. Whatever they think is missing at home they look for it somewhere else, all the while saying how much they love their wives. Because both Monica and Sean have a life away from each other they think they have the perfect relationship.

Monica and I are in the kitchen and since we're still alone, I started questioning her about Sean. "Sean and I are good for each other."

"Monica, I know you already know that he's not leaving his wife. I also know that doesn't matter to you since you've no intentions of leaving Dave either. I hope you gave serious thought about people getting hurt later though. And when I say people I mean your family."

"We're both happy to be married to the people we're married to but we find something in each other that they can't give us."

"Something I wonder about a situation like yours. I know you love Dave but apart from pushing him away aren't you afraid he might find out."

"No. Sean and I have the same to lose if any of our other half finds out, so each of us is as careful as the other."

"Do you love him, I mean Sean? Do you love him enough to take that chance?"

"Yes I love him and he loves me in our own way. We're in love with our lives, with our marriages but right now we just need each other to complete our happiness."

"I just worry about you."

Hearing her say that makes me wonder if Dwayne is thinking the way they do. Is he in love with his wife and have me on the side to complete his happiness?

"When he and I get together we just do things he can't do with his wife and I can't do with Dave. Well I should say things I don't want to do with Dave. Sometimes doing certain things makes some people feel uncomfortable."

"I know you and you were never afraid to speak your mind."

"Speaking my mind is so different from going to your man saying I'm bored with him. I enjoy being a freak but that's not how he sees me. Don't want to think every time he looks at me he sees a freak. He expects me to act a certain way so I stay that way."

"I guess you tried doing some of it with him, with Dave?"

"You really think I'm telling Dave my freaky fantasies for the bedroom."

"I can't see why not. You should give him a chance and find out. You've been married long enough for him to know that about you."

"Sean and I have the same fantasies and we fulfil them with each other."

"Girl, just remember that there aren't too many good men out there and you have one who loves you. Don't make the same mistakes some of those other women are making only to find your marriage lonely and you all alone later on in life."

"Sandy don't worry. I've got it all under control."

"Believe me. It's not hard to find someone out there he can get to fulfil his unknown fantasies. And might even be some of the same fantasies you didn't give him a chance to share. The way you're doing it means that you'll never know because you don't give him the chance."

"Sandy stop. Stop worrying about me and worry about Sharon. Now her situation is hopeless."

"What you mean? Did something else happen that I don't know about?"

"She had that idiot she's sleeping with moving clothes and other shit in her house."

"With her kids in the house?"

"Try not to say anything to her yet but talk to her later. I tried to talk some sense in her but she won't listen to me. She's just messed up right now and won't listen."

"I know. She convinced herself that he'll leave his wife and stay with her. He's probably doing that to convince her that he's serious about her."

With everything my sister been through, the last thing she needs now is that asshole playing with her mind. She's so gone that she can't even think, much less to think straight. Sometimes I just want to hit the shit out of her so she can listen to whatever advice we give her, but she's grown. We can't force her to leave him.

"Sandy I know that no sensible man will leave his family for someone with so many kids and none of the kids are his."

"I tried to tell her that but it was useless. She doesn't even want to touch the subject."

"I guess I shouldn't tell you that she might be pregnant again. This man is living two lives and getting away with it."

"I don't know where to start when it comes to Sharon. She needs to wake up and realize that this man is getting free sex and because he knows she's desperate, he know it won't take him much to win her over. I can't believe she can be so stupid."

"An understatement."

"You know what? I can't deal with her and her shit right now. I'm here for a party so let's leave it at that."

"Yah, the rest of the girls are here anyway so let's get started. We'll deal with her shit some more later! And try not to say anything about the pregnancy yet." Still talking to me while she's walking away from me.

"K"

Everyone's excited with what we're seeing. All the women seem pretty eager to please their man in the bedroom; the orders are coming in like crazy. We talk and joke about some of the items but all in good fun.

These are the people I can feel comfortable around and we're able to open up about our sex life and ideas to each other. I see a few things I can make good use of so I place my order also. I've all intentions of using them the right way. (Dwayne will love these for sure.)

The party is going on and too many times I find myself thinking about my sister. How the hell does she manage to put herself in the same situation with the same kind of man like all the others? The same mistakes using different men. In my heart I know it'll only bring her more pain.

Yes, it's with a different person and different circumstance but the end result is always the same. Of all the men she's been with, there hasn't been one good one. She had her first child way too young and by the time she got to her mid-thirties she has seven kids and no support or a man of her own. They all had their way with her and they all left her with kids.

There are many women who had their first kid young but didn't keep going back. There are also some with many kids but had a stable relationship in there somehow. She had or did neither.

If all these men leave after a while then she must be the one with the problem. She knows how to get them but for some reason she has too much trouble finding what it takes to keep them. That sounds terrible coming from me as her sister but she just won't keep her frigging legs closed.

Somehow she keeps forgetting about birth control which only shows her stupidity every time she gets pregnant. I can only pray that one day she'll wake up and live for herself and her kids without thinking she needs a man beside her.

My evening with the girls was great. I came home to get some well needed rest. Lately I've been losing too much sleep and feeling tired more than usual. All the drama with Jenny along with trying to keep Dwayne happy is draining the hell out of me. Hopefully it won't last too much longer.

With all that's going on, I'm also neglecting my kids and that I was too busy to see. They need my time more and I haven't been giving as much as I should and I've to do something about that too. I've made Dwayne my life and I'm realizing it now but I'm convinced that it's gonna be worth it in the long run. Anyway, it's too late to think negatively or give up now; he already owns my heart.

The kind of thoughts that makes me happy also forces me to find things to keep things interesting. I'll never allow Jenny to get ahead of me with the sex games. I've never had so much fun having sex before and I don't think he had either. I didn't find my kids' fathers worth the effort. Over the years, I've learned a few new things from other men I've been with which he knows all about. He doesn't seem to mind so I'm happy.

He's not worried about how many men I've had in the past just that he's the only one now. As things are right now, I've had no desire to go back and try any of my learnt lessons with any of them neither.

Dwayne is different and I look forward to seeing his face when we try new things; I really look forward to it. If I don't have his heart and mind, I'm sure about having that piece of muscle I own. He just keeps it between his legs for safe keeping.

The things I do will make him think twice before he entertains the thought of leaving me. I bring excitement to his life that he's missing with his wife. Everything I've done, has been all about keeping him happy and in the process I also do it for me so I can feel wanted.

Some days I say it doesn't matter if he leaves her and some days it's all I can think about. On those days all I do is plan for the day we end up together permanently. That's when I'll make sure he never has any reason to say he's sorry for making that decision to leave her.

I got a few things at the party last night that I didn't have to wait to have delivered. I called Dwayne to come over but he already made plans with Jenny and couldn't come right away. He said he'll come by and see me tomorrow. With all the time we spend together, those text messages she found still have him on edge and he tries to always think about staying safe.

I thought the explanation I gave her when we had our little meeting would've put her mind at ease but almost every time I call to see him, I hear tomorrow. Before, all I had to do was pick up the phone and he'd be here. Sometimes I didn't even have to call because he wanted to see me as much as I did him and ended up calling me first.

    A little while ago Dwayne called back to say he'll stop by tonight instead of tomorrow after all. I thought about telling him he couldn't stop because I already made plans, but I changed my mind.

Even though he didn't say, I keep thinking he's coming because Jenny changed her mind. It would be nice to think he's coming because he truly wants to spend time with me after all. I suddenly feel like I'm the 'just in case' for him. I'm the one waiting just in case he has nothing or no one better to see. Overwhelmed. (When did I come to this?)

I'm here to please him just in case nobody else is available. Even with all these thoughts running through my mind, I'm still standing here looking through my window pretended I'm fine. (Sometimes I even confuse myself.) I see him in my driveway so I meet him at the door. He sees that I'm not looking as happy as I usually am to see him. I guess I'm not as good at pretending as I've been in the past and without thinking, I hear my sarcasms taking over.

"I thought you're gonna be busy tonight with the misses?"

"What? You don't want me here?"

"That's not what I said. All I ask is one question. You get mad if I talk to another man and then you tell me you can't be with me because you have to do things with your wife. Now you come to me when you've nothing better to do. How do you think I should feel?"

"Listen Sandy, I'm here to spend some time with you. You complain when I don't come and now I'm here you're still complaining."

"Like hell I'm complaining. Dwayne I'm just saying I don't like feeling as if I'm not important in your life. I need to feel special too."

I think I hit a nerve. "I spend time with you that I should be spending with my family! I sneak around to see you! I lie to my wife about our relationship! What the hell more do you want from me so you can feel special?" Yelling at the top of his voice like he thinks I'm deaf. I know that what I said can't make him this mad. What the hell happened before he got here?

"Yes I know you do all that but let's get this fucking strait, you do it for yourself too! I'm not the only one getting something from this relationship! I do everything to make you happy, so I'm going out of my way just as much as you!"

I'm tired of this shit and I'm not backing down again. It's time he face the fact that I'm here because he needs me too. I do more for him than he does for me since all his sneaking around is to satisfy his sexual needs also. I'm the one doing what his wife can't.

"You're starting to sound like you're my fucking wife! If I want to hear all this I can go home! What the fuck do you think this is?"

"You should be here taking care of my business at nights instead of being home digging into that pussy that you're tired of, just to make her feel good. And when she doesn't satisfy your wants you come running, expecting me to open up without complaints and just enjoy."

"So what? You're the one that wanted to start this and at the beginning you said you had no expectation."

"Well I've been doing that for too long now and I'm putting an end to it. You've to start treating my crotch like it's important since it's the one you crave and the one keeping you happy."

"Let's just get this shit strait! I come here because we both want this! I don't come because I don't want my wife but because I don't have to explain to you about my life!"

"I'm sure when you're fucking me you're not thinking about her but when you're climbing on top of her, you're probably thinking about me while you're doing her!!

"If it makes you feel better to think like that then go right ahead, feel free. You just know that I don't have to explain anything to you about mine and my wife's relationship."

"You're so wrong Dwayne! You think because I love you so much I should take all your bullshit! I already know you're not leaving your wife and I've accepted that but you need to treat me better than just your sex treat. This isn't sex therapy and I'm not just the cure for your hard-on moments."

"Do you know how many times I've argued with Jenny because of you? I told her I stopped talking to you when I haven't. Do you know what'll happen if she finds out?"

"Maybe that's what should fucking happen then."

I know I don't mean it but it just came out. I'm just being sarcastic but he's taking it the wrong way. This won't turn into the 'I feel fuckish so I'll call Sandy for a treat' syndrome.

"What the fuck did you just say? If you make that happen then it'll be the biggest mistake you every made and you'll be so damn sorry! When you came into this you knew what to expect! You also knew that I wasn't going to put my family second and you first and you were fine with it, so why now!"

"Your wife doesn't know how long we've being sleeping together? What would happen if she finds out how long you've been lying to her? How much longer do you think I should go on like this? You keep fucking up and expect me to take it with a smile! No fucking way, no more!"

His nose flares and his eyes open wider than I've ever seen before. "Are we going there?"

"You've been doing this to me for too long now. I think we're at the point where we both expect more from each other."

"Fine! Lets talk! You want to talk? Lets talk!"

I need to calm down some. "You know I love you but I need you to act like you need me as much as I do you. And stop fucking around with my emotions."

He takes a deep breath, puts his two hands together as if praying, and relax his shoulders before talking. "I do need you and you should know that." He takes my hand to lead me where I can sit as we both calm down.

"Well I don't feel it from you except when we're in bed together and that's not fair to me Dwayne."

"Sandy you know that I love you. I try to take care of you the best I can right now. It's not a matter of how or when, I still do. The day you feel you want someone else is the day we call this quits."

I don't want to fight so I try to stay calm. "I never said I wanted someone else. I said I need you to want me more and to make me feel like an important part of your life; to make me feel important and not just when you're in my bed." We're both calm now and can talk without the screaming.

"Just think about what I just said to you." He picks up his keys and head for the door. "I'll talk to you later. I'm going home to get some rest." He holds on to the door handle and look back at me. "You should also know this, and listen to me carefully. What you give me I can get from any other woman out there but I chose to be with you. You or any other woman can't give me what my wife gives me at home. So if you think that you're one of a kind, think again." I jump up and open my mouth to say something but he stops me. "I'm not getting in another screaming match with you. Many like you're out there but I chose you. In my eyes, that's special enough and I don't want to hear any more shit from you about this."

I can't believe he just said that to me. Is he serious? "You fucking asshole!" I don't care that he's bigger than I am. I'm still up in his face even if it means yelling at his chest. "You think you're the only one who wants some of this? I chose to sit and wait on your ass so in my eyes that's special enough for you to treat me special" My neck's straining to see his face instead of his chest. "I shouldn't have to ask you to come to me; you should know your fucking job."

"If you feel the need to give it to someone else who wants it, then be my guess. If you want to turn yourself into a whore for everyone feel free. But as long as your ass is mine, you'll keep it quiet and get the fuck off my back about not doing what you think I'm not doing."

"You think you're gonna talk to me like that and I do nothing. You think I'm not tired of this shit also. Get the fuck out my house! Fuck you!" He opens the door and slams it behind him as he leaves.

With all that I've done for him I can't believe he had the nerve to talk to me like that. He left me with an overwhelmed feeling of loneliness. He's the only man I've allowed to basically do anything he wants to do with my body, to come to me any time he needs me.

I don't even look at other men anymore and he has the nerves to talk down to me. I know what I am and he has no right talking about me like I'm anyone out there. Describing me like a commoner he picked up off the streets. Not right. Let him go home to that dead pussy he's been fucking for too many years and that should remind him of why he's coming to me.

I've never felt so alone before. I can't see any reason for him to talk to me like that before he left. All I want is some attention without feeling I'm forcing him to give it. He's not anxious to see me the way he used to and I know his wife is on him about me again.

I get tired of trying to figure out what's going on with him but I want to know. For some reason he's acting like I'm the one stressing him and for what reason I don't know. I'm so confused about this whole shit. (Am I losing him?)

I can't think of anything I could've done to bring him to this point. No matter what, he always felt free talking to me about anything. Now I'm curious to know what changed between us or whatever is making him unhappy. I need to know if I'm the cause and how to fix whatever it is.

Evelyn Once Said:

"*If you don't want to be alone don't look for the perfect partner, look for your equal.*"

Evelyn Once Said:

"Only the strong has to struggle to move forward. The weak stand still and watch the strong with their struggle and ask why bother."

Chapter Ten

I woke up this morning still crying. I didn't sleep much last night. I was busting my brain all night thinking and still can't come up with any good reason for Dwayne's behaviour. All I can do now is give him some time to think about what happened and the awful things he said to me.

If I don't hear from him soon I'll call to find out what I did. (My head is killing me.) Because I was crying I couldn't feel relaxed enough to get any rest, and I still can't. My body and mind just can't find a comfortable space. Every time I dozed off last night, I woke up with the same thought; trying to figure out what caused the argument.

Waiting for what seems like forever to hear from Dwayne isn't what I want to do today. I can't even call him right now so I'll have to wait until later. He won't take my calls when he's still at home. He doesn't take any chances for his wife over hearing any of our conversations. If I need to contact him in the mornings, I let the phone ring once and hang up. He'll know it's me and call back as soon as he leaves his house for work.

Sometimes he leaves home earlier so he can call me back because he doesn't know if it's an emergency. I usually wait until he's out of the house to call if it's not important. Talking to him then will give us more time to talk at ease.

His schedule usually stays the same and if it changes he lets me know as soon as possible. If I send him a message now I probably won't hear from him until later and that's if he's not still upset.

Most mornings he calls before he heads out to check up on me and since I haven't heard anything yet, I don't know which it is. Because it's the weekend he might be staying home all day also. When he's home all day he usually find a minute to send me a message just to check up on me. Sometimes he tells me he sends it just because he can't hear my voice.

I think back to when I could contact Dwayne anytime without worry. Now we communicate by text messages and he erases them after so they won't be on his phone for Jenny to read; he learned his lesson. Now, my calls shows up unknown on his phone so he can always say it's a business call. If Jenny is close by he calls me by a man's name so I'll know that she's close to him and it also can confirm to her that it's business. After, he pretends he's going to the meeting or to see his friends and come to me instead.

I'm still tired from last night and my eyes are a bit swollen from crying. Sharon dropped by earlier and commented on how I look but I told her I had a fight with Dwayne and was very upset but it's nothing to worry about. The truth is that I'm really scared for myself now.

I'm starting to see that in the long run, nothing good can come out of this. I'm going to be the one getting hurt the hardest too. If he hasn't left his wife already then I'm only dreaming but I can't walk away; just in case. At this point I just can't help myself anymore. I need him and I've tried to walk away from my feelings but now it's just too far gone.

Dwayne knows I'll do whatever it takes to keep him and after the things he said, I see now that he's using it against me. I thought that was enough for me but I need more than just sex from him and the time we spend together is getting less, I doubt it'll happen like that again. I'm at the point now that even when I'm at work I can't get much done. I'm just doing what I need to right now until I get to where I want to be.

I stressed myself so much but now Dwayne calls to tell me that he's sorry. I was happily surprised. I'm happy he called me before I did him because it shows that he was thinking about what happened last night as much as I am. He said he feels badly about the things that he said and wanted me to know. He thought about it and wants to apologise to save me the stress.

I'm just happy to hear him so I accepted his apology. He's stopping by later and when he does I'll stay away from talking about last night. I just want some stress free time.

All I'm doing is making plans for when Dwayne comes later. I'm also trying to figure out what to do about my shitty position because even though he apologized, I still can't forget the things he said. But I'll try to work through it.

I called a few friends to pass the time and ease my mind while I waited on him to come, then I made something for us to eat. As soon as I stepped out the shower I heard the phone. It was him calling again to make sure I'm home and not long ago I heard his car outside.

I've been standing here looking through my window, watching him sit outside in his car for a few minutes now and he's finally coming inside. I'm just thankful for my parents that I can drop my kids off at the last minute most of the time.

    While we're eating I tell him I don't want us fighting like that again and he agrees. We also agree that we won't mention it again tonight. After we finish eating I suggest we go up stairs to relax and get comfortable. There we can lay in bed and talk and enjoy our evening together like a couple.

My feelings are still hurt but all I can think about are ways for us to make up. I want us to remind ourselves of what we mean to each other. I believe him when he says that he loves me. He proves it by going through all the trouble he does to see me, without complaining. I knew he was right when he said that last night but that doesn't mean his efforts always work.

It would've been so much easier for me if he had said some of the things last night without anger. The same words sound so different when you're angry but he was right about some. That shows my importance and I realize it now. But I still have to accept that he doesn't love me the way he does his wife.

I've loved this man more than I can say and I just want him to love me back just as hard. I know that he loves her but I'm willing to be whatever he wants me to be without him thinking I'm trying to ruin that. It's my heart and not my good sense talking but until I figure things out for myself I've to manage with this. How long I can go on like this, is a puzzle. I just know that right now he's who I need to make me happy.

 As soon as we came to my bedroom my instincts said to continue my plan I had for last night. I want to make him feel good and then we can relax in bed afterwards. It's more important right now what he feels when he leaves and he'll have nothing to give away to his wife. She can take some punishment when he ignores her since I'm sure sex between us is always better than between them. I'm sure that I'm better because the memory of our love making lingers in his mind days after. It's hard enough being the other woman so if I'm not happy why should she be.

He stays with me and when I made love to him I must always go the extra mile and that must mean something. I'm a single woman so I've nothing to lose. I'm still a little upset so I know I won't enjoy him the way I usually do but I'm not letting that interfere with satisfying him. I must concentrate on making him happy and stay comfortable with me, since every couple fights.

I make the first move and kiss his chest since I want him to know that I'm okay now. Then I kiss his lips. He smiles.

"Sandy, I'm really sorry for getting mad at you last night. Jenny and I were going out for her birthday but she went out with her friends instead so I decided to come and spend the time with you. I thought it was a good chance to come here instead of going home. I wasn't in the mood for what happened."

"I'm sorry too Dwayne. I felt so bad that you didn't want to see me because you had to be with Jenny. When you called to say you were coming over I assumed you were coming only because she was the one to change your plans and cause you to change your mind to come and see me. I didn't know what was happening but I felt unwanted."

"I want to make it up to you."

As soon as my body touched the sheets he removes his clothes to give me a better view of what I'm cravings; of what I'm fighting for. I release a quiet sigh. (I think I'll enjoy him after all.) His touch comes with his kisses as they travel the path between my breasts while arresting any bad thoughts from our fight; putting them aside.

He's giving me enough reasons to enjoy his love without any resistance. His touch so pleasurably assaulting my senses and his taste so satisfying to my hungry pallet overwhelms me.

Thinking of how much I need to enjoy him right now, removes any road blocks and the release to my pain allows me to enter in a space that I can comfortably occupy. Each of his touch reminds me why I love him so much. My body upset with my mind for ever thinking of not feeling him again. (What was I thinking? I can never be too upset not to enjoy him.)

The lengthy love making isn't possible right now as I know we both just want to use our bodies to say 'I'm sorry' and our clothes comes off in a hurry. I lay on my back watching him hovering over me and my sensual sigh show the relief that comes again with his entry. The feeling of delight running through me makes every push more intense, sending me in a blissful space.

My heart's forgetting its hurt and is welcoming him joyfully, bringing my thoughts to what's coming. The intensity from the feelings running through me with every push; going back to my arms, legs and head with every pull, is stronger and stronger every time.

The look on his face telling me that his body's feeling exactly what I'm feeling, forces my hands to grab the sheets. The feeling like my body's floating on air attacks; my inside muscles holds on and squeezes with such strangling intensity. His body welcoming each squeeze while it's pulling harder, looking for relief, all while his facial muscles talks; telling me what to do next.

My inner walls are fighting to release every built up feelings inside, to break away into different places. My toes are curling. My body still floating, almost crippling my breathing, sends a crowd of feelings running all over, as like a jail break. His body stiffens, fighting hard to follow mine. With our relief coming at the same time, we both share the sensation travelling, running between us as he slowly accompanies mine without a word said. The feelings crawl through at a snail's pace, as I slowly feel my body easing down back to the sheet that's waiting to save my fall.

The inside walls sending gratification signs, winking continuously. And I feel all the competing senses allowing my pulsating attacks to pull from his body every ounce of splash I feel, running from him and hitting my every wall.

He covers my body with his; resting inside while I enjoy his after kisses on my forehead. My sensitive feet touch the top of his as he accidently touches my foot bottom. The touch sends aftershocks as my inside blink, and my walls contract again and again. His tip shifts as if sliding off the walls. With no more words needed to say 'I'm sorry'. He pulls me closer to his shoulder and we both lie in each other's arms after he eases out and roll to the sheets.

A few minutes later his phone rings and it's one of the guys looking for him. He tells them he'll see them in a little while then he hang up and look at me and smile. We linger in each other's arms, not saying much before he gets dress and kiss my shoulder. He gets his stuff to leave and tell me to go get some rest. No long conversation needed as we both enjoyed his giving and my accepting of this apology. (That felt good.)

* * *

Making up with Dwayne brought me the peace of mind to ease into relaxation. To feel 'rested' the past few days is nice; finally. I felt more at ease this week than I had in days, which made it easier to work a double shift all week. I wanted to go away this weekend with friends but I can see that'll be out of the question. I use to have fun doing that before but lately I find I don't get the chance.

I don't see myself enjoying it as much. And working the long hours seems to get in the way of my already limited time with Dwayne and the kids. I guess it's the price I'm paying for having a married man for my man.

Beverly and I used to spend weekends together sometimes. She's planning to sleep-over here so we can spend some time together later. She seems to be having a lot of free time on her hands lately. Her husband leaves on out of town contracts now and she gets lonely in the house by herself. Maybe we could even take in a movie with the kids. Dwayne usually comes on the spur of the moment but I need to start doing things on my own again.

He knows she's here for the night so it's alright and doing things on my own will tell him that I still have a life without him. It sounds bad that I run anytime he wants me to and I'm getting tired but I'm trying.

Our argument made it clear that I must start looking out for myself and I've been thinking more about that statement about what his wife brings him. Even though I don't bring it up in our conversations, I never stopped thinking about it.

Making time for myself, it'll make him think twice about what I'm bringing to him when I'm not available. I'll also feel better since he'll feel the way I've felt so many times; neglected. Doing this makes me feel a bit more in control and that I'm trying to slowly pull my life back.

I can tell that Dwayne's friends are pressuring him even more about leaving me. They think our relationship has gone on for too long now. In my mind I thought I had passed the mistress treatment stage by now. More and more I've come to realize that he and I as a full time couple will never happen if it hasn't already.

Right now my feelings are even deeper but I'm praying that someday soon I'll have the strength to move on, to find someone for myself. Now even Beverly is also pissed with me for staying this long. She always tells me how hopeless the whole situation with Dwayne is. She even tells me how sorry she is for her part in getting me in this 'so called' relationship as she puts it.

She thinks that I've given up years of my life to him for nothing in return. At first I hoped he would choose me but now the reality of him staying with me indefinitely seems almost impossible.

I knew what I was getting into but I still went ahead and now I can't undo what's already done. The only thing I can do is just keep enjoying what I have until the day I'm able to leave comes along.

Sometimes I get the feeling he's thinking the same things about me. For some reason we both aren't able to leave each other alone.

I'm beginning to think we're both each other's addiction and I think we each bring something special to the other's life. Bringing something that has been missing between us and other relationships and people in our past. Maybe we didn't even know it was missing until we found each other. I just know that I love him with all my heart and until something else happens, nothing else matters to me.

Now I don't even feel stupid. When I think about the things his wife is going through; I just think she's stupid for staying. I can laugh at her since she's the one that looks stupid from my angle or from some others who knows what's going on. Some might even feel sorry for her and she doesn't even know it or why.

Verona J. Knight

Evelyn Once Said:

Best revenge, show no emotion.

Evelyn Once Said:

Good relationships aren't the ones without problems but are the ones where no problem is bad enough to force you to leave

Chapter Eleven

Everything I say now sounds rehearsed. Every time I talk about a future I end up with that familiar feeling, reminding me that I've given up my life. Dwayne already has all of me. I can't help thinking how crazy I am with each thought but I do nothing about it.

Over the past year I've heard from Jenny a few times and I still deny that I still have a relationship with Dwayne, even with all her evidence. As long as I never say yes to anything, Dwayne is happy. He's getting everything he wants and I'm losing myself while I lie about my feelings. He knows how to use me against me. He knows I can't help myself right now; my emotions are ruling me.

Whenever I complain, he talks about breaking up so I run into the panic room and change my mind, then ends up doing whatever he wants me to again. I'm never even sure of his words but I find myself getting panic attacks whenever we have a disagreement. I worry because I don't know when that break-up day's really coming. And even though it might be a good thing, I'm not ready.

How can I give so much of myself and give someone such a strong hold on my emotions. I've never done that in the past and I wonder what would've happened if I'd done it with any of my kids' fathers. I wonder if I'd be with any of them today. My thoughts are haunting me. (Was I stronger then than now? Am I more stupid now not to walk away?)

I've seen him lied to Jenny several times and sometimes I wonder if he does the same with me. Whenever he gets caught in his lies he talks his way out and she accepts it. Am I doing the same?

The night she caught him with his head sticking in my car window he lied right in front of me. Now I'm also a liar backing him whenever he wants me to. Another time he got caught right after we finished having sex and I lied for him. He got caught together several times and I denied that there's anything going on so there's nothing for us to get caught doing. I feel desperate.

I don't even think that Jenny cares if I'm sleeping with him as much as she cares if he's sleeping with me, if that makes any sense. I just mean that I'm not the one hurting her, he is; so his actions are what matters to her. Lie after lie. I told her we're doing nothing that goes beyond just a friendship while I stood there with him draining from my body between my legs. I stood there telling her to move on and not worry about me; all while squeezing my legs together to stop anything from run down my legs.

I do it all because I want to make him happy. I do what I can to make sure she won't find out about anything else. I'm sneaking around and telling lies just for sex.

I accept so much so far. She once said that I should listen how well he lies because after a while even the truth will be lies. He won't know the difference. (Would I know when it's my turn to hear the lies?) She makes me question how loyal he'd be to me if someone else comes along and strikes his interest. (Will he starts lying to me?)

For weeks I kept hearing Jenny's question in my mind. (Would I know?) I'm giving myself to him believing that he's with me and his wife only. If I'm giving and someone else is also getting how the hell would I know? His wife is questioning his behaviour but I know him and what he's capable of. With all the questions flooding my mind, my problem is to find a way without him knowing what I'm doing.

Whenever he's not home or with me I expect him to be with his boys. If he's not in any of those three places I want to know where and with whom. No I'm not his wife, but sometimes I give more that she does and I'm not doing all this work for someone else to come along and reap my benefits.

Sometimes I think back to when we started. I thought and still do, that he's a good man but over the years he has done things that surprised me. Back then I saw someone I had never met. Today I see a combination of what I thought he wasn't and what I thought he was. Since he does it for me it doesn't hurt, but if he starts doing for someone else, I'll make sure he doesn't enjoy it.

He's a good husband and father who work hard and because of that he believes he should be able to do whatever and get away with it. He's different from the men I've known and was involved with in my past. But with what I've been able to get from him and the things I've seen, how much so?

The person that I was then isn't who I am now. I never thought ahead to see that when he got involved with me he'd become a liar. Now to know the extent he goes to be with someone else, me, means my ex might have been not-so-bad. I convinced myself that since it's me, it's alright. I want to believe that he loves me so much that he needs to be with me at all cost.

A while back a few of my friends were talking at our lingerie party about cheating men in general. Some asked questions that I never thought about or ever wanted to hear. One question was, 'if we find out that someone we see as a good man is having an affair, would we see him as a bad person? Would we ignore the good things we used to determine that he's good? If he still does the good things for his family would the cheating wipe out all the good? After that, how would we judge their actions or would we ignore them?'

One of the other women answered saying that she would still see a good man, but with a dirty habit. She would still respect him for how the takes care of his family but nothing beyond that.

Another woman said that 'a good man can't turn into a bad one because he has a crotch weakness.' Another said 'he's just an asshole pretending to be good.'

The one answer that caught my attention, I still think about. 'Whatever good opinion we have of him is just what we're brain wash into believing is so. Our opinion was of the person we thought he was and not about the right person, the real one'.

I didn't have an answer then and can't come up with one now. Am I seeing Dwayne as a good man because I'm the one he's cheating with? Is that why I can tell him that and believe it? If I was the wife I wouldn't think of him as a good man since she's the one left alone when he's with me.

Are the wives calling them the same names we call our former men that hurt us? The men we looked at as bad ones, are they being looked at as good ones through someone else's eyes? I keep asking myself questions that I'm not ready to hear the answers to. I've never look at Dwayne as the type of man who willingly hurts someone; though he cares about his wife and is hurting her.

I believe he loves me so much that he got caught up with sneaking around and became someone else. I think his love for me caused him to lose himself along the way. If he loves me that much, how can I complain?

* * *

I tried so hard to make live between us stay on a good course but others in our lives are trying to make is hard. A few weeks ago Dwayne and I had another fight. I know someone wanted to cause problems between us even though I don't know who. For some reason they told him something about me sleeping with someone else. During the fight, the verbal stones were thrown hard and hurt just as hard.

They must've thought putting doubts in his mind would give him reasons to finally leave me. I was hurt that he believed them over me and we haven't talked to each other since that fight.

Now I've been putting all my time into my work by taking on extra shifts. I'm trying very hard to move on but I miss him so much that my body aches and it's only causing me stress. I don't want to lose him but sometimes I do want to leave. (I'm scared.)

With everything I've been going through, another New Year is coming to find me the same way as the last one. Having a man who doesn't belong to me and one I'm not able to stop loving. It's too much pressure on my heart.

Now I get satisfaction by causing trouble in Jenny's life. Why should her house feel happy when I'm here by myself? After all the time I've put in I still don't have anything. I say I want to end it just so I can sound sensible but it's a lie and I'm still waiting.

I'm just so depressed since all my hopes seem clouded at times. This holiday I've to work on spending time with my family and a few friends. If I survive it without concentrating on Dwayne, then I might be alright after all. But I still have hopes.

* * *

I got to work this morning trying to re-coop from all the excitement over the holidays. I thought about Dwayne every second but I decided not to call just to get my feelings hurt even more. Now I learn that he's belittling our relationship to his friends like I'm just a laugh. Then I find out he isn't saying good things about me to them either.

He's making me sound like a notch on his belt. I was beyond angry when I heard. Telling his friends the only reason he stayed with me all this time is because I'm a good lay. Now I come to work trying to do everything to keep my mind off him and without warning I see a text message.

The last time we had our fight things got so out of control that anyone would think it would get physical. He never touched me but I could see the rage in his eyes when he looked at me. I guess hearing that I cheated sent him over the edge and I guess if he didn't love me so much it wouldn't have mattered. I see the message is coming from Dwayne's phone so I forget about my anger and read them.

"Hi baby, going crazy thinking about you."

I'm so happy after reading what he just said. The first message already makes me feel better. It's been weeks since he and I talk to each other, and even though I told myself that I'll get through without him, I'm having a hard time doing it. I send him a message right away.

"Hi babe, I'm here going crazy waiting to hear from you too. You know how happy I get when I'm talking to you. I need you babe and I hurt when we fight."

"Okay baby, I'm sorry. I don't like it when we fight either. Tell me what you want me to do to make it up to you?" When I read that coming from him it's like winning something. (Finally my feelings will be considered.)

"I don't want anything special, I just want you to love and trust me when I tell you I'm yours only. I do everything you want me to but then you go telling your friends bullshit about me. Why are you telling them that I need sex all the time and that's why you're with me?"

I feel unappreciated when he continues to deny his feelings for me to his friends. I know they wouldn't run to his wife to tell her anything. If they know his feelings they would give me a little respect as his girlfriend.

"Sandy that's not quite how it was"

"Now they're thinking that I'm just a loose woman who goes around sleeping with married men. I don't appreciate that and I shouldn't be put in a position where I've to put up with it either."

Even though I love and want to keep him in my life I also need to take a chance to let him know that. I shouldn't have to worry about him disrespecting me to his friends.

"Sandy, I told you that I'm sorry and I meant it. Now we have to figure out how we can continue loving each other and not hurt each other."

"You know what Dwayne, it's okay. I love you very much but I can't take this bullshit anymore."

The fact that he contacted me shows that he's also unhappy that I'm not around him. Knowing this, I can give him my demands and he'll give in to me.

"No Sandy it's not okay. I've hurt you and that's making me hurt too. Baby I just need to know how to make it up to you."

"Dwayne we've gone through this so many times before. I tell you what I need you to do to make me happy and you do nothing to change things so why try anymore. You're selfish."

"Sandy I'm trying to do my best. You know how things are for us."

"I spend my holiday alone while you're with your wife and family and you have the nerve to accuse me of sleeping around on you. I told you so many times that I belong to you only and you still accuse me of cheating. Do you ever think of how I feel when you're with your wife at nights and what you're doing to her while I'm alone in our bed?"

Does he believe I lie in my bed at night and don't think about what he's doing to her? Does he think I stay in my bed at night and not wonder if he's doing the same things with that bitch as he does with me? Does he think my feelings aren't hurt and I feel no pain from my thoughts? I'd like him to explain to me how he thinks I feel.

"Baby I know that you miss me and I do miss you too. Like I said you know our situation. It's not that I don't know what you're going through. I know that our time together is important to you and I try to spend as much time as I can with you."

"I need to feel like I'm important to you Dwayne and sometimes I don't feel like I am."

"You are Sandy. I love you baby and I get scared when I'm not with you, you'll do something crazy. You know what I'm going through here. How can you say that to me? I just need you to give me some more time."

"Dwayne we're on two different pages here. You keep thinking everything is about me wanting you to leave your wife. I can't tell you what to do about your wife, you must decide if you should leave her but we have to spend more time together somehow."

I'd never come out and tell him to leave his wife but if he decided to do it, I'd have no problem welcoming him as mine. My intent is still to do whatever I can to get as much time with him as possible. I'll be watching where we can go from here but still with my silent hopes. The fact that he's contacting me gives me hope again.

"If I leave my Jenny how do I know that after a while I won't be sorry? Starting over now won't be easy for either of us. How can you make sure I'll be happy with you more than I am with her?"

"Dwayne you know how much I love you. I've told you so many times that I belong to you only. I'll do anything and everything you want so that you can be happy with me. I'm yours and will be yours forever. I love you babe, forever."

I'm getting nervous and my heart is racing waiting to hear what he has to say after my last message but it's taking awhile to come back. I want him to think about what I said and hope that he'll think seriously.

The long pause in our conversation makes me think he'll call me later to talk about us. Knowing that I'm waiting for him to come to me is going to need processing. He knows how much I love him but he's never given me this kind of reason to think it'll happen. Asking me how he'd know if I can make him happy. (Finally!)

I've been waiting a little bit too long now to hear back from Dwayne. Maybe Jenny's there and he can't talk anymore. I can wait until later to hear from him though, but he just made my day. For weeks I've pretended that I didn't care but I was going crazy not talking to him for so long. We've never gone this long without talking to each other because we were mad.

I'm already starting to make plans for us. I know he's missing me so I expect that he'll come over later. That'll be his next move.

We haven't made love to each other in weeks and I'm anxious to feel that. We have a lot of catching up to do. I want to take the lead and tell him to meet me at home later so I'll do that on my next message. Finally his message is coming in now. I guess he finally got away from her.

"I just woke up and I wasn't the one texting you. You were getting text from Jenny before, not me"

My whole body is numb and I want to fall to my knees and hold my stomach. My heart is hit hard, never so hard before in my life. I want to cry and scream at the same time but I can't do that here. How can I handle this now, at work? I can't handle it. I need to go to the bathroom and release the tears that are fighting to come through.

I know if that bitch was close to me she'd get hurt so bad. I don't give a shit that he's her husband. She had me pouring my heart out thinking that I was doing it to Dwayne. All the time she must be laughing at me. I feel like shit right now and I can't do anything about it. I can't believe that witch used his phone to send me messages and had me think that I was getting them from him. Holy shit am I ever hurting right now. (That bitch. I just wanted to fuck her up seriously.)

After Dwayne saw Jenny's hurtful prank, I expected to hear from him but haven't heard anything all day. I waited expecting he would've called me with an explanation about what happened. I think I at lease deserve that much. He shouldn't be so mad that he doesn't care about the hurt he must know I'm feeling right now.

He should know me well enough after all this time and know how I'm feeling. And for him to ignore me like this, I'm finding it hard to deal with. I need to get over him and move on; but how, how?

Reading those words that I thought were coming from him sent my heart back to him right away. The messages reminded me of how much I love him and no praying can help me get over him. All I can do is cry beyond tears and look up to the sky. (Help me.) I'm hurting for him so bad; this pain. (Help me.) I'm hurting real bad.

Evelyn Once Said:

"Faith is when we see the light before the solution; especially in the darkest hours."

Evelyn Once Said:

"Love in every way feels good. The one using your love against you is the one who hurts you. Love doesn't hurt."

Chapter Twelve

I'm still feeling pain from Jenny's prank yesterday. I went to bed with a hurt heart and every time I think that Jenny was the one sending me those messages from Dwayne's phone, tears falls. The messages gave me hopes because I thought he was missing me as much as I am him. When the one real text from Dwayne came telling me he wasn't the one sending the messages before, I felt weak. I wanted to disappear. Just crawl under something and hide from myself.

Now I sit here looking at my phone receiving messages coming in again but from Jenny's phone number. It's the last thing I need this morning. After what she did yesterday she thinks I want to picture her laughing at me again. I know she's sending messages to harass me even more.

I should be the one with words to piss her off. He's her husband but I'm not holding a gun to his head, forcing him to come to me. The length of time we've been together says that he's enjoying me. I've told her before that there was nothing going on, now the text messages yesterday tells her the true story. What the hell made her pretend to be Dwayne sending them?

Any excitement I had is gone and won't come back. It never crossed my mind to think that it wasn't Dwayne. Even the tone of the messages didn't give me a hint. He never talks to me about our sex life unless it's in person because of Jenny snooping but I just wasn't thinking. After those first messages she found to make her suspicious, we stopped taking any chances. I was so sure I was talking to Dwayne. That's why I was so open with all my feelings and said the things I did.

I should've been more careful but I was tricked and I can't say I feel badly that I unknowingly told her everything I have. I'm sure she's hurting now that I confirmed it all. The hurting will come from her disappointment that Dwayne has been lying to her for so long. I'm sure she's more concerned about her husband lying to her than with me.

The things I think are running through her mind right now, gives me comfort. Everything I said should put some pain in that heart of hers. What will give me some gratification, is her reaction when she finds out the extent of Dwayne's friendship with me and how long it's been going on.

Thinking about all of it makes me curious to know what she wants, why she's sending me more messages. I don't want to answer but I might get a chance to gloat after all. I'm too curious not to read them.

"Sorry to ruin your day yesterday. He's not leaving me, so you can continue to be his sperm disposal."

"Never told him to, never asked him to."

"No, you never told him to leave me, you're just waiting and praying while doing whatever you can to make trouble between us to try and make it happen. He tells me I should stop upsetting myself because you're not worth it and now he can't stop begging me not to leave him."

"You can say whatever you want. I don't care what he tells you."

"I do understand that when free samples are given away many will try it, so you can keep giving yours away. After my husband you'll have many more waiting to sample you the way your kids' fathers did."

"You're talking from both sides of your mouth. One day you're leaving him, the next he's your man. I don't call and bother you so please go on with your life. I'm no threat."

I know that Dwayne will hear about this conversation sometime and I won't say what I really want to. This way he'll know how civil I am to her and how disgusting she's been to me. I'll never let him see or hear that I'm disrespectful to her but it doesn't stop me from thinking of her as a bitch that can't hold her man.

"I never thought of you as a threat just as a sperm bank holding my husband unwanted donations. I was planning to leave his ass but for your sake I plan to stick around a little longer. I'll also keep you updated on our love life, bitch. You were never thought of as a threat. Your kind is very common, just a menace like a rodent. You're not able to hold a man of your own so you try to take what's not yours such as other women's husbands."

"If you didn't think of me as a threat why were you sending me text messages, pretending to be him sending them?"

"You're the one telling someone else's husband that you'll love him forever. You drink, smoke and donate your body to other peoples' husbands for them to experiment with. Many would see that as very sad. That speaks of your character. You know what? I won't waste my time fighting with you because you're not worth it."

"Sandy will be fine thanks, please don't worry about me, I'm a big girl."

"I've no doubt that you'll be fine. After my husband I'm sure that you'll have many other women husbands going through you. If you had put the same energy into keeping your baby daddies as you did trying to take away a married man from his wife, you'd have had a man for yourself. Good luck and have a nice lay, bitch."

She has the nerve to be calling me names. She should know that if she was any good he wouldn't be coming to me. She's telling me to have a nice lay. What I wanted to tell her is that I do every time her husband is climbing between my legs. To tell her how he screams my name and not hers when he's in me. I'd like to ask her if she wouldn't like to know how much of a good time he has when his face is between my legs.

Maybe one day I'll tell her just how good her husband works me; especially those times he was suppose to be somewhere else with the guys. And if she didn't think of me as a threat, why the hell did she feel the need to contact me. She's calling me a bitch?

I'm not going to her house to see Dwayne. He comes to see me because what I offer is better to him, not hers. Now she wants to blame me for his straying. He does everything to see me, sometimes without me having to force him. That's what should be telling her something.

All I need to do is pick up my phone and he's ready for me. I should've told her that I'm holding her husband balls in my hands to do with when and what I please. I should've let her know that I'm the one putting life in it so even when she gets some, she should thank me.

I've got more control over him than she does. Everything I told her should prove to her that he loves me more. Let her get angry because that'll send him to me. I'm sure he'll be calling me soon after he hears what she's up to. Without knowing, she may have just done me a favour.

I remember Dwayne coming to my house one night with a bottle of wine. Before we made love that night, I laid my naked body down and he dripped the wine on me slowly and sipped. I remember lying on my back and feeling the wine streaming. The wine was chilled and my body was warm from the shower I had just taken. Remembering the way that man drank the wine while it ran off, damn, I still react. After awhile I couldn't tell whether it was the wine or me running between there.

I can't ever imagine doing the things I do with Dwayne to anybody else. That's one of the reasons I worry if I could ever find another man to take his place. That's why I put up with all that I do so I won't have to face that reality yet.

One day I'll let her know why he needed me for such a long time. I can imagine the look on that bitch's face right now. I'd give anything to see it, I'd feel good. I'm not feeling it right now but one day I will. When Dwayne and I settle our disagreement I won't put any more pressure on our relationship.

Dwayne isn't just a want he's also a need. I know that he enjoys me. She calls me his sperm disposal holding his unwanted sperm but one day I might make good use of those sperm and give her the shock of her life. If I ever decide to do anything like that it would force her to leave him to me.

In my heart I know I won't do that since I know it would change our relationship and definitely in a way he wouldn't want. I also have two kids with part time dads so I'm not looking for another. He trusts me and because of that I wouldn't do anything to betray him like that. Because he got jealous and angry to the point of accusing me of cheating, I know it's his love for me speaking or he would just move on without saying a word.

Her actions might be what'll push him away. I know that he wants me even when he pretends not to and he has my body on a timer and as soon as it's ready, he's back. She thinks that sending me messages will stop that. Now I don't have to keep hiding anything. I can even stop caring even if she sees him in my bed. The only reason it mattered before was because of Dwayne's worries.

Maybe that's the push she needs. I've waited long so I can wait a little longer. I sure as hell would love to be a fly on the wall in their house at nights, especially the last couple.

I'm sure Jenny will be all over him about what happened. She's not the type to let him apologise and move on just like that. Beverly tells me things. I'll just have to wait and of course be ready when he calls. Like I said, I want no one else and these past few days are making me more impatient waiting for him to come.

* * *

It took a couple of days but I heard from Dwayne. I told him about my last text conversation with his wife and he wasn't too surprised. He didn't get mad or anything but he did say he'll take care of it. I know he only said that to calm me down but that's alright with me too. That was yesterday and now I'm getting another message from Jenny. At first I didn't want to read it but again my curiosity gets the better of me.

"Good morning Sandy. This is just a reminder for you to keep your disposal clean. It's usually hard to keep dirty places clean when it has

heavy usage but it can be dangerous when my husband dump his deposits off. I wouldn't want him to bring anything infectious home. Please keep clean at all times. With my appreciation, thank you."

"You fucking bitch." After reading her message I'm sorry I didn't just delete it instead of reading. And responding to it just makes it worse but it's like reflex.

"Well thank you. It's always nice for an apprentice to get acclamation from the pro. I can't reach your status so please take comfort that I'll never catch up to you in your profession. And like I said before, please have a nice lay."

"You might think it's dirty but your husband thinks differently."

"My dear, even a garbage man works in garbage all day but he's usually glad when he gets home to clean up and really relish in cleanliness."

"You're a real bitch."

I called Dwayne and told him he should make sure his wife stops calling me. I told him I'm not bothering her so I don't think he should allow her to bother me. Because I called him, he thinks I'm bothering him and got pissed then told me to leave him alone. Our conversation ended on a bad tone again.

Before he hung up he asked me if I thought Jenny was going to send me flowers when she found out about us. He once said that she isn't as quiet as she seems so I shouldn't underestimate her.

Now I can see that I did do it but that won't happen in the future. That bitch will not be comfortable in her so called 'happy life' now that she knows about me.

Evelyn Once Said:

"My body is made to heal whether it's broken skin or heart."

Evelyn Once Said:

"Worry not about the words they throw behind your back. Success brings criticism. Success pushed you forward and you hear them less along the way."

Verona J. Knight

Evelyn's Once Said

"Forgiveness is not to make them feel better; it's to save our sanity."

Chapter Thirteen

After Dwayne finally believed me that I'm not having an affair with anyone else, he started to act normal again. It's been a long few months. I just want to have some space for myself and not think about anything upsetting right now. With all my work this week I don't want to deal with anything else but I'm praying that somehow it will be getting better.

I keep going through the same things over and over with Dwayne but he's basically sitting back and ignoring it. Sometimes I think he's having too much fun at my expense but at least he's back to normal.

I'm spending more of my time reading as he thinks I should better myself and I'm also planning to go back to school. Dwayne started me on that track and I do want to better my future so I do plan to continue.

Recently I read several quotes in a book A MIND NOT LOST and a quote I read said that *"we shouldn't search for our happiness in other people"*. It said *"if we can't find what makes us happy, how do we expect someone else to do it for us? To find one's happiness in another person is guaranteed to be temporary; leading to a rough path to dependency. We need to make ourselves happy then we can look to find someone to share it with. We must make sure to find our comfortable place and not go searching for someone to comfort us."* The book says "*by finding it on our own, those who come and go in your life can't hide or take it from us if or when they leave."* Now I need to find that happiness and not depend on Dwayne for it. I should've read that before I got myself in this mess.

Today Monica came over so she and I are spending the day together. I need someone to help me clear my head but we just casually talk about my problems. I don't want to spend all my time talking about Dwayne as usual so she's telling me more about Sean, her married man she's been seeing.

I worry a lot about her even though she tells me not to. Listening to her talk I can see how excited she is about her sexual escapades between her and this man. She and he apparently had a threesome a few days ago and she's still smiling.

"What you mean you had a threesome?"

"Yes, three people having sex with each other, at the same time."

"Don't be silly. You know I know what a threesome means. But do you mean him and another man or him and another woman?"

"Me with another woman and Sean. I'm not ready to do the two men thing. That's out of my league and I couldn't manage that."

"Okay. What happened with this threesome?"

"Sean and I talked about a threesome several times and that we'd like to try it one day. We never thought about when or with whom but just that we would. Sean called and said he wanted us to spend some time together so we made plans several days before to meet that afternoon."

"I've thought about how it would feel to be in a threesome. I wonder what it would feel like but I didn't ran out and do it."

"Anyway, I mentioned it to a friend and she was curious."

"Why'd you felt safe talking to her about something like that? So personal."

"Actually, I mentioned it jokingly and she responded in a way I never expected."

"What?"

"She said it was something she also wondered about but didn't know anyone she might want to try it with. After the first talk we laughed about it a few times in different conversations. It came down to where we didn't know if the other was serious or not. After mentioning it too much over the past several months she eventually asked if I ever really seriously thought about it. All the times we joked about it, I was honest and we both started taking the other more seriously."

"I don't know if I would trust someone with that kind of information if I were married."

"I did since she and I have been friends for years. Finally one day she said if I ever got serious enough she would be interested. I guess it came to the point where she also felt safe to trust me. She said she's tired of her husband coming home just to give her an orgasm then leave her on her own until the next time. He thinks as long as he's in the house it means they're spending time together, even if all that time in spent in different rooms. She was just tired of that. I believed she was sure about it so I thought about it for awhile before deciding we should go ahead. I thought it would be a good surprise for Sean so we all met a few days ago. I wanted to do it before either of us chickened out."

"Sean had no idea?"

"No. No idea. You should've seen the look on his face when he came in the room and saw my friend sitting on the bed beside me."

"I guess he got very happy thoughts after he figured it out."

"I didn't have to convince him of anything. He didn't have to say a word when he saw us. She was sitting on one side of the bed and me on the other; both of us naked."

"Every man's dream, haw?"

"My plan was to make sure none of us needed to dream anymore. When he stepped in the room, I told him to stand by the foot of the bed but away so we both can see the specimen. With a smile on his face he had no problem showing off his great body. He's not one who works hard to keep his body looking great but he's very active and it shows. Looking at his six-foot height standing there, slowly exposing his chest going down to his pants coming off was intoxicating."

"Damn, girl."

"Damn, is right. Both Jasmine and I sat there watching while he put on a strip show for us to enjoy and sitting there watching him had my body going crazy."

"Holy shit!"

"That's not even the good part, seeing the look on Jasmine's face sent my crotch crazy. A kind of excitement I've never had before."

"Are you serious?"

"Yes. That's the main reason why I love my relationship with Sean. He's not going to say no to anything."

"But is he worth your marriage?" I don't want to put a damper on our conversation but I must ask.

"No, but it won't get to that. I can enjoy the attention I get from Sean's and not worry about doing anything out of the norm because he also enjoys me. We sat there watching Sean continue his striptease and she and I looked at each other and smile. She was just as anxious as I was, watching our plan come to life. Finally he finished stripping and we were about to do something to satisfy our curiosity."

I feel my body reacting to Monica's story and I wasn't there. My imagination is taking me in that room with them. "I wasn't there and my body is excited waiting to hear what happened next."

"I know I can trust you so I'll tell you who she is."

"I guess it's somebody I know?"

"Yes. Jasmine."

"Oh my gosh! Are you serious? I know Jasmine and you've been friends and work together. I know her marriage had some tension but nothing like you're telling me." Finding out who the other woman is, gives me some reassurance so I told her to finish telling me about their night.

"We both have something to lose if it gets out. We both feel comfortable with each other so I knew both of us would enjoy him and have him enjoy us. It was both Jasmine's and my first time doing anything like that. Sean on the other hand I wouldn't swear for. I can only speak for me and Jasmine not doing anything like that together before."

"Girl I believe you. I know that."

"Okay. You know she and I been friends for years now but I had no idea she was willing to put herself out of her marriage like that. Until she and I talked and laughed about it enough I really didn't take her serious before that. We double checked and made sure it was what we both wanted and we took it from there. The day we all met at the hotel, watching her face was such a turn on."

I'm listening to Monica and my mind drifts back to some of my first times with Dwayne. I understand her excitement about what she experienced and hope that she'll not get her heart tangled so bad that she'll feel pain along with the excitement. Sean being married is no guarantee that she won't get hurt by him. My mind keeps absorbing the details.

"We watched Sean dance and afterwards he joined us on the bed. I moved back and pulled my leg up to lie on the bed and Jasmine followed me. He climbed on the bed between us with a 'what happens next' look on his face. He looked like he didn't know where to start or which one of us to touch first. I thought I had to make it easier and let him know I wasn't jealous which one of us he wanted first. I leaned towards him and kissed his lips, then touched Jasmines lips and slightly pulled her head towards his. My body felt a different kind of excitement, not like any before. I felt my inner walls clapping and jumping, getting uncontrollably wet like the first time I was with Sean. I watched his body when her lips touched his."

"Girl I think I'm wetting myself."

"I'm getting wet again thinking about it."

"From what I'm hearing, I don't see where you or she could do anything to disappoint him."

"Both of us were all over him at the same time. Girl he went crazy. When he felt Jasmine lips on his legs and mine on his nipples, he just rises with each touch. His body went wild, convulsing. When I started kissing going down his stomach and she kissing up moving to his other nipple I saw the confusion with his senses when she and I passed to switch place. I watched his body go out of control."

Monica looks at me as if she thinks I'm judging her. "I was just starting to wonder when the ladies got their turn."

"We eased away and he got up and allowed us to lie on our backs again. He was so excited that our bodies felt whatever he was feelings flowing through us also. We laid there anxious to see what would come next. With a smile and a pleasurable look, his face says so much with so little time, but in no haste."

With a smirk on my face I let her know what I'm thinking. "I'm sure."

"Then his lips touched between my legs, heaven. Watching him massaged her between her legs with his right hand while kissing mine, had my body twisting. With every look and every movement my body reacted in a different way; but always almost too excited. As she and I looked in each other's eyes, her hand touched as if to solidify the moment in our minds. I've never kissed a woman before and I wasn't ready to go that far but before I realized she eased up and was kissing my breast."

Damn. My body's losing control. I can't believe Monica really did that. "Are you kidding me?"

"No, I'm not kidding. What surprised me the most was that I enjoyed it. My hand went to her nipples then down her legs. I felt Sean lips going, kissing my then sensitive inner thigh and I touched her. I thought 'holy shit I'm there, I'm going to explode right here'. I didn't want to go yet but I lost all control when they both kissed my body at the same time, watching me quiver."

"That's it."

"No. After my body stopped jumping, I eased Sean head from between my legs with whatever little energy I had left. Jasmine laid back for Sean and he kissed her going to her legs. Without thinking I leaned towards her and returned the favour to her breast. I've never touched a woman's body sexually before that and I was excited.

Sean moved closer to Jasmine and I watched her 'beyond excited' body react. She eased her head and looked up toward the ceiling with her twitching body, raising the curve in her back and her shoulder rocking from left to right. With all three bodies responding to each other's so well, we felt the need to go even further."

"Oh . . . my . . . gosh."

"I watched him slide inside her trembling excited body. With every push and pull, I find myself touching her while she bit her lips. Her body gave out and she lost control and within minutes her body took on a seizure like attack as her soft screams turns into strong moans before going rigid."

"Holy shit!"

"Wait girl, there's more. After she got hers, by then my body was ready again and Sean and his attention moved back over to me. His kisses on my face before he penetrated me, was like normal. I surprised myself some because I let him enter me after he just pulled out of Jasmine but I didn't have time to think. And my body was still so sensitive I couldn't tell how much longer I could last before exploding again."

"Oh my gosh."

"His entry opened that door in my mind of our first time together. My body screamed I'm telling you. Jasmine recovered enough to join in again. My body gripped on to every part that was close; hold it in place. And then, I lost it. My orgasm was creeping through like it wanted to flow through all of us and I could see Sean couldn't take it anymore. Jasmine kissed his back and I felt the splash on my inside. His body went rigid. The intensity sent a blazing fiery rushing like it's pushing every other senses aside; exiting through every pour."

"Holy shit! Monica I swear I just got off."

"Definitely. Holy shit is right. I tell you it was an experience that I've never had before and one that I hope to have again."

"So what happened with Jasmine after?"

"We laid there afterwards with each of us on his arms and laughed. Neither of us could believe what had just happened. She and I made sure we were okay with it and we both were. He just listened. Jasmine and I agreed it was the most enjoyable sexual experience for both of us. We also told each other that our regular friendship after leaving will never be the same; it will be better. We figured our friendship would be fine and that it would bring us a tighter friendship. We even plan to do it again in the future. No set date but it'll be happening."

"The safe thing is that both of you have something to lose so you'll protect each other. Now you definitely have a friend for life. That's if none of you get divorced." That statement got us both laughing some as she nudged my arm.

"We'll be fine. Now we pass each other in the halls always with a smile on our faces and I'm sure we're both thinking the same things. She asked me what Sean thought about everything and I told her he enjoyed us as much as we did him. I told her that he even mentioned that we should do it on a regular; both she and I are thinking about it now."

After Monica and I finished talking about her and her sex friends, we talked about Sharon some more. We're worried about the struggles she got in her life and think it's taking too much of her energy right now. Sharon has a problem with making good decisions and fails to learn from her mistakes.

She's a mother and a grandmother who's single and laying all her hopes on a married man. She's hoping for something that she has no control over and with no guarantees from him; she's giving all of herself. Now Monica and I think I should go over to her place sometime soon and talk to her, so I will.

Evelyn Once Said:

"Sometimes the right thing to say isn't the right thing to say. It might be coming from a kind heart to comfort someone but might do more harm in the long run."

Verona J. Knight

Evelyn Once Said:

"So often people say the right thing instead of saying the truth."

Chapter Fourteen

The things I must deal with but, in the long run, it's worth it. I make myself sick sometimes though. By now I'm probably making my friends sick also. Now some of them say I plan my life around Dwayne and they're also wondering how long before he gets his divorce. They won't come out and ask me that but I can tell.

His wife's insults also don't bother me anymore and I'll deal with her so called reports on their sex life my way. Now she sends a message telling me I'm not doing much since he's going to her for sex. Telling me I should do my job and be useful in this relationship. Saying if I was doing my job he wouldn't have to look to her when she wants nothing to do with him. She wants me to know that as long as my crotch is in the relationship it should be working harder.

I'm pissed enough but I won't let her know just how much she's getting to me. I accept that he'll go to her sometimes but if she can't accept my part in his heart that's her problem, not mine.

I don't think she wants him touching her as long as he still talks to me but her doing that is in turn doing me more of a favour. My answer to her was that I'm clapping for her since she's finally getting some. In her words, she's just keeping me informed of her husband activities when he's home. She also wants to notify me that if I'm not doing my job he might find someone else to do it for me.

I had no idea that she could be such a bitch when I met her. I just want to feel my hands around her stinking neck choking the living crap out of her. Release the tension she creates in my life. She tries to get me jealous and I pretend it doesn't work but it's working.

I send back a message telling her I don't have time to waste with her. That I'm very busy with my life and I don't have time for this foolishness. Tell her I'm doing quite fine and won't get jealous over a husband and wife fucking? Every time my finger hit a key while I'm writing, I wish it was hitting her in the face. I am jealous and hurt.

I thought about turning my phone off but I read her response instead. "Not busy enough. You're sucking and kissing his ass and it's not working anymore. Step up!"

"Obviously my crotch is working harder than yours." After I press the send key, I turn off my phone even though I don't want to. If Dwayne should call and don't get me he can call my house line.

She can be such a bitch and I can't say all I want to because it'll piss Dwayne off and I can't bother with arguing with him over her. With everything she said, she got me thinking again about Dwayne and if he would ever leave me to find another woman. I've invested years in him now and it'd be a big blow if it ever happens. Damn. Do I ever want to kick the shit out of her right now? She got me doubting my abilities.

Why would I want to think her and Dwayne aren't sleeping together; I can only hope. That's the last thing I want to think about even though I can't help myself sometimes. (She has no right messaging me to tell me that.) I've a hard enough time dealing with him leaving to go home to her every night.

I don't need her reminding me of that all the time. I'm just tired of her and all her bullshit. He wasn't kicking and screaming when I invited him in so why's she haunting me when he's the one who made his decision. I'm not the one she's married to. And with all the shit I must put up with, Dwayne didn't show up for our date, again.

Dealing with Jenny's bullshit for the past few days means I don't feel like company but I'm meeting some friends later for another sex party. This is just another chance to buy and try a few new things and share our experiences and ideas with each other. Everything I've tried, Dwayne seemed to enjoy.

Again I'm running from boredom when we make love. Each time should feel different from the last or from what he has at home or eventually, it won't be worth it for him to come to my bed.

It's special to know that the things we do together aren't the same as with anyone else. That's why it's my job to find new things. That's our special bond. The last time we made love I allowed him to do things that my body took days to re-coop from. I was uncomfortably for days but I did enjoy him.

That night I saw the look on Dwayne's face and it was worth it. It was so intense and felt like nothing before. I can't complain about something new that allows me another new experience. It drained every life from his body but when he told me how much he enjoyed me, it was like pay day for me.

I get here and see Karen's house with about fifteen women and a few tables set up around the room. We chat for a while and then got into a big discussion about anal sex after I brought up the topic. I'm surprised to find out how many of the women tried it at least once.

They were talking about things to do before trying anything like that. They all agreed that it can be enjoyable if you prepare yourself. I've no plans to do it again in the near future so I only took mental notes.

My mind drifts off but even though it's not my favourite, I'll be prepared just in case he comes to me with it again. (Who knows how I'll feel by then.)

I also have a few things I want to try with him after hearing about Monica's little session. Looking at the beads and scented oils are forming many ideas in my mind. I'm a bit excited thinking about it all so I called Dwayne. I walk away from the crowd going closer to the front door to talk where nobody can hear me.

"I baby. I'm at my party and do I ever have plans for your ass next time."

"You're not tired of me yet." I can imagine the smile on his face right about now.

We talked for a few minutes before I rejoined the party. Not too long after that the door bell ring and I hear someone apologizing for being late. Kimberly is Karen's sister-in-law and Karen told us at the beginning of the party that others were coming. I've seen Kimberly at a party before but we aren't great friends so I didn't turn around to look when she walked into the room with her friend walking in behind me.

Without seeing Kimberly's friend I hear someone introducing herself as Jenny. My head is now moving in slow motion to see which Jenny it is. I turn to see Dwayne's wife and I froze in the chair. I couldn't say or do anything.

Jenny and Kimberly walk in and after a few steps she recognize that I'm the one sitting here but she doesn't say a word. Ignoring me, they both look at the products to see what they missed and seem very interested in some of the toys. Of course Jenny announces her husband Dwayne enjoys sex and she might have some new things for him to do. She's also asking the women their opinions on some of the products displayed on the table. I think she's doing it only so I might know her plans.

"Now ladies!" Talking loud enough to make sure that I can hear her ask. "Who's the expert on these vagina trinkets?" Everybody looks around laughing. "I guess nobody needs to explain the vibrator since that one I don't have use for but some of the other things I want to hear about." All the women are joking around about the items and laughing with everything Jenny says.

Since Jenny came in my interest in the products is gone. Kimberly's stares got so intense, leaving me to believe that Jenny told her about me before and she just realized who I am or told her some time during the party. Now she realizes that I'm the same Sandy; Dwayne's mistress and her attitude changed. After a while she's also asking questions and joking along with Jenny.

The other women in the room join them in the fun but without any idea of what's going on between Jenny and me. They're very friendly to her while they answer her questions; which is making me a little jealous.

Karen is Kimberly's family so I know sooner or later Karen will also know that Dwayne's still married and living with his wife. Kimberly on the other hand couldn't wait to take it to the next level. She held up a vibrator with a clitoris stimulator attached and shows it to Jenny.

"Hey Jen, I think you and Dwayne might have a really good time with this one." They both laugh while Kimberly looks over at me.

"Naugh. Might be fun having two at the same time but the clit stimulator, don't know? Girl what you think he has his lips and tongue for, eating?" They're joking and playing around; all laughing. With every word, Kimberly looks at me. "Dwayne's mouth is good for something else away from lying. He's my stimulator. He goes crazy watching me enjoy myself."

I'm sure Kimberly is also talking loud enough for me to hear their conversation. "You might be right. We wives should leave something out there for their bitches. They should use their mouth to satisfy our men while they cushion their egos; telling them what they want to hear. Afterwards they can use these toys to satisfy themselves while they think about what the husbands are giving at home."

"What I can do with, are some oils. I haven't had a massage in a few months. The last time I had one Dwayne came home and we took a shower together. After that he gave me a massage with some oils and, damn, my husband slowly licked that oil off my body going down, sending me to O land." All the women sit listening to hear what he did next. "We're all girls here so we can talk. That night he rubbed my body and massaged my muscles so intensely, right before he slowly drizzles and spread the oils evenly. Going into places only his lips can massage well. Because he told me to close my eyes, I had no idea where he would be touching next. When his tongue, oh yes, over my nipples, then I felt him on my navel then back on my breast. Damn. All the while I expected him between my legs."

One of the women has to comment. "It's always nice when they appreciate having a good woman at home."

"Girl I must admit. I was pissed at him because of some slut he has out there but that night I had to give in. Was I ever glad when he moved down my body again and finally tastes me. And with those fingers inserted while he ate, every touch, every glide and every slide, made me forgot why I was mad. I just laid there waiting to see what's next and left him to eat what his heart desired."

One of the other women joins the conversation. "Girl I know what you're talking about. All of us married women should remember that there are women out there who don't have what it takes to be a wife so they must settle for the mistress position. We shouldn't worry though for that's all they'll be."

I know Jenny's trying to piss me off but I'll survive this. I'm a big girl.

"I must admit he felt especially good that night. He begged me to forgive him and said he'll make it up to me. He told me that nothing out there is worth him leaving me and I'm not to lose any sleep over things that aren't important; trivial things or people. I did start off angry at him but after he started I couldn't resist and he did calm me down"

Kimberly tries to really slap my feelings. "Well, now that he's begging for your forgiveness you could bring some more excitement in the bedroom. You should believe him when he tells you he couldn't leave you for something that's willingly giving it away to a married man with no hesitation."

"Well he did say those women aren't wife material. He thinks because they give themselves away freely, they end up giving it to sample takers, nothing more."

Another one of the women jumps into the conversation. "Those women aren't smart enough to understand that the man will say anything to help them open their legs. They'll even say the love word until they have their orgasm."

Beverly is also here. She's also hearing everything and we both look at each other watching these women go off. She finally jumps in. "Sometimes these women see themselves as a potential keeper. I also believe if the woman continues with their relationship for years with no kind of commitment then it's not worth it."

Kimberly and Beverly met before but Beverly had no idea Kimberly knew Jenny. After Beverly made her statement Kimberly's expression says she's not very impressed but she continue with what she wants to say and cut Beverly off.

"These women sleeping with married men are pitiful. The fact that they can't get one of their own should tell them to do something with themselves."

Beverly seems to be defending these women as if she's defending me. "Just because they sleep with married men is no confirmation that something is wrong with them."

Kimberly looks at me, pissed since Jenny isn't saying much. "There's something wrong with a woman who gives her crotch freely knowing that she'll end up alone."

Carol jumps in with her thought. "If a woman is at a certain place in life and decides she doesn't want marriage, she'll still have a man if she chooses to. If she does have one, more than likely it won't be a married one. I think if she's staying away from the drama of marriage then she won't want to take on another person trouble and their marriage." She and most of the women agree with what Kimberly's saying.

"Some of them get the man in the end." Beverly is trying to make me feel better; going back to Kimberly's statement.

The statement gets to Karen. "Yes some do but, how many? And how long before she herself is looking over her shoulders to see who's coming to take her place?"

Kimberly and Karen look at each other before Kimberly laughingly says something. "Now you're sounding as if you've had some experience and I think it's something the family knows nothing about."

"No experience either way. I just can't see a woman with any respect for herself or with high self-esteem treat her body that way.

It pisses me off to know that some women are fighting for respect while some freely throw theirs away. How could someone think so little of herself? She opens her legs with just a wish. Giving away her body with all the risk of catching a disease and no guarantee she'll get the man in the end. Our crotch we have control of, and giving that control away tells the value we put on it."

Melanie now steps in with her own story. "My husband and I are married for ten years now. We've had our bad times and managed through, but if I found out he's having an affair after all that, now he'd end up crippled. Somehow he would have an accident."

Karen is surprised to hear her friend say that. "Why the hell would he end up crippled?"

"Yes. I'd cripple his ass and leave him with his memories. Let him enjoy that while his dick stays where it should be. Let him figure out if it was worth it in the long run."

"So what's going to happen to you after he's crippled?"

"That I'd have to figure out afterwards." She laughs. "I'd make sure he hears every way that someone else is trying to take care of business to torture his ass. I agree that too many wives are prim and proper in the bedroom but I'm his bitch in there. He has no excuse to cheat unless he's tired of life."

Another woman, Grace, said she wonder if there are enough men out there to supply every women. Wondering if some women checked and without telling the rest of them decided that's why they have to share.

Sara now wants to give her opinion. "My husband works hard seven days a week and if he feels he needs for some outside service I wouldn't leave him just for that. If one of the good ones trip and fall into another woman, does it mean he turned into a bad one? When he begins to lie, sneak around and cheat what is he? Even if he works beyond hard and covers his family's needs in every way but still cheat, what is he? Does he fall into the 'all men are dogs' category? Who decides if he's still a good man? Is it the wife who still gets the financial attention along with the lies? Is it the other woman who sees how well he takes care of his family's need and also gets his time? Many times the same man is good in one situation and bad in the next. If my husband is cheating, then I see him as an asshole but the bitch he's cheating with sees him as a good man. Which is he? What makes a good man?" After she finished talking she throws her hands in the air and look at every one.

(My thoughts exactly.)

Karen smile then comment that she often wonders some of the same things. "Many times these women decided to be with someone because they're tired of the assholes they're used to. If they were smart then they should figure out that they're helping to turn the ones they see as good into the assholes they say they're running from."

"I doubt if these sorts of women are smart enough to recognize that. If their previous men cheated on them then you would think they'd recognize all cheaters as assholes. I guess since they're now the ones turning the good men into the assholes category they see nothing wrong with it. Now I guess the ones they thought were assholes might actually have been good in someone else's eyes."

(They're wondering the same things I do.)

The woman that said she would cripple her husband if he cheated tells a story about what happened to her friend when she found out about her husband's affair. "She talked to her husband on several occasions to stop with his shit and nothing happened. One day she got fed up and wrote her husband a note and left it on the table before leaving the house for days. He sent her several messages and she didn't respond to any of them. When she finally came back he changed his lifestyle because he realized how easy it was for her to step out on him and didn't. She told us what the note said *'you are but one man trying to please two. Since I'm feeling like the third, I'll go find a fourth. Prepare to be a square'*."

With all the women laughing after that story, Karen tried to end the conversation about all this cheating so it wouldn't put a damper on the evening. But before that she throws some info on the table. "Listen ladies. If you have a cheating man who think it's okay for the man to cheat but not the woman, then leave him be, let him keep thinking that. They've the notion that it's different for a woman because she's a receptive who takes home what the man lets off. Men like that are too easy to deal with. Just leave them in their world."

One of the women questioned Karen with a puzzled look on her face. "What does that mean, easy to deal with? It's not right for them to believe that they can get away with it and a woman can't!"

"I agree. What I mean is that they're easy to deal with because what they say isn't what they mean. They talk about women being receptive and all the other shit because they're possessive. They don't want anyone touching their women even though they want to go out and do it. Now, once a woman knows that, then she can handle her man well. She needs to know that she only needs to challenge the manhood of a man who's like that."

"Challenge their man's manhood? How are they going to do that?"

"Yes. A man don't want his woman to think about another man much more be touched by one. If you tell your man that you masturbate while thinking about another man he'll go crazy. You're now in the position where you can enjoy another man without being the receptive. He can't do anything about it and he'll go mad thinking he's being cheated."

"Girl I never thought about it like that."

"A man's greatest boost is in knowing that he can please his woman sexually. If he thinks that someone else is pleasuring her, even if it's in her mind, he'll lose it. If you want him to really lose his mind, whenever he comes to you for sex, take a little while to respond. If he asks what's wrong, tell him you masturbated and it's taking you a little longer for your body to respond to him. Now if he knows you masturbate thinking about someone else, the pain he feels will make him understand what you feel when he goes out there and you've no control. He'll always be wondering who you think about when you do it, mainly if you think about any of his friends. Remember, you don't even have to masturbate, just tell him you do."

"Oh! . . . my! . . . gosh! This is so mean! Karen you're so bad!"

"I'm not bad but I've some experiences in life that taught me well. Revenge doesn't have to be physical. You can enjoy another man without having him touch you. The thing is, your man will have nothing over you because another man never touched you but it'll get to him more than if you were touched by someone else, all because he has no control over what and when you do it."

"Girl you're so bad!" Laughing.

After Karen finished her lesson on getting back on men, Kimberly took the floor because she wants everyone to meet Jenny. Karen had met Dwayne before but like I said she has no idea that he has a Mrs. She thinks he's just a friend of mine.

"Come on ladies. Let's continue with our party and not with conversation about bitches and whores. Some of you are beginning to scare my ass." While she's looking at the woman who said she would cripple her husband.

Kimberly turns around and look at Karen because she just needed to let her know who Jenny is. "By the way Karen, I didn't properly introduce you to my friend here. Ladies this is Jenny Wesley, actually Mrs. Dwayne Wesley. My sophisticated friend who can calmly look at her husband's mistress and not rip her eyes out." Those who don't know Dwayne look around wondering who the mistress is.

Karen finally understands the whole conversation that's been going on. Some of the women cover their open mouth with their hand and some smile maliciously. It seems most of the women are now aware of the past hour of conversation about cheating men and their whores. The whole room just goes silent since they now figured out that I'm the whore who caused the whole conversation.

Without thinking I just stand looking, wanting to leave. I've gone to places with Dwayne before where many of these women were also. I've never felt the need to tell them that Dwayne's married, so except for Beverly, none of them knew much about his life. Now they all know that Dwayne's married and that the whole conversation was directed towards me.

I didn't have much to say about anything so I pick up my things to leave. I was heading towards the door when Jenny walks towards me. I've no idea what she wants to say but at this point there's nothing more hurtful left for her to say. I'm walking to the door and she comes up behind me and without raising her voice she calmly talk; but I don't know if any of the other women heard.

"By the way Sandy, if you have any intentions of using your items on my husband tonight get rid of the idea. I've plans for him tonight. You should always remember that you're welcome to what's left over. What I don't want. That's what disposals are for.

Good night and don't forget this." She hands me a vibrator and tells me she pay for it. "My treat." Then she walks away.

I can't believe she went there. "There's only one thing I want to say to you Jenny. I've no intention of sitting here and listen to you trying to embarrass me because you know you're only upset that someone else can please your man better that you can." Now I know the women are hearing me.

"That's okay. You just remember to know your place. You get after I'm finished, always. Sometimes we can't go at home and even though public toilets are dirty, it comes in handy those times. Men often like using the freeway instead of a quiet path. Have a good night, Sandy."

"And if you keep harassing my phone I'll report you."

She stops, turn, looks at me putting one arm across her chest, holding up the other by the elbow. Her finger, her pointer finger, is covering her lips as if trying to stop her from getting upset.

"Do you think I can't afford a phone?" Now she's walking back to me. "Why do you think I've my phone on my husband's account? You go ahead and then explain why you're reporting the number that's registered to the person you call several times a day. How stupid are you? Maybe that's why you're in the position you are."

As she turn and continue to walk off, the silent room got even more silent. Some of the women turn their head with smirks on their faces as I walk away. I've no intention of standing here and listen to her anymore.

As I walked out, I walk in shame but with my head up high. I'll not give her the satisfaction of knowing how much her words hurt. Lately all I feel when I think about her is doing something bad, but Dwayne's saving her.

I came home and called Dwayne. I asked him to come over but he told me that he couldn't until tomorrow. Said Jenny wants him to do something later so he'll have to stay home with her. Now for the rest of the night I'll be here, by myself, thinking about what she's doing with whatever she bought at the party. (Why do I do this to myself?)

Evelyn Once Said:

"*2 intelligent minds, reason.*
2 aggressive minds, debate.
1 intelligent and 1 aggressive mind, argue.
2 ignorant minds take comfort that none is better than the other."

Evelyn Once Said:

"Safety doesn't mean not to do, it means to do but be prepared for whatever can go wrong; works the same with our emotions."

Chapter Fifteen

Jenny showing up last night turned my time at the party and after into misery. I expected that my whole attitude would change after she showed up and I should've left as soon as she came through the door. I don't know why I didn't. She had the nerve to come attack me like I was the one going to her house and not him coming to me. I shouldn't have to go through this every time while Dwayne sits back thinking it's not a big deal.

When he and I made up, after Jenny started sending me those awful messages, he promised that he'd take care of her harassing me. Since then I can see that he's done nothing and I don't know if he has any intension to.

It felt even worse than I thought I could after they started talking about women who're giving themselves freely to other women husbands, knowing that nothing permanent will come from their relationship.

I've said so often that I'm willing to wait but more and more, I can't avoid thinking about ending up alone one day. What's going to happen to me if he decides to stop? I honestly hope that we'll never do, but I have no guarantee. When we talked he said he'll come by later and I'll try to work in the subject to see how he responds. I must start thinking seriously about mine and my kids' future.

    Beverly called me this morning to tell me what happened after I left the party last night. All the women there were surprised to know that Dwayne's still a married man. They told Jenny they don't know him well so they don't know much about any of this. Beverly said many of the women, both single and married, didn't like the idea of Dwayne and me since in their eyes, it could be any of them in Jenny's shoe.

Some didn't have much to say since I'm their friend and they didn't want to pass judgement. She said the whole cheating conversation ended with one of the women telling the others that instead of giving themselves headache about whether or not their husband is cheating, just throw a damn phone in his vehicle and track it. If she calls and he says he's somewhere and the phone she's tracking says somewhere else, then he's cheating; so simple.

The night ended with all the women laughing about men and what they think they get away with. Concluding that if you have to track your man then he's not worth it but before you decide that he's cheating, make sure before throwing the relationship away.

I told her it doesn't matter to me what they said since their confirmation isn't something I'm looking for. After a while I didn't want to talk about it anymore so we talked about other things instead. She mentioned some of her concerns she has about her marriage but ones that she doesn't think are serious enough to worry about.

Her husband is a nice enough guy but in my mind I wouldn't trust him either. I'm learning that men are men. I've seen the way he looks at other women when Beverly isn't looking. Bev and I talked for awhile then I told her I had a few things to do before my plans for later.

Along with everything I've to deal with today, now Sharon's calling me in tears. Even though she's my sister I get pissed when she comes to me crying and not take any of my advice. I warned her about the things she does that might mess up her life and there's not much more I can do for her. I can listen but that's about all I can do.

A few years ago I read a book that touched on people in abusive situations and I told her about the book. At the time one of her baby fathers was notorious for verbally abusing her; always using the worst words that comes to mind. I gave her the book and she read it and that was when she made up her mind to leave him.

A few years later she told me that it literally saved her life because she felt like the book was talking to her. The section in the article where it talked about the voice of verbal cruelty being the worse for the abused family got her attention.

She read how *verbal abuse leaves 'hidden scars' that affects one's future ability to love. The abused person hides the truth from others to protect their abuser. They don't understand that because they hide the truth from others, it only gives the abuser strength to abuse them more. Many abused people make the decision to keep quiet because of their fear of loneliness. They put themselves under pressures and aim to get some kind of approval and attention. They work hard to please their abuser but it only results in disappointment from more negative criticism. Abusers tend to blame the abused for any wrong doing. They try to play the victim since the real victim remains quiet, mainly from fear. The abuser is the first to shout in a conversation intimidating the abused rights to speak.*

From that article my sister discovered what she was doing to herself and decided to change it. One day she came to me and said, 'I identified myself'.

After that she left him; even though they already had two kids together. I was happy and at the time I thought she learned from that. Now my fear is that it already did too much damage to her since she still makes the same mistakes by choosing the wrong men to love. She still doesn't know how to love and who should be deserving of her heart. She keeps looking for men that end up using then leaving her. Now she's giving Luke the same chance as the others and when he's finish he'll go home to his wife and live happily ever after.

It does surprise me that he's still hanging around after all this time though. I found out about him a couple of years ago, not too long after she and he started their 'whatever she calls it'. I wasn't happy when she started since she was barely out of another abusive relationship but with all my concerns about Luke, he's still there.

I heard he's a religious man and my thought then was that he conveniently forgets his religion when he's out of church. I also noticed I haven't heard of him going to church. Even though they argue a lot he always goes back to her with an apology and of course she accepts it and takes him back. She told me once that whenever they argue he tells her that she's only good for one thing; which is sex. In his apology he tells her anything bad that he said to her was said out of anger and he didn't mean it.

I gave her the advice a friend of mine gave me once. 'If someone says something bad to you once during an argument then you can accept that it was said out of anger. If that person says the same hurtful things in another argument, then you must accept that the first time they meant it.'

I always try to give her the same advice I get but none of it seem to work with her. I remember being told that 'to lay my heart down for a married heart to enjoy, is to send my heartache air mail to be delivered later'. At the time I was getting that advice I also shrugged it off as nothing. That was when I just started with Dwayne and my friend at work told me that.

This woman was like my mentor and I confided in her. She used her years of experience to direct me but I ignored her advice and now I understand more what she was talking about. When I started with Dwayne's married heart I was setting myself up for my heart break, hence sending it air mail. Now it's starting to hurt and it'll hit me even harder in the future. I know the road that I'm on with Dwayne will not last forever no matter what direction it takes but I just can't let go. I feel trapped even though I'm holding the key.

I was also told to stop wasting my time crying over someone I think is bringing me joy and start looking at the only one who can bring it constantly; me. Now I sit and think about that statement more than I had before, especially with the constant disappointment when I want Dwayne's time. I try to be patient. I acknowledge that now I'm weak to him and his needs, and in the process stifling my own needs. More and more I get scared when I think about Sharon and her situation. Am I becoming like her; handcuffing my heart to the pain and disappointments?

I must meet up with Sharon sometime in the next few days to see what I can do to help. I've no idea what I'll say to her but someone must talk some sense that she might understand. Monica and I talked earlier and she thinks she should come with me when I go to see her.

We all have our problems but Sharon has gone overboard and we can't help but worry about her more. In the long run we might have to be the ones running to the rescue when she's on her own again. We might as well do what we can for her now.

One thing I know is she must start using better birth control. (I'm just glad she's not pregnant after all.) If she hasn't learned by now then she must be told. A single woman must always believe in birth control whether she wants to or not. I think when she went to nursing school they would've taught her more about nursing kids.

      Dwayne got here and the night was good. I told him about the party and what happened there with Jenny. He isn't angry but he showed some affection. He said he's sorry that I had to go through it. We also touched on my future and what I need to do to feel safe. I was surprised at his response to the future part of the conversation. Since he had no comment about Jenny I couldn't get into details about any plans.

I also still had Sharon on my mind and I don't want to get into a fight with him so I let the topic go. I intend to continue with him and the discussion another day though. I also know that he can't walk away from me as easily as he would want me to believe.

I couldn't get angry at him since he did send me a few comforting words after he left. And a person who's not in love wouldn't care to find time to send messages and leave romantic voice mail when he's at home with his wife. I know that she's in the house when I hear his whispering messages on my voice mail. Telling me that he 'loves me bad'; if that isn't love, what is?

After Dwayne left my life must continue. I called Sharon. She had nothing much to tell me since she had already calmed down some. I still want to see her though so we can sit down and talk, that way I can know what's happening with her now. I'll call Monica tomorrow and decide when.

* * *

Today I'm at Sharon's with Monica. We don't want to come down too hard on her before we get the full story about what made her cry when she called me a few days back. All I could tell from her hysteria then was that it had something to do with Luke.

She's taking too long to tell us and I can't wait any longer so I asked her what's happening with her and him. She won't volunteer anything and we've been sitting here more than half an hour. Even though she told me there's nothing wrong, I can tell if she's lying when I look in her face.

"Why were you crying on the phone when you called a few days ago?"

"I'm alright now. Everything is good again."

"Everything is good again. I could barely understand what you were saying then because you were crying so much. You had me feeling bad for now coming over right away and now everything is okay so soon."

"Luke and I made up. He came over yesterday and we're fine now."

"What? He broke up with you again. Did he apologise yesterday and you ended up in bed again right after his apology."

"It really isn't the way you make is sound."

Monica is sitting here listening and I see how annoyed she's getting. I also can see how anxious she is to say something to Sharon but she's holding her tongue.

"You know that idiot is using you right?"

"If he is it's my business."

"Yes it's your business but it still concerns us since we're your family."

"Well I'm fine so no need to be concerned."

I don't want to hear from her that we don't have to worry and think that's all there is to it. For her to think we came to her house only to be told that she's fine now so go back home, is crazy. If that's the case what'll happen the next time she's not fine. I've no intention to leave without saying what I have on my mind either.

"You might think you're alright and need no support from us but you're wrong. You must start thinking about yourself. Your main concern is about his feelings and how to please him. You go out of your way for him thinking he'll leave his wife for you." Sharon is sitting here listening to me come down on her harder and shock me with her response.

"Is that what you're doing? Are you going out of your way to please Dwayne hoping that he'll leave his wife for you?" Yelling at me because she doesn't want to hear the truth isn't going to stop me from telling her.

"How did this become about Dwayne and me!"

"It did when you started telling me what Luke is doing with me!"

"Dwayne and Luke are nothing alike!"

"Why! Does he cheat on his wife! Does he sneak around to see you! And does he also lie to his wife about you!"

"That's not the same thing! Anyway, this is about you and Luke not about me!"

"Monica you're standing in one corner while Sandy stands in the other like you're my two psychologists. Dr. Bitch and Dr. Mistress! Coming over here pretending you're in a different position than me! The only difference between us is Monica you're married, with a good man at that. You went into your relationship with Sean knowing it would be temporary but you're still a cheating bitch"

Monica's frustration is getting to her. "Sharon you listen to me. I'm not getting in a shouting match with you. You can call us any name you want to but it doesn't change anything. Sandy and I are just concerned about you. You have seven kids and you've been here in the same situation before."

Sharon put her hands up with her palms facing me. "Don't say another word." She backs away from me and moved to the other side of the room. "Okay I'm done with the shouting but that's just it. I've been here before and I'm surviving with my kids." She looks over at Monica. "You on the other hand haven't been in a situation like you're now with Sean. Now you're acting like you can just get up and walk away. Monica if you could do that you wouldn't be still with him. Even if it's just for the sex it's holding you there. That alone should make you understand how I'm feeling."

"Yes you're a survivor Sharon and your kids are happy now. What you need to ask yourself is how happy are you and how long before it starts affecting your kids?"

"I work hard to give my kids everything they need mainly because they've no father beside them every day. I wouldn't jeopardise that for anything."

"That's just the problem. You won't recognize when it starts to happen. You're too busy thinking about what Luke wants and how to please him." I'm keeping quiet and watch as Monica gets her attention. "I know it seem like Sandy and I are coming down hard on you but we're not. You need to hear this so you can watch for signs now that you know we're seeing them. Do you think you're hiding it from the kids when you're crying? You can't do it all the time."

"I protect my kids. I don't cry when they're around."

"You might not cry with them around but that's no guarantee that they'll not know when you do. What do you say to the older ones? You have granddaughters and do you want their mom teaching them what you're teaching your daughters?"

"Listen. I'm not a child so stop talking to me like one. Yes I know I've made too many mistakes in my past and this might be another one. All I want is both of you to say you're not doing the same as I am. It might be on a different scale but it's no different."

Now she's pissing me off again and Monica is playing the diplomat. We're here trying to help her get some sense-of-order in her life and she keeps referring to what Monica and I are doing. I have two kids and she has seven. Monica has a husband and she has part-time baby daddies but no husband. What's she thinking when she keeps telling me that we're alike.

"Listen Sharon, whether or not you want to admit it Monica and I are here to help you. We can't force you to take our advice but we can force you to listen to us."

"You both can talk all you want but all you're doing is avoiding your reality. I might not be the smartest one in the bunch but I know you're kidding yourself as much as you might think I am. Both of you're missing your signs that you can't see, just as you say I can't see mine. Just know that Dwayne, Luke and Sean are the same and both of you're the same as me."

"There you go again."

"Yes, because you're both hypocrites. You see and judge my life and don't judge each other. You say Dwayne's a good man but you helped turn him into one of those assholes like the ones in our past. He's a liar and he cheats just like the rest. He might not have been one before he started with you, but he's one of them now. What'd you expect after you got your claws in his ass?"

"The difference between Dwayne and Luke is that Dwayne's in-loves with me. He and I have a better chance of having a future than you and Luke. You and Luke broke up so many times in the past couple of years and then he comes back because you give him love better than his wife."

"So you want to go there. Do you think Dwayne would be with you if you decide to stop sleeping with him? Do you think he would love you without your crotch holding him? You stop sleeping with him and see how long it'll be before he stops loving your ass. Without that crotch of yours you might not have much to keep him coming back."

Monica is pissed at both Sharon and me now. "Both of you shut the fuck up. Sisters shouldn't talk like that to each other. Listen to you and what you're saying to each other and all because of these men. They're both assholes from one end or the other. As a matter of fact, all three of them are. They might look like good men to you but they aren't to their wives. Do you think their wives don't know that something is wrong every time they leave their house to go to the store or to have a drink with their friends? Try to stop kidding yourselves."

Monica said that and both Sharon and I feel like idiots. Sharon and I don't usually fight and we never fight because one of us is trying to help the other. I love my sister and I want her to be happy but I still know that Luke isn't going to be the one to bring her that happiness. We all calm down a little and allow Monica to finish what she wants to say.

"Now, I've been listening to both of you and now I don't want any of you to interrupt me until I say what I have to. I love both of you with all my heart and wouldn't want to see any of us get hurt. We have to look out for each other and make sure the other knows when they're doing something wrong. We mightn't want to hear it but we must. Right now I know that I'm in a place where I shouldn't be but I'm finding it hard to leave. I love Dave and if he were to find out what I'm doing it would kill me; hurting him. Sandy you're in the same place and Dwayne won't leave his wife for you either. You're also where you shouldn't be and won't be happy for much longer. You're in love with him and he does love you. He's more in-love with his wife no matter what he tells you or what you've convinced yourself. Sharon you're in the worse spot. You have more than a family of kids. I love you and I'm not judging but it's a fact. The hardest thing to expect is for this man to leave his family and to come stay with you. He would be deserting his kids for your kids. On the other hand why should they even think about doing that when they can have their wives and us freely waiting on the other side?"

"Oh fuck. What are we doing? Monica, Sandy, I'm so sorry for getting upset with the both of you. All I want is to know you're not thinking that you're better than me. Yes I've made more mistakes than both of you but I want you to admit that you've made them just like I have. I might be the most fucked up one but we're all fucked in our own way."

Sitting talking with my sister and my cousin, I must admit that they're right. We're all fucked up. I know that I've given so much of myself in the years since I've been with Dwayne. His wife cussed me with no support from him. I've had my house damaged with the inability to do anything about it. All I can hear from Dwayne is that he'll take care of it.

All the three of us can do now is agree that we'll not get angry when we try to help each other to see our mistakes. For now the most important thing is getting Sharon to take better care of her life. And now that we know she's not pregnant we talked about her not getting pregnant again. She's never been a fan of birth control but she agrees to get something done.

After our fighting period we move on to talking about what Beverly said happened after I left the party. Monica and I talked about it before but I never told any of it to Sharon. I tell them that I know when Dwayne said he'll take care of it with Jenny, that deep down I know he says that to calm me down, but I accept it as fine. I tell them Beverly is on edge that something is going on in her marriage. As soon as I mention Beverly Sharon jumps in.

"Did she find out about his girlfriend?"

"What! What girlfriend?"

"Okay. I guess she didn't."

"What girlfriend?"

"A few weeks ago I was at the mall and I saw Felix there. He was walking with a woman and a little boy. This kid was about three years old, a cute kid. At first he didn't see me but it didn't take long for him to notice me after I tried to go back the other way. He saw me and I think he wanted to say something about the woman and the kid and not let me go saying anything to Bev."

"A kid and a woman, I can tell this isn't going to end right." Suddenly I'm getting nervous.

"No it's not. After he saw me I figured my curiosity wouldn't let me walk away. He introduced me to the girl as a friend of his that needed a lift to do some shopping, so he gave her a ride."

I'm sitting listening and I know I won't like what I'm about to hear. "He never goes to the mall. Bev always calls me when she wants company and always complains that he won't go with her."

Sharon's anxious to tell us more. All the attention is off her now and she's going to keep it that way. She tells us about how nervous Felix was when he was talking to her. She said the woman was also a little nervous since she was sure by then, the woman figured out that she and Beverly are friends.

"Wait. There's more to it. At first I thought I jumped to the wrong conclusion when I saw him and her together and I was glad to know that my first impression was wrong. I had no reason not to believe him, especially when he mentioned Beverly in front of her."

"I can't say that sounds bad. Maybe he really was just helping out a friend."

"I agree that it doesn't sound bad and I honestly believed him also. I told them bye and was about to walk off when the little boy ask who I was and called him daddy. He could have pissed himself. And the look on the woman's face told the whole story; another bitch."

"What the hell! I'm sure Beverly has no idea or she would've said something to me. The only thing she said is she has a feeling something is wrong."

"I couldn't wait to leave them. I didn't know what to say. Before I left I promised him that I wouldn't say anything to Beverly. He wants to be the one to tell her when he thinks the time is right. I dread the thought of ending up being the bearer of that kind of news. I shouldn't have to be the one to give her such bad news so I agreed."

Monica was never a fan of Beverly's. She always thinks of her as a friend but not onc that she would tell her business to. She doesn't look very sympathetic when Sharon gave us the news, but she has her comments.

"Listen. I like Beverly but she needs to know what her husband is doing before she decides to help others get into situations. If she was watching her man she would've known he was out there making baby with some other woman."

"Monica you shouldn't be like that. When she finds out she'll need us."

I know Monica wouldn't want to see Beverly hurt but she won't be too sympathetic either. She always said that Beverly talks too much about other people's business. Sharon continues telling us the rest of the story.

"Sandy hold on. That's not the end of the story. I found out that he lives with this woman part time. When he's away on business trips she's his business. Other times he makes sure not to sleep at her house so he leaves her before morning to go home. If he and her has to do anything special that he needs to dress up, he already has clothes and everything else he needs there. He leaves his house in his casual clothes and then goes to his and the woman's condo downtown to shower and change. When I saw him they were coming out of a suit store looking for something. That weekend he was supposed to be away on business."

"Bev said that he used his parents as excuse to leave the house sometimes, saying they need his help more now that they're older. Are they also covering for him? He has it all planned in a way that Beverly won't have to find out."

"This woman is willing to live like that as long as he stays apart of her life. They have a kid together. They're his other family."

"Bev does complain about him coming home late many nights. She always admires him for the way he takes care of his parents. This man is living two different lives with two complete families. Has he really convinced himself that she'll never find out? Talk about assholes. Whose good man is he?"

"Listen to me Sandy. Both you and Sharon seem to think that there are good men out there. All men including my husband have the ability to cheat. And as for the women we all do have the same ability since we're the ones these men cheat with. Those of you who're single might not consider it cheating but it is if the man is married."

"I'm not really thinking anything like that. Beverly might be a lot of things but she's not cheating on him. I'd know if she is."

"Yes I'm a cheater and I'll deal with my God about it. If Dave's cheating on me I'd still feel some anger but not enough to leave him. Sean on the other hand would probably die if his wife cheated. Right now, the only thing I can see that'll make Beverly get pissed enough to leave Felix, is the child."

Monica shows signs that even though she cheats it would hurt her if Dave did the same. That I expect from a man so she surprise me a little. Now I'm worried about Beverly.

"That, I can't know. You guys are closer to her than I am. We just have to wait and see. If he's not man enough to tell her what are we going to do about it Sandy?"

"I really don't want to be the one to give her that kind of news. But I wouldn't want to see her looking like a fool especially if others know about Felix's secret life. She should have the choice whether to stay or go. Who knows if she'll be like Jenny and accept everything the husband says." Now I have someone else to worry about.

Monica is also thinking about me and Sharon more that she is Bev. "I don't know what'll happen with Bev and Felix but all I want you both to understand is that you Sharon should find a man who wants you for more than just your body. One that wants your kids along with you and not just when he wants sex."

"I do understand what you're saying and I agree. My heart hurts so much for this man and he's not mine." Sharon finally gets it.

"None of you should have to leave yourself behind to gain their love. I'm in love with my husband but I love Sean and that's the difference. I'm with Sean because of the physical pleasures he gives me. Still I know I've got another life away from him and this story hits home, my home. All of us need to find our futures." Even though Monica is still lecturing us about our lives she takes responsibility for her life also.

"Then we can cheat?" We all couldn't help but laugh when Sharon came out with that sarcasm. I was getting tense again from everything that's said.

"That's up to you. Just don't let a married man keep you away from making a future for yourself with a slight hope of him being there with you. I'm not ready to give up Sean's sex but if I ever find my marriage in jeopardy, I'd leave him. Yes it would hurt but I wouldn't think twice."

The three of us sat and talked almost all night. We wanted to let the other know that we'll not criticise but we have to keep looking out for each other. We often recognize someone else's mistakes when they're making them but can't see our own even when it's the same ones looking back at us.

We listened to each other and were encouraged, but in our hearts we knew that after we leave we'll go back to our same lives with these same men breaking us down. Our conversation did force me to acknowledge that I lost myself in Dwayne. My world revolves around him. I love him, but as like Sharon and Monica, all our emotions are fighting in our minds; unable of letting go. Now looking back over the years, I really should've been too tired by now.

Verona J. Knight

Evelyn Once Said:

"Just because somebody say they don't remember hurting you doesn't mean their conveniently forgetfulness stops your pain."

Evelyn Once Said:

"There's nothing wrong with following your heart as long as you let your good sense lead and your intelligence steer."

Chapter Sixteen

I'm too drained of thinking now. I've gone over too many hurdles but I've survived them. Since my intervention with Monica and Sharon, I've had some nights when I was hurting and, all by myself.

I'm used to Dwayne changing his mind and putting me on hold every time Jenny says she can't manage with whatever it is by herself. Tonight I'm alone. I thought I should find somewhere to go since he changed our plans again but before I made any plans, he called telling me he's on his way over. Even though I'm pissed, all I said to him was okay.

He showed up here a little while ago acting as if it's not a big deal and without an explanation; but he could see that I was mad at him though. My kids are spending the night at Sharon's since they wanted to spend some time with their cousins. Since I was planning to pick them up tomorrow anyways I'm free tonight.

Now, I go above and beyond to make sure he doesn't do anything unnecessary to get Jenny angry but what about me. If he falls asleep here I wake him to make sure he leaves and gets home at a decent time.

Tonight I didn't act as head-over-heels as I usually do; running to his arms. He came and I hardly greet or acknowledge his presence. I didn't know what to say without sounding too demanding but before he could sit down my sarcasm takes over. I just can't help myself right now.

I sarcastically said "so the misses changed her plans again? I thought you had plans with the wife." He heard it as me saying he isn't welcome right now and he got very defensive, which of course caused another argument. He wants me to feel guilty that he comes to spend time with me but I'm giving him a hard time, again.

In my mind I knew that the only reason he came is because his plans with his wife did change and he decided to use me to full that time slot, again. And, again, my thought is, if it was plans that he could've changed then, why wasn't he here without all the drama in the first place?

Instead of saying something to make me know that it's not like that, again I hear the speech how he lies to his wife and sneak around to be with me. Now he's sounding like he's doing me a favour and not getting anything from us being together. I must stop allowing him to believe that. He should remember he gets as much out of our affair as I do. He's gone as far as accusing me of sounding like his wife when I'm defending myself.

For him to compare me to his wife is an insult in my mind. I know that all his statements like that are said to scare me into shutting up. If he thinks of me like he does his wife then he wouldn't keep coming to me, since he's here to get away from her.

Honestly, I worry about his reaction sometimes but I still let him know that I won't take his bullshit to get his love. I've got no reasons to do anything to jeopardise what we have but it's passed the point where he needs to start treating me right. I've done everything for too long to make it easier for us.

Whenever I lie, it's to make his life easier, not Jenny's. It doesn't matter to me if she knows that he and I are still sleeping together and that it hurts her, but it matters when he hurts. I even took her insults which was hard for me to do.

I think what pisses him off the most is when I say anything that sounds like I want Jenny to know more about our affair. I said it but after thinking about it I was sorry because it comes from my anger.

I didn't expect to fall so hard for him. In the beginning I accepted having his wife around but after we fell in love things changed and my way of thinking changed also. By then Jenny suspected that Dwayne and I were sleeping together but with no solid confirmation, there was nothing she could've done. Now it's too late and I'm too far gone; unable to turn back. That's why I think I deserve more but even so I just can't break away.

I haven't kept the extent of my love a secret from him and I know he's taking advantage of that. Any comments were only meant to make him think about my value but instead it brings anger.

After my comment that Jenny should know, his anger gave me insults and threats about what would happen between us if I made the mistake of telling his wife. I indirectly gave my own warnings which didn't help the anger. I can tell how much he's upset with me but right now it doesn't matter to me. I hold some cards now, even if I have to cry while holding them.

He grabs his keys and walk out of the house leaving me sitting on the couch. I didn't want to put much pressure on him but I want him to understand that I'm not feeling right about the way he's acting. We both knew what we were getting into at the beginning and that things could change. I'm not the same person who cried every time we had a fight and now if I do, it's not in front of him.

I sure as hell expect him to show me he can put other things aside for me once in awhile. What I need is for him to bring me comfort when I need it and not make me feel like his charity case. But even though I'm standing my ground, it scares me to think that I could start sounding like his wife.

I want him to feel safe to come to me for comfort so I usually try not to press the issue too hard. This time was too much and that's what caused me to break down and said what I really wanted to. Even though in my heart, I didn't want to say out loud. But I think tonight I painfully made my point.

I stood my ground last night but my tears couldn't stop after he left, even though I thought I wouldn't cry. Every time I thought about the pain I've endured because of him, the tears flowed harder. Now I'm sitting by myself thinking how my body, my soul, and my mind feel damaged. I'm sorry about the argument but at the same time, I'm happy. I just have to wait to see how long it takes him to call me. The length of time it takes will tell me how much he's planning to change.

If he calls early today then I'll assume he'll be thinking I'm going to do what I usually do; forgive and forget. If he calls later then he would've put some time in thinking about what I said, but can't stop himself from calling me. If he waits a few days I'll know he was trying to end what we have but his wants for me won't allow him to. I'll just have to let his timing tell me.

I've been through this enough to know the difference. Now I see he's 'just a man' so he'll do like 'just a man'. When I do hear from him I'll be happy but informed. Whether or not I might be still feeling the pain from our fight I can't say but it's just the way love goes.

* * *

Dwayne called me as I knew he would, but not in the time frame I was hoping since it's now too many days after. I told him how he kept me up all night because I kept thinking about our fight but I didn't tell him about me crying. I don't have to make him feel bad. Before I could tell him to come over, he said he'll stop by and see me.

In his words, he's sorry for getting angry with me and he wants to make it up to me. I think I can make this visit fun. Still, I know I still have work to do but he also knows he has work to do too. He loved it when I used the oils before so my plan is for us to have an oil treatment. I figure it'll be fun for both of us and can relax us.

When we talked I accepted his apology without hesitation. I don't want to let our fight get in the way of us having a good evening so I'll just put it aside. I'll meet him at the door when he comes the way I'm used to. Just to remind him of us, the way we used to be. I want to see how happy it makes him.

Earlier I prepared something for us to eat so we'll have it then go up stairs to my bedroom where the oils are ready. I'm looking to enjoy it as much as possible and my memory is making me feel good.

    Dwayne got here even earlier than I expected him to and I can tell he feels good being here. We didn't eat but instead came upstairs to an already fragrant scents and candles glowing through its glass casing, leaving the glimmer from the light flickering; overwhelms the bedroom. The glitter and the fragrance floating in the air is very seductive and pleasant to the nose. He throws himself on the bed without undressing as if he's tired.

"Mmmm." He's pleased with what he sees. "That smells nice."

"What's wrong with you?"

"I'm fine. Just want to relax tonight."

"That's not like you. What's wrong?" I'm a little hesitant trying to find out why. I can't help but wonder if he's losing interest after the things Jenny said. That witch! She's gonna have me wondering all kind of things with every little thing he does now. Why the hell did I listen to her?

"Nothing's wrong. Just came to spend some time and relax with you tonight. No sex."

"What? No sex. Why? Now that's weird for you. I don't mind us relaxing but that's not like you." I'm just so puzzles. No sex after all this time, I'm not his wife.

For some reason he's not as eager for sex tonight as he usually is. Usually as soon as he sees what I have planned, he's ready. Why's he acting so strange? Sure isn't normal. What's happening? (Is he losing interest?) I've to change this mood.

"Get undress baby so I can give you a message."

The massage and everything else I've planned will send a different message, will make him feel better. He seems to enjoy the unknown when it comes to pleasuring his body so I got up to go into the bathroom. I can feel his eyes watching my ass as I make sure it's visible while I fill the tub with warm water and turn the jets on. After undressing, I told him to come and he walks over and step in. I watch him sit and eased into the water with his head also easing back, allowing him to relax there.

I plan to go in with him but I just want to allow him some space for awhile so I sit on the edge of the tub watching. After, I start to massage his shoulders from behind while my hands purposely reach slightly too far down a few times; passing over his nipples. Every time I touch a nipple I feel his body jump slightly, responding to my feel.

I can see he's ready to enjoy us, after he's been enjoying my massage for the past few minutes. I'm making sure my body's always telling him I'm ready also. I can see that he's forgetting about his no sex request he gave when he came earlier. So, I slide my body in, slipping slowly in the tub to join him allowing my body to do all the talking.

Using my foot, I massage his thighs, slowly, going between and up his legs. He releases a pleasing sigh. I enjoy seeing that safe pleasant look on his face each time his toes touch me slightly between my legs while he try opening them even more. My head tilts backwards; resting on the tub.

With all of it, my mind's trying to brush away any thoughts of our fighting and why he said no sex. My body claims calm and my mind says I've got nothing to worry about so relax. I'll try. (Did he have sex with his wife before he came here?)

Slowly I lift one leg from the water, using my toes to teasingly play. My foot rising up to his mouth and my toes touching his lips gives him access to nibble. My other leg still under water, massaging between his legs; loosens his concentration.

Our playful teasing becomes a stimulating foreplay. His toes are between my legs, touching my lips; without words, just smiling gazes. My body's in an eager place. I'm hardly able to wait for satisfaction while last night fades, bringing a sense of comfort; making way to appease my appetite.

Leaning forward, the jets still going against our bodies has my senses floating with us both in the tub. My parts plead to my body to hurry. The smile and look on my face tells his eyes that I'm okay and a bit impatient. Without much hesitation, he pulls me towards him and our legs wrap around each other, bringing him closer for my lips to touch; then I take him in.

With the jets hitting, he takes my knees as he stands in the tub, exposing his body. I hold on around his neck while giving anyone a view through the low windows. His gorgeousness is exposed to the outside. Without hesitating and wondering who can be watching, I move my face towards his groan. As he lowers me back in the water to tip touching my lips, any self control remain unseen.

He eases me up, allowing his body to go behind mine; adjusting me to lean forward. The water bubbling around us feels so good. I'm feeling for something else to hold on to, easing forward towards the edge of the tub. His hands slowly feeling my skin, glides over my breast. My heart's racing, knowing the feel of one hand leading down my stomach, heading between my legs. The other, continues its work over my breast; slowly massaging my parts.

The feel of hardness conforming between us, sends chills flowing. Touches on my breast, tightens my skin and I feel my nipple going firm. My nipples. My body. My senses. My man.

My legs are fighting the forceful water while I'm trying to open wider to welcome whatever comes close. My body calmly searching, working with the swirling water. It's waiting to feel which hand can bring the most pleasure, both equally winning.

My legs opening some more from his nudge tells me to give him more access. (Have mercy.) His finger casually enters. Both of us losing our abilities to control beyond now but that's ok. His body takes charge and from behind, he covers me. (Damn.)

I can feel my entrance playing tug-of-war with the water and him; fighting there with every attempt. Pushing through, my inside slowly tries to grab on to whatever is busting through to take possession. The sliding feeling going on around inside, against my walls, sends a message to my brain. (It's about to collapse at any time now).

In a 1-2-3 grabbing system, my inside says it's too much and as soon as he broke through, it holds on for life and my over ready body feels relief fighting to come out. He breaks through with a push, coming in harder than expected; hitting my right spot. His body reacts to his entry as he travels deep beyond; almost convulsive. I can't wait any longer. His hold says not yet and sinks in hitting deeper. (There.)

The water's massaging outside, his hand, holds on tighter; feeling of ecstasy flow every time he touches deeper. Each push touches a right place, allowing the intensity to crawl or rush in. Coming to my peak I feel my inside opening to allow whatever wants to come out, my release. I feel him. My inside; he's painting. His splashes send orgasmic impulses straight to my head while forcing hiccups from between my legs. (Yes!)

The pleasure's creeping through going to my toes. I'm confused as the pressure from the water prolongs the floating. This lingering delight's drifting through, says it won't leave soon, encouraging my body to scream again.

My inability to move, tells his body not to either. Each of us going deeper and deeper in a state of collapse, he holds and hugs me from behind. Neither of us wants to move. I stay leaning forward over the tub with him over me, resting inside. The sensation's fading while I try to find the energy to get out of the tub. (Have mercy. My inside is still jumping.)

I can barely move. We listen to our bodies then he eases and my body release him. I turn the jets off. The water drains, leaving us to sit, searching to find some energy. Watching, we leisurely wait for a few minutes. After, we moved to the bed to re-coop. The feeling flowing in embraces my minds desires. Every touch is reminding me that we haven't had sex like this in such a long time.

This is one of the most pleasurable nights we've had together in a while and all from him wanting no sex. My plans for tonight failed but I'm glad. The only problem is that now I'm thinking again why he didn't want to have sex in the first place. Maybe this is it; he wants spontaneous sex instead of planned sex time.

Our arguing turned into a most memorable night though and after a night like this, the arguing doesn't bother me as bad. I'll make sure we have our 'make up' sex time, just like tonight if we need to. (Here I go again, planning.) Make up sex is good though. It's amazing how good we are together.

Ironically, I can understand how Jenny feels when he's not there. It's just that I hate when I've to wait on him all the time, feeling neglected. But even though I understand, what she feels isn't important to me; better her than me. (Did he make love to her before he came here?)

I know when I had my little intervention with the girls, I thought hard about what I'm doing. I'm still thinking about it but it's not going to happen overnight. In the mean time my body can't take care of its self all the time and there's no rule that says I can't get him to satisfy my needs while I think. (Did they have sex before he came here?)

Evelyn Once Said:

"We cannot force another to give us love or respect and if we demand it, it comes not with sincerity. Then it's just a joke and not worth the effort."

Verona J. Knight

Evelyn Once Said:

"If you need to hide to do him you should be questioning your self-worth."

Chapter Seventeen

I think back to that day when I sent Dwayne the text messages that started this whole mess. I only did it because I was lonely; I still get depressed when the holidays come. My family just wasn't enough for me that year and without thinking I sent the messages and that was it, the troubles with Jenny started.

I wonder now what things would've been like for us if I hadn't sent them. If Jenny hadn't found them, where would Dwayne and I be now? Back then I didn't give a shit, but if I'd known the trouble that would follow, I would've 'think twice'.

At first I pretended to care so Dwayne's would think that I was concerned. I needed to reassure him that I didn't intend for her to see them. I was doing what I thought would make him feel better about us. I really didn't mind that she found out someone else loves her husband and that he loves someone else also. But I mind the result from it. If that hadn't happened I would've missed out on a lot with him though, since all her nagging and whatever else she does, pushed him closer to me.

All the hiding and the sneaking around was worth it for me in the beginning but it's been too long now and it doesn't feel the same. Even though it feels good to know the extent he goes to spend time with me, it's still getting tired.

Maybe it would've been better off accepting everything the way it was and not try to change it. Maybe I should live with the way things are instead of putting a strain on Dwayne. I think of all the things I've done to get her angry and yet she still stays. The constant conniving I've done just so he'd run to me is draining me.

We're at the point now where she's probably blaming me for making trouble and not concentrating on him bringing the trouble. The fact is, my needs won't allow me to give up. We depend on each other for that missing piece of life.

He constantly talks about how smart Jenny is but in my opinion, she's not as smart as he thinks she is. If she was, then she would've allowed him to get me out of his system but instead, she's giving him reasons to want me more; giving him ultimatums.

One of his favourite phrase is 'you can catch more flies with honey'. He complains about her nagging him about me and even though he never gets into a deep explanation, I can tell that their arguments get quite heated. Sometimes I wonder if he's waiting for her to ask nicely. I clap for her smarts since that's all she has.

It's not keeping him happy. She looks like a novice when it comes to the bedroom and that I'm not. I don't have to worry about her taking my place in there. But other places, I don't know much.

Eating the same thing and at the same place every night can make you lose your appetite after a while. With me it's all knew. Even if I do the same as she does, it's new since I'm new. I know what I'm doing and obviously she doesn't. I've some experience in the field of how to get a man while she seem to be learning the field of how to lose her man.

She thinks because he's her husband she shouldn't have to compete for his love when the fact is, if she was able to keep him happy I wouldn't have to be in this. In my mind she's worthless when it comes to keeping her husband happy. Even though she's the wife I can always say that I'm the one keeping him, he's more my man than he's hers.

With all the troubles that she caused she should know by now that it's a full time job trying to keep him away from me. She followed and found him in my house and after a few days, he's back in my bed.

I know she listened to his messages I felt on his voice mail before and I'm sure there're other things she's doing that I don't know about. Just because she's his wife it doesn't give her the right to listen. How pathetic it must be for her life to be chasing a man that she can't keep happy.

I still leave him messages and sometimes even hoping that she might listen to them. Dwayne tells me not to leave any, but I still do. I like to imagine the look on his face when he listens and if she does, I imagine the frustration on hers. Picturing that look on her face when she hears the explicit details in my messages; priceless. They're also a reminder to him of what he has waiting with me here.

Over time, I've left messages telling how much I miss 'my man'. Ones saying I'm looking forward to seeing him. Tell him how much I love and will always belong to him. Sometimes I even ask when I'll get to taste some of him and have my aching body taken care of. If he gets angry, I know how to take care of that too. I talk about body aching, juices flowing and other things she might not want to hear. I also told him how thankful I am to have him in my life and that I had to let him know how much he helped changed my life. I must always show appreciation.

In one of the message I ask him to explain why my man's so good, putting great emphasis on 'my man' part. I wanted my messages to trigger his imagination so they're as vivid as possible. At the same time I play on her visual as much as possible, just in case she listens.

I relished the thought of her hearing how good her husband is with me. How good he makes me feel while I rob her of his affection, it gives me comfort and power. I want to make her angry to the point where she hurts the way I do when he's with her.

Doing it through my messages, I make Dwayne feel good, while she suffers. I can hope for more but in the meantime, what more can I ask for to make me feel better. That's the only delight I can have for the pain I feel when he isn't with me.

* * *

I heard Jenny is out of town so I'll make good use of the time. I don't have to use a machine to tell him anything while she gone, I can in person. Whenever she's away on business, which has happened a few times now, I can get him to stay here much later than when she's home. And the time we have together is my make him forget that she's missing time, maybe he'll even get used to her not hanging around.

Since Jenny came back from her trip days ago, Dwayne and I haven't seen each other. Today I called and he didn't answer his phone. I've no idea what's wrong or if I've done something. Now Bev tells me that Jenny has been away more times in the past months, more than Dwayne told me about. I'm wondering now why he never said anything about those trips. I can't take it as simply nothing even though he never really talked much about her to me. I'm curious to know what that's about but I can't dwell on it.

Today I called Dwayne again and like yesterday, he doesn't answer. My curiosity really has me going now and growing greater and greater by the minute. Why isn't he answering my calls? I called him several times already today and he still isn't answering.

I need some idea, an explanation. I need to hear why he isn't returning my calls. (Why isn't he returning them?)

I finally got a hold of Dwayne. "A week now I've been trying to get you and you're telling me that you can't talk. You have no explanation to give me?"

He said he'll call me in a few days to talk and he'll explain what's happening then. Now days after talking to him still nothing. I'm still doing everything I can to keep busy.

Finally he calls and said he's coming over later this evening to talk. For the past few weeks things have been different and I feel a strain. It'll be nice to finally know why. I try to come up with ways, how to find out what the problem might be but without any success. So many questions I need answers to. I need to know what I've done to cause him to act the way he's been acting towards me. (I'll just have to wait.)

Bev needs to talk and I've got some time before Dwayne gets here so we can. Since I found out about Felix's second life I've been waiting to hear something from Bev to tell me that she knows. Now she finally feels like talking about it after all this time and I want to hear if he told her the full story.

I'd to force Felix's hands by giving her a heads up on what he's up to. I couldn't sit and wait on him since he didn't look like he was going to. Finally he had to tell Beverly about his girlfriend, Debra. He figured he had no choice but to confess before she found out the full story from me or Sharon.

She said they worked things out somewhat and that she's staying with him. After they talked about their feelings and how to work it out, he asks her to stay. He's giving her some stress free space that she needs; to think about whether or not to stay or go. Now she's telling me that they decided to have an open relationship where she can have other friends if she chooses to. His only restriction is that it's done without a community notice, without people knowing. He also doesn't want her to throw it in his face every time.

She also blames herself because she can't give him a child and now that someone else has, she feels useless. She said when Felix confessed about his outside life, along with living with his guilt, she was surprised but somehow not. In the back of her mind she had many things running there because he spent so much time away on business or at his parents; she just didn't want to believe the worst.

She's forced to accept that he can experience fatherhood now though. She and I use to spend all our free time together before Dwayne. After I found out about Felix and Debra I just felt she'll need me so we've been spending more time together and I'm glad she was ready to talk to me.

After everything I've done all I can do is sympathize. I don't want her to think I'm judging her for staying or accepting Felix's behaviour and I'm in no position to judge after Dwayne. I remind her of that and let her know that it's all up to her what she does, I'm here for her.

She tells me it does bother her and I'm sure it will for a long time. She knows that one day she'll lose control and ends up finding someone to give her some comfort. But, she's not going to search for someone and she'll figure it out if she gets to that point. She's sure that with some more time she'll learn to handle it better but for now, she's struggling.

Before Dwayne came over tonight I kept thinking that I'll finally know what's been going on with him. I worry if he's planning to tell me that we're over. He gave hints of break-up with me once before but I changed his mind when he came to my house to tell me. Now that I think about it, it was one of the times I heard Jenny was out of town.

That night I could tell he had something serious to talk about but I diverted his attention to pause his mind from thinking. By the time I was finished with him all he had left on his mind was coming to see me next time.

I had plans to go to a party my friend was having that night but when he told me he was coming over, I changed my mind. I remember he was acting strange and mostly trying not to touch me. He was giving me the wrong vibe so I told him about my plans before he told me he was coming by. I could see he wasn't enthused; I think he was trying to find the right way to let me down without hurting me.

I spent most of that evening trying to figure out what he had to tell me but not giving him much of a chance to do it. That was the first time I felt I didn't want to be alone with him. I was so afraid to hear what he had to say and I had to come up with something fast.

I decided then to use what always works; sex. I got some wine and we sat and talked. After he got the nerve, he told me that we had to cool down and stop seeing each other as much as we'd been in the past. At the time, I wasn't going to pretend that I was fine with it and I didn't. I didn't get upset and I did restrain the anger. I had already figured out that it was something like that and I also knew that he didn't really want to end us but was trying to please Jenny; again.

Now, here I am again, standing looking at him and feeling the same feelings I had that night; that he's about to do the break up speech again. Yes, I'm here listening and listening to him giving me reasons why we must stop.

"What do you expect me to do now Dwayne? You want to say that to me and expect I'll say okay?"

"I don't know what I expect to hear from you right now. I just know that we can't keep going on this way anymore."

Next thing I expected to hear from him is how much better it'll be for me. I know he isn't saying anything that he wants to but he's telling me because his wife does. "What'd your wife find out now? Every time she tells you that she's leaving you, you feel guilty."

"It's not guilt talking right now. I know that it's time we end it. It's time for you to move on also."

"Like I told you and your wife, I'm a big girl. I can decide what's good for me and when I want to move on."

"I don't want to upset you Sandy. I really care about you. Actually I didn't realize how much until I decided to tell you this."

"The only thing I'm ready to do with you right now is help you relax. You need to get your mind off whatever it is that's making you talk like this."

I'm listening to him but the major thing on my mind is sex. I'm glad he told me a head that he was coming since it gave me the advantage; to plan for whatever. I can get my way with him here. All I need to do is get him in bed and I'll have him and all this talk will be over.

I control his mind when he's in me and I'm very good at doing that. I've got that control and know how to satisfy his needs. I can get him to do whatever I need him to, as long as he's in my sight. His phone's ringing and he's not answering it. (Yes!) I know I have him now. Dwayne loves me. I know the feeling is still there and I'll take advantage of it as long as it gets to him.

I still can't see myself with anyone else. I don't want to think about any breaking off anything right now. I can't handle it again. Watching him talking, I move in closer. I'm sitting and he's looking at me agreeing to everything he's saying.

Moving even closer I kiss his lips. "Keep talking baby." (Slowly go to his neck and shoulders and chest.) "I'm still listening baby."

His body's reacting and I know I have him again; he's mine. His body says I've nothing to worry about right now. Using my sex to change his mind again shows that I don't have to worry about him thinking anything like that tonight. He won't want to break the mood so I just open up and show him what's his and that he should enjoy it right here. Tonight we both can feel good and forget this nonsense. And I'll be comfortable in my bed after he leaves me later.

After my episode with Dwayne and his break up talk last night, I've to talk to Sharon this morning. I know that he's not leaving Jenny. Unlike Sharon with her whatever she wants to call it with Luke, she can't face that and she can't be fine with it. She still has hope with Luke. Since our intervention I've been waiting to see if our talk had any impact and if she would end it with him.

Luke isn't right for her. Seem like we know it and she doesn't want to admit it. He'll not be leaving his life with his wife to go and move into hers and I think I'd feel better if she could at lease accept that. In my eyes, he's better at cheating and is a better liar than Dwayne.

After I met and seen him a few time, I found out a few things that turned me off right away. He tells his friends that his wife is his life right before he goes and climbs into Sharon. He probably makes his wife feel like she's the best thing to happen to him but then turn right around and tell Sharon his wife is the worse; that he needs Sharon to make him feel good.

I've heard rumours of domestic abuse and he still tells friends he couldn't manage without his wife; but like I said I've heard rumours. From what I found out Luke has always had other women and does other things that he shouldn't. But no one takes notice because he functions very well. He has nothing good to bring to make Sharon's life better and it's still surprising that she knows all of that, but still has her hopes of getting him. That only shows her desperation; she's working so hard to be miserable.

I've walked away from my loves in the past and now I'm in a relationship that I can't lose. Walking from lovers is easy but relationship is not. I accepted now that Dwayne and I living happy ever after won't happen. I've a problem walking away and I think that's the only thing she and I have in common; fear of loneliness.

I'll stay for now even with my doubts of my future but unlike Sharon, I accept there might not be one with Dwayne. I know he finds it hard to leave me also and unlike my many mistakes in my past, I recognize this one was also a mistake but I'm working with it. I told him once that I'll belong to him forever and I know now how much I meant it because even when we break up, I have a feeling that he'll still have my heart.

It's hard to walk away from our years together and it makes me understand why it's so hard for him to leave his marriage after decades of him loving her. My worries get even greater for Sharon and the life she's living when I think how hard it is to leave.

Over the past few years Dwayne's gone through everything in my life with me. He's helped me through some emotionally draining battles and I've helped him through some of his, even before we started sleeping with each other. With all the past ups and downs, I honestly wasn't sure if he'd come back to me, but he did. (He's not going anywhere.)

Verona J. Knight

Evelyn Once Said:

"It's easy to walk away from a bad relationship but so hard to leave as your memories travels with you and traps your mind back there.

Evelyn Once Said:

Walking away is just taking steps, one after the other and another. Leaving is when your heart takes each step with you and not fight to stay".

Chapter Eighteen

It's only been a few months since the last break-up talk and here I am again; where something serious is happening but with no idea what. The breaking up sex isn't working like it use to so fixing it is not as easy any more.

Today I got this note from Jenny and I've been staring at it since it came. But I just can't decide if I want to open the envelope or not. It's puzzling why she'd be sending me anything in the mail. I was surprised to hear from her and I know it can't be anything good but the curiosity is killing me. Okay, I got to open it.

{**Quote**}"*You entered my life and brought me years of turmoil. You stayed in my life and induced instability more than all. The comforts of my home crumbled because of you. You crushed hearts that you had no rights to. You took the path of destruction. The time has come for you to change sides but keep looking back for your trouble might not* *hide. With all that I have and will gain, I say thank you though you know not why. Also, I will say good-bye."*

I'm even more surprised; actually shocked. I've no idea what this note means but I must call Dwayne and ask him to come over. I know they're having problems but I had no idea it was this bad. Right now I'm more curious about the goodbye part. (What does it mean? Damn. Girl you might have done it after all.)

Dwayne got here a few minutes ago but he's not really in the mood to talk about Jenny. After I showed him the note from her, he said she's leaving for a few months to work in New York. She got a transfer to live there for a while and she can work from their offices there to make it easier. My first thought is that she'll be out of my way and for the time she's gone, we'll be free to do anything with each other; that's a sense of relief.

* * *

Dwayne and I are spending more time together since Jenny left for New York but I can see that it's not as happy as I thought it would be. Sometimes I get the feeling that even when he's with me his mind never is. In some way he might be missing her since they've never been away from each other for so long before. That I'll try to be more understanding about. The fact that they've never lived apart will be hard.

Months before she left I've known he's been staying with his friend Mark and I figured it had something to do with me. Now

I feel that the reason he moved out is also the reason why Jenny really moved. He left Mark's and went back home after Jenny left but it still doesn't feel right with us. She's not here and nothing's standing in our way but it's not feeling right.

I keep thinking about something Sharon said to me in one of our fights. She asked me what would happen if my good sex left the relationship. How much longer after that would Dwayne stay with me? That memory instigated my controlling urge to do everything I can to revive our love life again; I'm still trying.

I've done everything I thought he would like to make every moment an adventure but everything I tried seems like a waste of time. He just isn't enjoying it the way he used to. Since Jenny left, he still comes over when I call but not every time. Now I'm not always sure if he'll show up when he tells me he will.

He said he's coming over later. I've got this haunting feeling; thinking that final 'goodbye' day is creeping in. He's at my door and I'm really nervous. I always knew that using sex to change his mind might stop working one day and I don't know if this is that day. Stepping through the doors not giving me a kiss the way he's used to. At lease he gives me a hug and a soft embrace as in friendship. Now he sits down not wanting to go upstairs to relax and be comfortable.

His action is talking to me. This time won't be as easy as all the others. I feel my body going numb before I hear the words I'm assuming will be coming out of his mouth. I feel like I should be using the bathroom since my body isn't feeling right. Those lips that said all the right things to me in the past years might be about to tell me the most painful things they ever can.

My knees suddenly feel weak and my heart's racing. I close my ability to hear when I heard 'it's o . . .' I think the rest of the sentence say 'over with us'. Did he really say the bad words 'it's over with us'? My chest's hurting. I can't control my breathing. I'm suffocating. (Oxygen please, I need some fucking oxygen.) My lungs feel like I'm not feeding it air.

I'm talking but my voice is hiding while I feel the tears rushing to come. Flowing from my eyes, the tears meets whatever is running from my nose, as it both runs to my mouth; quietly. My knees give way and I fall to the ground and hold on to his knees and rest my head without any thought about dignity.

I've never experienced this feeling before, never. Before my brain could fully process what he just said, the first word my voice will allow is "please". My vocals only saying what might embarrass me later. "I'll never leave you and I won't let you leave me."

I'm begging him to think about what he said because I know he doesn't mean it. I need him to understand that he wants me the same way I want him. It's like déjà vu. I thought he didn't mean anything he said to me talking on the phone yesterday, but I only pretended not to have heard it. He said we had to end our affair but I told him he needs to say it to my face, in person if he really means it.

I was sure I'd convince him he doesn't want that. He said it a few times in the past but I never thought he meant it then either. And he usually changed his mind after he sees me. This time I can feel the coldness in the message, in his voice. No matter how much he says he's not trying to, he's only making me feel pain.

Right now I'm not too proud not to beg him to stay and to try and make us work. "Dwayne I'm willing to live anyway you want and I'll do whatever you say. I'll never make any demands on your time and cause Jenny any trouble."

I'll do anything he wants me to so I can keep this. He must know that he's the best thing for me, the best man. He's changed my life in ways nobody else has. I've become a better person, mother and friend because of him. The things that should be important to me are now, because he helped me to mentally grow. I'm not acting like it right now but I've matured along the way.

Everything I do and say isn't having any impact now. He thinks he's made his decision and his mind's made up. And his face says he has no intention of giving in to me.

"Sandy you know I love you but not enough to keep my family fall apart any longer."

"Dwayne I know that Jenny isn't a part of your life anymore as your wife, so you need me."

"No. I need to get my life back in order."

"I can help you and support you however you want me to. I want to help you to accomplish that."

"No you can't Sandy. You're just a reminder of what I've done to ruin my family. Jenny's my family."

"Dwayne how can you say that? How can you say that to me?"

"Listen. I'm not blaming you for what I've done. It's my family so I was the one who should've protected them. Instead I allowed sex to get in my way, and now look. Look what happened. I'm not blaming you. It's my fault."

When I hear him say that I'm a reminder of his pain, I feel worthlessness. The ideas that every time he looks at me I'd just make him think of Jenny's pain is a blow to my heart. I expect to have him look at me and see all the great moments between the two of us. Not his wife's pain. I expect him to see me and want me. I expect him to want me to help ease his pain. I expected many different things but not to hear that I'm his biggest mistake. To think that he regrets the times he spent with me is the blow of a lifetime. I've never felt so scorned. Never!

Evelyn Once Said:

"*A real friend knows when you need to be carried so you can meet up with your strength.*"

Chapter Nineteen

Since Dwayne threw his heart crushing news weeks ago, I haven't heard from him. I called him the following days to talk some sense into him but he didn't answer any of my calls and hasn't taken any of them since. I wasn't surprised though. Lots of times in the past he ignored my calls for the first few days after an argument. He usually calls after he's not pissed anymore then come by to see me anyway. This time, I'm still waiting.

I called him too many times today already and I'll keep doing it until he answers; I can't help myself. I know every time he sees my number on his phone, he'll think about me. Those thoughts will eventually bring his mind back to having some sense.

Yesterday I called Dwayne a few more times, and the day before that, I called him three times. Today, who knows? I've been calling for five days now and finally he took one of my calls. I knew he'd give in to me eventually. I knew he would come around. I know he's sorry for the nasty things he said to me and I also think that he loves the chase.

Since he took my call a few days ago, he's taken several. The first one he answered tells me things will be okay with some work. I've said some nasty things to him when I want to sometimes. Lately I find that I don't frighten when I need to say what I have on my mind; I just don't when it comes to Jenny.

I know he's angry with himself and that's why he said the things he did. Nobody is giving him love right now and he's a healthy man. No matter how much he thinks he wants to walk away, he's not going to start with someone else right now to make it worse with Jenny. He knows that I'm it if it's not her. I mean it when I tell him that I love him; it's my truth. I even stopped thinking about the bad outcome sometimes when my heart speaks instead of my questionable good sense.

Dwayne and I've been talking again for a few weeks now. I remind him that I'm trying to give up but it's too hard. He said it's not as easy for him either but it's a must. I also reminded him that even though I know that we'll have to end, it doesn't have to be now. Jenny isn't here and he needs me just like I do him and since I'm not ready to go to someone else, why not give and take with someone we do love; each other.

All the convincing got me a temporary agreement, meaning it doesn't have to end now. I want him to know that everything I said the night he broke up with me, I meant it. I told him that we can go on and no one has to know and everyone would think that he and I are done; including his friends.

We won't have to go out in public and I'll be here when he wants me and come to me when I need him to. I've no intention of losing what only he can give. And if he's not getting from someone else, what does he have to lose. I know it's my desperation talking but I don't care.

We've been doing the phone calls for weeks and he and I talk sometimes several times a day. We always end up talking about the things we've done together. Even though we haven't done any of it in a while, there's no way I can allow him to forget. I keep reminding him how we enjoyed making love to each other.

Months without sex is getting me frustrated but a few days ago, he called me instead of me calling him. When I saw his number on my phone, and he initiating the call, I almost dropped it. The first thought was what to do when we see each other again. The second was that he's back. We're back to talking every day again; the way it use to be, so long ago.

I was talking to him and I asked him if he really want me to find someone else to do the things we use to do. I already knew his answer since I know how possessive he is and he couldn't stand the thought of someone else touching me like that. I know when he tells me we're over he's not thinking about anyone else doing all that to me if I move on.

His arrogance tells him if we break up it'll affect me more than him. I know it would devastate me but I also know that it wouldn't make him happy either, whether or not he wants to admit it to himself.

Today he called to come over. The past year had too many ups and downs, full of emotional turmoil for me with him. I found out about his and his wife's problems and that he was staying at his friend Mark's house. Then I got that message from Jenny telling me thank you and goodbye a few months ago. Now, I also found out that she moved out of town and not just for her job. He and I didn't get into any deep conversation about it but Beverly filled me in on the whole thing. I don't know how she gets it all, but I welcome it.

When Jenny left he was living at Mark's and I gave him his space to get Jenny out the way, but he still broke up with me. I used to think if she's living by herself wherever she is, then she's the one who made the decision to leave him. Then I was thinking my work would be half as hard here if she hurts him, but again, he still broke up with me.

Why would she want to move to another city to work, so far away from him and she didn't have to? She went back to work, then she moved away and she didn't have to. There's so much more to the story. But do I really want to know?

    I'm feeling good right now and I gave Beverly a call since she's always been a great support for me. The way she held up through her troubles with Felix's amazes me. Yes, she sometimes has her problem dealing with it and even though she talks to people, she's not having sex on the side. Home is fine for now also; that's where her heart is.

She actually thinks it was one of the best things to happen to her since the strain of not being able to do something she's wanted to is off her now. This way none of them will stifle each other and do whatever without any guilt. She wouldn't have done it this way but now, it's a good way.

She even enjoyed an episode with Felix and his baby mama. They now have a relationship and the child almost seems will have two mothers. Bev loves the kid like her own in that short time, since she doesn't have any for herself. They worked things out and now they're living like one big happy family most of the time.

She hears my voice and the first thing she said is that she was planning to call me. She couldn't wait to tell me about her night, last night. Felix's child came over and the child's mother didn't want to stay home by herself. Bev gave the okay for her to stay and hang out together until she was ready to go home. They already worked out their problems and been living as 'Felix and his two wives' like a TV show. (Weird.)

During dinner they had a bit too much to drink and she started explaining to Bev about why Felix happened. It sounds like me and Dwayne and I'm almost feeling sorry for the baby mother, Debra.

"Anyway, before we got too drunk Felix came in the room and was ready to take Debra home; he didn't want her to drive like that. In my state I thought what the heck, let her stay. I thought what else could happen after they done had a kid together."

Debra decided to stay even though Felix wasn't too keen on the idea at first. But since they all decided they'll work on their relationship for the child's sake he figured if he sees them getting along then it would be good. What she said happened next sounds like a porn movie.

I've to wonder if that's the way it is with those men with many wives. She told me they had a couple more drinking after Debra said she'll spend the night and since Felix was the sober one he could take care of anything else.

"Girl at first I thought it would be fun to have her in the next room hearing what's going on in my bedroom."

"You're sick. You know that right?"

"That's okay. I couldn't wait to start on Felix and he had no trouble taking some of me either."

"You're sick and your man is worse."

"Might be but it turned out better than I expected."

"You're sounding like you never had sex with your husband before."

"I've never had sex with my husband and his mistress before."

"Are you serious? You sick shit. All three of you are sick shits. Okay. Now what happened?"

"It was late and everyone was in bed. At first I thought Felix was going to give some story why he should sleep in the family room or something but he was fine coming to bed. He actually went in the bed and left us because he thought we were both drunk."

"Which you both were of course? I can only see you doing all that if you were drunk."

"Girl I had a few but my mind was working fine. All I kept thinking about was having sex with my husband and letting his mistress in the next room lay there in her bed and listen to us. I actually thought it would bother her but I was surprise to see her standing at our room door watching us. It was a bit dark and I was about to snap until I saw her touching herself."

"Oh shit. Are you serious?"

"I swear to you. She was standing there touching herself and that's when Felix saw her there too. He didn't seem as surprise as I was and I was at a loss for words. I had to turn the lamp beside the bed on to make sure I was seeing all of it right. I still can't believe it."

Bev's telling me about her night and all I keep thinking about is all the things she's been going through and now to get here; to be civil to Debra.

"Bev I don't know. Those kinda shit never happens to me. All I get is stress."

"Well Felix was laying there and then I'm sitting in the bed with my mouth opened. I hesitated for a minute after she asked if she could come in."

"Have mercy. You all sick I said."

"You might be right because we let her in the bed with us."

"Every man's dream; having his wife and his mistress in the same bed with him, at the same time. Was he pinching himself?"

"Whether or not he was I don't know but I can tell you it wasn't long before he was pinching my nipples."

"What'd she do? I'm curious to know if she could perform with the 'wifey' by her side."

"I've always wondered what happens when he's with her and I can now say I know some of what they do together. At first he was giving me most of the attention until she took over. She kissed his chest and his stomach. I almost forgot who she was when I joined in. I've never had a threesome before so I didn't know exactly how to react to her."

"I'm feeling like I'm having one from the story I'm hearing. How'd you feel watching someone else making love to your husband?"

"Surprisingly, I was turned on. When I put it out of my mind that she carried his kid, it was alright. The thought only crossed my mind when we started. After we got into it all three of us were enjoying it. He was in another world. I was afraid to touch her until she touched me and I felt my lips sliding and my thighs slipping against each other."

"Damn. This sounds unreal."

"Imagine how I felt in bed between my husband and his, not just mistress, but his baby's mother."

"Never in a million years would I think that you'd forgive that much."

"As the saying goes, 'if you can't beat them join them'. My situation has already gone so far that I can't change anything so what the hell."

"So what else happened?"

"Okay. Imagine my husband laying there enjoying her lip over his body while he's lips are doing me. She watched him with me and felt no way about it. While it was all happening my mind was thinking but after, I thought it was the perfect job for her and it felt really good. In my mind she was the help cleaning. But I can say it was exciting for all of us."

"Now that you had a chance to think without the liquor, how you feel about the whole thing?"

"Now I think it was great. I don't think of her as the help now and I figure it was the best way to do anything like that; a threesome. There's nobody involved who has someone to tell on so no secrets. Perfect. It was an experience and whether or not it'll happen again, who knows. We actually smiled at each other after she and I got sober; so she drove home."

It'd be in the year never before something like that happen between me and Jenny. Dwayne would probably do it with me and another woman but not his wife. I don't think I could be in the same room watching her with him either. That kind of freedom is serious.

I told Bev that I'll call her later because I need to do something. She doesn't know that Dwayne's coming over and I didn't want to get into it with her right now. She knows that he broke up with me and didn't seem too sorry. She thinks it's time I move on with my life and not sit waiting on him also.

Dwayne and Jenny's problems aren't a priority to me anymore. All I know is that he's coming to see me. Maybe he's realized that his attempts to fix his marriage won't work. They might even be ending their marriage since he's living in their house and she's in another city. After all that I've gone through with him I can't allow him to end his marriage right now either.

All he's done since she left is hurt me. I don't even think he himself knows how much. If she leaves him it'll open the door for other women to come in. If he stays with her it's just going to be me.

I won't have someone else reap the benefits of what I've worked for all these years. But, if I get any signs that it's me then hey. She's still a part of his life but not the way to bother me so I'm good.

I was gonna take a shower but changed my mind. I'm hoping that I can get him in there with me, but I won't force it. Now that he's on his own I'm pretty sure he's not getting the attention he's used to from anywhere. When he comes I must jog his memory. Remind him that I'm here for him and there's no need to be lonely. Also that there's no better place I'd rather be.

I know he said I remind him of the things he did wrong to his marriage that caused him to put pressure on his wife. But, this is a chance to show him that he gained in the process also. And since I have no doubt that his feelings for me are still real, I can't see it being a big job.

He still has his key for my house and I told him to let himself in when he comes. He never gave it back even though he said we're done. I want him to feel ownership over whatever is inside these walls. Using his key should give a feeling of belonging, a feeling of home.

I decided to go ahead and take my shower after all. I stood in the shower with the water flowing, running down on my face. I was looking out for him and from a glance, I see his shadow walking into the bathroom but because of the water I didn't hear the door.

I watch him standing, admiring me with such care as if he was on a bad vacation and is happy to be home. I stepped out and leaned towards him with a greeting kiss going softly on his cheek; pulling the towel off the rack in the same motion.

I figured he's watching me because he wants to feel what he's been missing so he reached and I give him the towel. He took it without hesitation and slowly taps my skin, going over my shoulders, leaving going down my back, towards my legs, stopping to kiss the middle of my back. Then he continues down to my legs from behind, almost tapping my skin dry. We seem to have a love hate relationship and right now it's time for love.

Without drying the front of me, he drops the towel and takes my hands in his. Walking backwards, he leads me back to the bedroom with our eyes looking in each other's. Playfully, I push him to fall on the bed behind him. I didn't hesitate either since I know that we're both sorry. It's as if we like fighting so we can make up. That might sound like I'm sick but right now it's not bothering me.

He lay with a smile covering his face saying 'I'm sorry' and I unzip his pants then slowly bend over to pull them off. He unbuttons his shirt and I climb up on the bed with him. Him still lying but between my legs, I kneel to help him with the buttons. Leaning forward I whisper in his ear.

"It's fine if you think about someone else tonight."

I want him to feel both of us making love to him tonight. After my talk with Bev it doesn't sound that bad. I kiss his nipple and I see the look of reassurance on his face saying I'll be alright; so I ease up and smile. I kiss the other nipple and I ask him another question. "Does she do this?" I nibble on his nipples then I kiss going down his stomach. I admire my sculpture and ask him again "or this".

The reaction of his body tells me he's at ease and that he knows he won't have any need to pretend. I watch the pleasures flowing, engulfing his mind while he relax; knowing he can think about anyone tonight. He can do it with no guilt, feeling my kisses down to his legs. With every kiss going to different parts of his body, I ask a question or tell him something to make it easier. "Allow us to make love to you tonight."

I move closer, positioning myself so I can ease down and sit on his perfect spot that's ready and waiting, and again I lean forward for his kiss. This is the first time our lips are touching each other's for a while and it feels right. My first kiss in months and it feels good. I whisper in his ear again. "I want to be both your wife and your mistress tonight. Enjoy both of us and I'll enjoy you."

I need him to know that I understand. I've to let him see that I'm not jealous of his love for Jenny even though they aren't together. I can give him his space and the time he needs to ease his pain. After all the years they've had together, no one would believe that he can get over her so soon. He has to know that I accept that. And that I treasure the years we've had together also.

I've always known the right words to say to help him do whatever I want him to. I know what to do to make sure he enjoys me as much as he can. I must now learn how to help him forget the pain he's feeling from his break up with Jenny.

He has no idea that I know as much as I do, so he'll know that my efforts are sincere. His wife once accused me of kissing his ass while sucking his dick to get him to do anything I want, and I'm fine with doing that. Now he's here with me and she's wherever, and I'm not crying about it.

Whatever I do to his body and whatever I say to support his confidence will have him coming back. Those thoughts are the ones that takes over my mind and helps me slide down on his extra rock hard muscle; so sweet.

My inside hugs every inch like a loved one who's been missing and showed up out-of-the-blue to surprise me. (Mmmm. Yes. Relief.) Welcome back.

Evelyn Once Said:

"There's one problem it's best to deal with sooner rather than later because we can't run from it; ourselves."

Chapter Twenty

Weeks ago I couldn't get Dwayne to answer my calls and now he calls me instead. Beverly told me that at the last party someone asked how Jenny's doing and Kimberly told them she's doing great working in New York. The women said they didn't know she lives there and she told them it's not permanent. Apparently Jenny's decision to transfer was made on her own. It tells me more about the note I got from her months ago among other things happening with Dwayne.

Many scenarios are going through my mind now. Since we got together that first time after our so called brake up, we've been together many other times. Although for the past week we haven't spent much time together but we talked on the phone. I know mine is the only sex he's getting right now but how long before she comes back, and what'll happen then?

I'm sure I'll still have some time before I've to think about that. His mind sometimes wonders off when we're together; I assume it has to do with Jenny. I'm living in someone else's life and can't find mine anymore. When did I come to this? Why did I let myself come to this? Our time together is usually about sex now but we still have good talks on the phone.

I'm meeting up with the girls at Karen's house for another lingerie party later. I've gone to parties but not any at her house since the one with Jenny there. I know sooner or later I've to face those women again but I can do it now with them thinking I'm not still with Dwayne. They can respect me for ending it with him after the incident with Jenny.

Only Dwayne and I have to know we're still together. When they see me buying they can only wonder why or think I found someone else already. I'm back to keeping up with my bedroom assets and I can still enjoy them.

    The party started before I got here and even though I was greeted well, I know some of the women are thinking about my last time. I'm having a good time and the other girls seem to have put my last episode behind them.

An hour or so after, Kimberly walks in which cause my heart to race a bit. With my damn luck, again she has Jenny walking in behind her. Then I look and behind Jenny is her friend Madge walking in also. This time I'm not staying and then later tell myself I shouldn't have, so without saying a word I'll walk out. I got up to get my purse and turn to go towards the door. Right then I heard Jenny saying something.

"Sandy if the only reason you're leaving is because I'm here, then stay. I'm over all of that and I wouldn't want you leaving for my sake. You're my past."

Again I hear the room go silent. Kimberly opens her mouth and was about to say something but Jenny stops her. Both Kimberly and Madge aren't pleased to hear Jenny say that to me. The other women in the room are basically the same ones from the other party so they all know what it's about this time. I change my mind and decided to stay, mostly out of curiosity but also to show that I've moved beyond that also.

The party isn't going as bad as I thought it might and during the show the women all got to talking about every item. We're laughing at some of the women's expressed imagination and ways of using the toys. One makes a comment about having the right man to use the products with. She talks about trusting the right person to use them with. That way we won't have any inhibitions or worry about safety. Right then Jenny jumps in the conversation.

"Having the right man is not the problem or even one you can trust. The problem is we never know how clean the person he's stepping out with is."

Right then Kimberly gave her opinion. "I still believe in loyalty and without that I've no intention of doing many of the things I'd want to do."

Mary, one of the other women who's not married but has a boyfriend she's been with for a couple of years, gives her thoughts. "I believe a man and a woman should be careful who they sleep with. Anything can happen that they didn't plan for. I love my boyfriend but if I found out that he's cheating that would be it."

Jenny continues. "I was married forever as you all may know and my husband did the unexpected. Now I've learned that there are, in my opinion, four kinds of men out there for you to identify when you're looking."

"What have you discovered madam?" Madge asked with a smile while everyone listens almost in silence.

"Well even though I'm no expert. Over the years I ran into some that you'd never give the time of day. Those are the ones that keep you walking when you hear their voice because you simply don't want to hear what they have to say. Another kind, are the ones that you know and respect but couldn't see as a lover. Even though they might be attractive there's something about them that turns you off. In their mind, they feel they're so good that you must want them but you just can't picture yourself with them in your bed; egotistical."

All the women sit in silence while Jenny continues. "The third kind, are those ones you wouldn't want to hurt their feelings. They seem nice enough but you feel no attraction what-so-ever so you compliment them and tell them you can't have a sexual relationship with anyone right now. Let them know it's not because there's anything wrong but because you're searching to find yourself or something like that. But you would love to have their friendship."

Now even I'm waiting to hear more. "Now the best ones are the ones you see and you give a second look. And then the third look comes because you can't stop yourself. They're the ones you need to watch out for. Those are the ones that you can feel admiring your outside without you seeing them do it. They're the ones with the confidence and they know they're worth looking at. And they're the ones that can have you looking at faces on the street hoping you'll run into them without you realizing you're doing it. The ones you might get naughty with without thinking of the consequences and your inside jumps just with the memory or that look."

Madge looks at Jenny with her eyes wide open, surprised. "Damn girl. What happened to you in New York?"

"I discovered a few things about myself. If you're in a committed relationship you can look at that kind of man and they can look at you, but with distance between you. And without saying a word you both know that you want each other and your bodies react to the silence between the two of your imaginations. Now if you're not committed to someone then that's another story and you keep looking. Then you can give a second look, and then the third can even turn into a steer. And when your imagination takes over, let it. Even if those slutty thoughts are visiting your mind about having that person in you, enjoy it. Feel him there and move on or do the introduction."

Jeneze, one of the women holding the party, continues the conversation. "I totally agree with all of it. The only thing to remember is that a man like that has lots of stares coming to him. Just never lay your heart out."

Of course Kimberly thought she should bring Dwayne in the conversation. "I guess that's how it was for you and Dwayne."

"Yes. We were young but we knew at first sight that we belonged to each other. We had no need to try and change the other since we each thought the other was perfect. But like I said, we were young. We just loved each other. Now, decades later we still feel that way even with everything that happened in the past few years. I recognize the blessings I've gained from the past few years so nothing I say now is to hurt anyone because we've gone on with our lives. I've found myself because of it all, I've grown."

I move into the kitchen where the snacks are. Just couldn't sit listening to all that talk. I figure some of the women were thinking about me while Jenny was talking. Even though she made sure to let them know she wasn't dropping words and she was enjoying her new life now, they might not hear it that way. Now I'm standing in the kitchen out of everyone's way and Kimberly walks in. She comes over to where I'm standing and lean closer so nobody can hear what she's saying.

"How does it make you feel to know that even though she left him, she can just pick up the phone and she can have him anytime she's in town? How do you feel knowing that your love for him isn't enough to prevent it from happening? Are you looking over your shoulders yet?"

"What are you, her body guard or her manager? She seems to be having a good life so what's your problem."

"You're my problem. And no I'm not her manager or her body guard, just her friend watching her back. Who's watching out for your back? Do you wonder who she'll enjoy those toys with? He's still her husband and she's the one saying no."

"Please leave me alone. She's fine with everything. What's wrong with you?"

"Did he tell you he's having dinner with her tomorrow night?" Her with that smirk I want to slap off her damn face.

"You bitch. You feel better now? Just get the fuck out ma face!!"

I can't take it any more so I walk away and try to leave her standing in the kitchen but she step in front of me.

"If I was in her position you'd be so fucked up right now. Actually you would've been the first time I found those messages on his phone. I heard the whole story and you wouldn't still be here."

This time Jenny's friends are all clawing me with their eyes. As I pass some of the women and said bye to everyone, her friend Madge looks at me as if she knows exactly what Kimberly was saying to me in the kitchen. It's as if they planned the scene without Jenny knowing. I've no idea how they knew I'd be there. I guess they came just in case, since I was there the last time Jenny was.

She seemed happy with her life and they seemed to be getting some kind of pleasure from making me hurt. Dwayne didn't say anything to me about Jenny coming this weekend but what worries me most of all is that he didn't mention he's having dinner with her. I didn't let on to anyone at the party that I'm affected by any of their conversations, but I was. Now I'm back to the other woman again.

For the first time in years I feel that she's in control of my live. When they were a couple, he couldn't wait to spend time with me and now they're separated and she seems to have the last word. I told him it wouldn't matter but what a lie.

    I'm thinking that maybe Kimberly and Madge were just having some fun at my expense last night. But this morning I gave Dwayne a call and asked him to come over later and he said he can't. He told me he already made plans for the weekend so it would be impossible to find time but he'll call me later.

Listening to him confirmed that Jenny's friends were telling the truth about his plans with Jenny. I must wonder if I should be looking over my shoulder after all. The past six months with him has been with struggles and yet here we are with me still with my trapped heart. How can I continue with this? How do I let go?

With all the time we spend together, and all the years we've been together, we still haven't spent a full night together. In my heart I'm afraid to admit that I know the answer and maybe that's why I'm afraid to ask him why. Whenever he comes he leaves in the middle of the night as if he had someone at home waiting for him. And the pain I feel tells me that he leaves just in case she gives him reasons to be at home.

This morning I woke up still thinking about Kimberly's warning. When Jenny found out about me, Dwayne didn't care enough to stop seeing me so I thought I was in a good place in his heart; for years I did. My confidence got stronger when he still did everything in his power to continue finding time for us to spend together. I thought if he did all that for me then everything would be fine.

Because of all that, I hoped she would leave him since I knew it would be hard for him to leave her. Every time he went against her wishes it raised my hopes. Now she's gone and I still have the same hopes but it's not in his reality. Sometimes I think that they should've stayed together since my life now is harder with him than it was then. All the pain he caused her he's passing on to me.

My mind's screaming the question, thinking what Jenny and Dwayne are planning to do tonight. I know they're having dinner together but what else is in stored. The question from Kimberly 'who is Jenny planning to use those toys on', is sitting in the front of my mind. The thought of him making love to her after all this time is killing me. If they haven't made love for so long, will it be like new? The way it was for us after only a few months apart. The last thing I want is for him to be reminded of what she has and what he gave up.

When they were a couple he showed no appreciation but not having her now might make him want her more. He used to ache for me whenever we stayed apart too long but is he now? Am I just the crotch that's available without working for? I couldn't handle it if he turns out to be the same with Jenny as he used to be with me.

On the other hand, she's an attractive woman so why wouldn't she find a man by now? I want to believe that she bought those toys for her and her new man. I must believe that she has one. I'm still curious about all her reasons for living in New York but he won't say anything to me apart from she's working there for awhile. I'll have to keep listening to the rumours and keep asking Beverly to find out whatever she can.

(What the hell are they doing with their evening together?) I'm going crazy thinking about them. (What the hell are they doing right now? Why didn't he tell me she's here? Have mercy on me.) My body feels weak, so helpless.

Evelyn Once Said:

"Some lives can teach us how to move ahead while others can be an example of what can prevent us from moving ahead."

Chapter Twenty One

    Things been a little rough for me and I've being trying to reassess my life. I'm actually now starting to accept that I'm just a sex thing for Dwayne. My other failures added to this makes me question myself; why so many failed relationships? What is it about me that's causing this? I'm the common denominator in all the relationship. Dwayne's and my on-and-off relationship is consuming me and now he comes only when I call and sometimes he doesn't come any more.

The kid's fathers only come when they call or if they have to do something specific that involves the kids; and sometimes they don't come either. And even though the fathers provide money they're not there to say 'good job' to them when they need to hear it.

Dwayne was the one doing that for them. He's shown that there's more to being a father than doing what the Courts says. If he's not there for me I'll lose more than a lover. He's brought too much to my life to give up. He helped us all grow.

Since he and Jenny had dinner together a few months ago, he's been acting stranger than even before and he hasn't said anything to me about that night with her. It would've been nice to hear something without me having to ask but I'm not in a position to.

I pretended that I didn't know anything because the last thing I want is to get into an argument. I console myself when I need a hug. I tell myself that he avoids giving me details about their lives because he cares too much about me and don't want me to feel more hurt or make it something more than it really is.

* * *

I'm here with the girls for another party tonight. This is just to make sure they know that I'm doing well and feeling good. I also want to pick-up the stuff I ordered a couple of months back at the last party here. Without them knowing, I also want to make sure I've got something to show off to Dwayne when he and I finally get together; which have only been a hand full of time in the last couple of months.

Kimberly is here but I'm ignoring her. I can't let Jenny and her friends keep me from going places I enjoy going. I won't allow them to be a warden in my life. I've already imprisoned my love and that's bad enough.

I didn't say anything but I looked around to see if Jenny is also here though. I never know if she might be in town again and he decided not to tell me. I'm in a good mood and not about to let anyone spoil my evening. I enjoy these parties and I won't let them control my time and what I do with it. I like buying things and using them to make statements. Anyways, by now all the girls know my story so there are no more surprises.

Good thing I ordered before Jenny got here the last time. I think it'll be perfect for us and the scents I ordered will drive his senses wild. I can't wait to let him see these. Even these dolls are looking kind of interesting right now. Maybe I should buy one of the dolls and give him his threesome. (Sometimes I make myself laugh. Dolls? Right.)

I called him from here after I surveyed the place and told him to come over to my house later and that I've got a surprise for him. He didn't confirm but said he'll call me later. He said if not tonight, he'd come over sometime when he gets the chance in the next few days.

I wanted to get Kimberly attention and rub her for the last time so after looking at some things, I said to the girls that I'll be having some fun with all the things I ordered. Let her mind wonder for a change. Let her wonder if I'm talking about using them with Dwayne.

Kimberly seems to think I'm going overboard and decides to take it on herself, again, to make me feel uncomfortable. She seems to resent everything about me, more so than Jenny does. The last time I saw Jenny she said she was over the whole thing and she holds nothing against me; she had moved on.

I think Kimberly is out of her frigging mind and I don't care to figure out what her problem is. I've tried to ignore her all evening but she finds ways to get my attention. Now she backs me in a corner in the kitchen again like she did last time, thinking she can get to me; upsetting me for her own pleasure.

I know any movement will have the women's attention again. I'm not in the mood but she insists and since I don't want another scene I give in. I assume she doesn't want to cause a scene either. She walks up close enough that nobody else can hear what we're saying. But I know from the women's memory, any movement with she and I so close together will spark their interest.

"So I see you're still trying to keep Dwayne happy. I heard that the last time he broke it off with you, you starting begging."

"What the hell are you talking about?"

"You crying and begging like the pathetic loose thing you are; crying until you tasted your own tears. Was your nose dripping instead of the other end?"

"That is such a lie. Ha ha. Whoever told you that is a liar. I don't act like that, sorry."

"I don't know you well enough to say what you would do in that situation but you're cheap. All I know is that you sleep with married men and sell yourself for nothing. I can only go with what I've heard. I wonder where people are hearing things like that from. Now, how many are looking at you and seeing that?"

I don't know how she would hear something like that but the only person away from me and Dwayne who knows is Beverly.

"I'm not the one who needs Dwayne to survive. I can take care of myself so I don't need a man to make me whole. And a married one at that, someone else's husband. I'm not as stupid as you might think."

"No, you can't keep one so you figure sharing one is the best you can be good at. Don't need a man? You need other people's husband."

"He's the one that came to me. I never held a gun to his head."

"Any man would run to you. You seem to be every man's type. The types who open your legs and welcome men without getting any commitments before you open up. The kind who finds nothing wrong with breaking up families knowing there's nothing beyond scx in it for you. You convince yourself that this man wants you for the rest of his life and sit for years waiting. How long now? Three, four, five years?"

"I've never told anyone that. If you heard that I did, then whoever said it is also a liar." (Could Dwayne have said anything to his friends and they're talking about me?)

"You don't have to say anything since your actions are speaking loud and clear for you. Do you think Jenny did all she did because she was afraid of you taking Dwayne away from her? If that's what you think then you're kidding yourself. She loved her husband and he loves her. You're just something that happened and that couldn't be washed off. She left because of the scorn she felt towards him because of your stain."

"The way it's upsetting you, one would think that you're sleeping with Dwayne."

"I can promise you that if you were sleeping with my husband you wouldn't be here able to talk to anyone right now."

"Are you threatening me for something that has nothing to do with you?"

"I don't threaten anyone. If I wanted you hurt it would've happen without you knowing it was coming."

"You're sick. You're really sick."

"No, I'm a friend of someone who allowed you to get away with too much."

"Listen, I have no time for you and your crap. I've a man to take care of and you can't make me feel any guilt."

Even though she's getting to me I won't give her the satisfaction of knowing that. I don't have to explain what man I have to take care of and I want her imagination to take over. I just know I never said anything about it being Dwayne.

"I can see that you're not used to having decent men in you. The fact that he even tried to help you better yourself is evident. You needed him more than he did you and that's why you couldn't let go. What he didn't know is that you walk with your profession between your legs and you're very good at your job."

"How is he encouraging me to better myself? I was always taking care of myself and my kids. You and your friend are gullible if you think that's what he does for me."

"No sweet heart, we know what he did for you. What you should be doing is finding someone else to do it since he won't have time for your sorry ass anymore. And find a better way to hold him since your asset should be worn now."

"I don't see where my life has anything to do with you. I'm not your concern."

"It doesn't really, but it does have to do with my friend. It just pisses me off when I see women like you. You're so pathetic that you actually think he loves you."

"You're calling me pathetic. Listen to you fighting someone else's battle."

"What do you think would happen if you stop sleeping with you? How long do you think he'd keep telling you nice things without sex? That's all you have to offer but you'll never believe it even though the evidence spits in your face. Don't you ever wonder why he's not divorced?"

She's going on and on and I want to kick the shit out of her. Telling me Jenny is Dwayne's wife and that I've no say in what she does or doesn't do with him. Saying I must remember that I'm only his appointment mistress. I only see him by appointments.

I'm so pissed. I want to scream and kick her ass at the same time. She has the nerve to tell me that whatever I do isn't important since my job is to keep my legs open. Going as far as telling me I should always remember that I'm the one sleeping with someone else's husband, not the other way around. Saying that I must live with whatever happens next.

"Kimberly, just fuck off and leave me along. I don't want to hear or see you anymore."

She accuses me of pampering Dwayne because I'm in a losing competition. Saying Jenny doesn't have to compete since she's the wife; then and still is.

If that's what she wants to think about and get pissed then that's not my problem. I don't feel any guilt because he makes me happy.

The fact that they think I pamper him is also fine with me. If Jenny wanted to do the same it was her business but she chose not to so anyone blaming me for their breakup should look for someone else to blame.

Anything she wanted to do for Dwayne would've made me jealous but she also knew that I couldn't stop what goes on in her house. Even though I did everything to stop them from sleeping together I knew that they still did; he was her husband. If she did all that she was and he still came to me for love, then that say I was giving him more. The fact is that he came around me even though it upset her and that can only mean he loved me more.

He wasn't with me then just for the sex he loved me and still does. Yes if I stopped having sex with him it would've created some problems but he wouldn't have left me because of that.

She's telling me that people like me journey is to become a leech. And what the hell she means, people like me; maybe someone that makes a man happy? Even though I can't show her my feelings, it's upsetting. She thinks I get pleasure out of making others' lives miserable and that's not true. All I want is to be able to do as I wish. And I don't want to hear anything about what I'm doing and that it's wrong for them if it feels right for me.

I want to go wherever I want with whomever. I want to enjoy that without hearing that it makes me a slut. Whatever people want to say means nothing since I'm the one with the man. If and when I decide to do whatever, it's my choice. I don't mind him keeping up with Jenny and her life either since I'm the one keeping him happy among other things. There's nothing more I want to say to Kimberly after listening to her going off.

She has a problem with me and she should mind her own fucking business. She has a husband to take care of and if she continues I hope that someone comes along and give her something to really worry about.

I'm tired of listening to her going on and on so I try to squeeze by to get her out of my face but she walks away instead. I make a step to walk off also and she turns to look back at me with a pleasing grin on her face. Then the words I didn't want to hear, her final words.

"By the way Sandy dear. Did Dwayne tell you that Jenny's moving back soon? You've been like the movie trailer with the highlights but now Jenny, the full movie, is moving back to give the complete story for the full satisfaction. Bitch."

Evelyn Once Said:

"*The hardest to overcome in a relationship is when one says 'I love you' and the other says 'I love you too' but it's a re-action instead of their feelings.*"

Chapter Twenty Two

Last night even though I had plans, I ended up alone again. Of course my plans were with Dwayne but right before he was supposed to come, he called and said something came up and of course without an explanation. He said he would explain later and again he leaves me wondering what the explanation will be and how long 'later' will be. This hard time he's being going though might mean he's accepting his marriage is really over.

The past year since Jenny's been gone should've given him enough time to think and his actions lately say it's hitting him hard. Now is the time to reassure him that he'll be alright and that he'll never be alone. To manage through the hard times I must help him to settle his mind and move on.

At this point, I'm tired of being disappointed and I'm sure he must be with her too. He must be wondering if she's sleeping with somebody else or if she was.

Now how much support he'll allow me to give him is what I'm not sure of. I know he can never get what he needs from anywhere else; even though he told me he could during an argument. I'm realistic so I also know my grip has loosen some but he also knows I'd never cheat on him.

    I talked to Sharon yesterday and her life isn't going well right now either, but that's not new. Now she has no one since he broke up with her. She's falling apart and there was nothing much I could've done for her. I just felt helpless and couldn't even advise her since I'm going through my own thing.

Today I'm stopping by her place to spend some time with her. Monica is on her way to pick me up so we can go together and cheer her up. I don't know what the hell more I can say to make her feel better but I'm sure I'll find the right words when we get there. Somehow we usually find the right words to cheer up the people we love, at the right time.

She jumped right in that relationship without giving any serious thought about what could happen, even with the warnings we gave her, and doing it knowing he was still married. Yes he had his problems at home also so he made her believe it was finished with his wife but even with all that, she still should've been more careful. (That sounds like me.)

Monica and I are in different situations but she constantly tells us we're the same every time we try to make her see what's happening. She has her kids to think about and having this man take over her life wasn't safe for us to see. But we couldn't convince her otherwise no matter what. Now we're not losing any sleep thinking that he's not there, just sorry for her hurting.

Even though Monica enjoys her out of marriage relationship she told us she's prepared to move on if they ended it. When it comes to a choice between him and her marriage there's not much to think about. If she sees any indication that her husband suspects anything, she'll end it without even saying why. That's satisfying to hear since the last time we talked about it she wasn't ready to let go. Sharon's break-up on the other hand wasn't done as one would expect.

Monica and I got here and the state she's in tells us it'll take some doing to help her through. As soon as we walked through the door she broke into tears. She really fell hard for Luke and he convinced her he felt the same for her. He had also gone out of his way to please Sharon in the past and that assured her that he did love her, he was believable.

Neither of us wants to say 'we told you so', but we're both thinking it. She has a habit of not listening to good advice and she's one of those people who can't seem to learn from her past mistakes. She believed him when he told her he'd be with her for the rest of her life. She was desperate to believe in him after all she'd been through and thought she finally found true love. Monica and I already knew he wasn't telling her the truth.

Any man would think twice before taking on someone else's responsibilities of seven kids. She wasn't married to any of her kids' fathers. Normally, that could make a person think she isn't smart enough to take care of herself by taking precaution and preventing pregnancies.

If she had one or even two baby daddies for her kids, that might suggest she stayed in a committed relationship. People might even think she tried for a while but gave up. Now her situation says she can't find what it takes to keep her man. She's my sister but if I try not to think like that, it doesn't mean others aren't.

Some might see it as stupidity why she couldn't foresee the result with not using a condom. Not doing it more than one or even two times, shows carelessness and the fact is she's not stupid. Women who divorce or widowed with seven kids are looked at differently; as strong. They got commitment through marriage and they didn't go in with the intention of ending up a single parent.

Now, the fact that we're here again, I've got too much anger. But she's my sister so I can't tell her exactly that I'm thinking that way. It would sound too cold and would only break her heart more and I couldn't live with myself for doing that.

Monica and I are sitting and talking to Sharon trying to help her ease her pain. There wasn't much we could say but we spent our time so far talking about everything and nothing. She told us that Luke actually sent her a message to break up with her. I'm thinking that he could've at least faced her and let her know that he wasn't intentionally trying to hurt her.

I know it wouldn't have changed anything but at least it would've shown compassion. But on the other hand he might have felt he would've been doing his wife an injustice if he showed her that. I think she deserved that much after all this time. She wanted us to see the message so I took the phone and read out loud so both Monica and I could hear it at the same time.

"I couldn't say what I wanted to before. I'm at a new point in my life and I want to start it off right. Any plans you and I had for any relationship in the future stops here. It's my last chance to fix and keep my family together. As of today I want no more contact with you; meaning no more phone calls or messages between us. If you decide to ignore what I'm telling you then I'll be ignoring your calls and don't even think of harassing me. I wish you only good for your future since there's nothing more to say to you I'll just say I'm sorry if this is hurting you."

Reading it out loud while she's listening again, I can see the pain on her face. I can also see that she's trying to be strong and pretending that everything will be okay for her. She also showed us the massage between them after she read his first one.

"I'm fine with that and I completely understand. I had no intention of going on like this year after year. I'm starting to see all the bullshit coming from you. I wish you all the best also. I won't call at all so you make sure you don't change your mind and call me either."

"I've some things at your house that I'd like to get some time."

"You can pick up whatever I have here and the sooner the better. That means ASAP and in case you don't know what it means, as soon as possible."

"You can put my things in a box and leave the box in the garage. I'll pick it up within the next few days while you're not there."

"That's not a problem. Since we'll have no contact, have a good life and don't fuck up anybody else's. It's also good to know that your wife recycles."

I read the sarcasm in her message that shows her pain because of how he said sorry.

"I'm sorry for hurting you but more sorry for what happened between us because I ruined my life because of you."

He also kept stressing the need for him to get his belongings back. She told him that she won't be shedding any tears over him like she had done several time in the past. I know that she's only pretending that she'll be fine. I know without him she won't be okay and I know in her heart she also knows that's far from the truth.

He kept saying he's sorry for hurting her but I can read his ego busting through in the message saying that he knows she will be hurting over him. He also told her that he made promises to his wife and intends to keep every single one.

After we finished reading the messages from Luke, Sharon confessed that she was expecting something after she got some text messages from Luke's wife. That's when she shows us a conversation she had with his wife. She sent them after she found out that she was Luke's mistress.

When his wife found out she was harshly verbal and they ended up having a nasty text fight. Sharon was surprised she found out about her much more so to be getting messages from her. I read out loud, again, so that Monica can hear.

"So you're the rodent still eating away at my marriage."

"Who the hell are you talking to? Do you know me?"

"I've heard enough to know that you and your family are two who go into marriages and try to eat away at families."

"Woman I don't know you so I don't care what you have to say."

"You should take notice since you're sleeping with my husband."

By now I'm thinking who the hell does she think she is? How the hell would she know about me? And why the hell did she get me in their conversation. I've never met Luke's wife and never had an interest in knowing who she was. Now I'm curious to know about her if she knows about me.

"If I'm sleeping with your husband then it's you who should take notice. That would mean you're missing something if he has to come to me."

"It's not what he's missing at home but it's that he's addicted to doing whores. He likes the fact that you're mouth does and says things perfectly."

"Why do you feel the need to call me and disrespect me?"

"You gave me the right to do and say anything I want when you opened your legs for my husband, by doing that, you signed that contract. If you think this is it, you'll be surprise."

"Listen I really don't know what you want from me but you should be talking to your husband and not me."

Sharon said she turned off her phone after she sent the last message and didn't talk to her any more. Anything that came in after that, she didn't open. After I finish reading the messages we talk about what happened after they had the text fight. I wanted to take her mind off the wife so I turned the conversation back to her and Luke. And like Dwayne, his wife got Sharon's number off his phone. These men and their damn phones.

Later in the night, after dealing with the text messaging, she drifts back to her memories. She tells us that she was at home one night and Luke was there with her. He got a call but didn't answer after he looked and saw that it was his wife calling.

"He was already half dress and I had the water running in the tub for us to get in to soak and relax. We just wanted to calm my nerve a little before we headed to the bed. About half an hour later the door bell rang and neither of us moved to answer."

Monica didn't like that fact that she was at home and not answering her door. "What if something happened to any of the kids out there?"

"The older kids had sleepover at their friends and the younger ones were already in bed. I knew they were alright."

"So none of you were curious about the door?"

"Honestly, I was but he didn't want me to answer, as if he already knew who it was. The person knocked about three times and neither of us answered since we both had better things on our minds anyway. And since he didn't care I didn't either."

"So what happened after that?"

"Well he was in the room getting undressed and I was easing in the tub when I heard the banging getting louder. At first it sounded like someone was using something heavy to hit the door and it frightened me."

"What'd Luke do?"

"By then he was naked and by then he also knew it was his wife. He grabbed his things and tried getting dressed as fast as he could so he could tell her some lame excuse why he was here."

"And did she believe him when you finally opened the door."

"Maybe she would've if we opened it."

"You mean after all that you still didn't open the door?"

"No. I mean after all that we didn't have a chance to open the door. That loud banging was her damn foot kicking my door off."

"What the shit! That's why your door was broken! You lied about it too!" I can't believe she lied to me about that.

"Yes I lied. The bitch kicked off my door. After the door flew off she ran upstairs and found him in my room and he was still not finished dressing."

Monica's jaw dropped. Mouth wide open. But, looks like she's also stifling a laugh. "What'd she do after that?"

"Well she started throwing things. I kinda loss track of everything since I was naked. I felt something hit my neck and I saw things' going at him like there was a tornado going through my room. While it all was going on, Luke kept getting dressed along with the hits. Finally he couldn't take it anymore so he grabbed her arms and held them in place. He started screaming at her to stop while he's yelling 'I'm sorry' over and over to her. I grabbed my robe and cover myself and watched him trying to take her outside."

"You stood there watching them and said nothing."

"It hurt like hell but if I did anything Luke would've been pissed. Plus I had to go tell the kids to stay in their room since a crazy person broke in our house but Luke is taking care of it so don't be scared."

"Are you crazy?"

"He always said he'll do anything he wants without causing her wilful pain. After all of it she picked up her phone which was in pieces. The battery, the cover and the phone were in different spots in the room. I figure that's what hit me in the neck. That seems like so damn long ago."

Monica's looking at Sharon surprised. "What the hell happened to you? You just let some woman come up in your house and caused a ruckus and just left it at that. All that shit happening with your kids around? You know you're fucking up right."

"See, that's why I didn't tell you all anything. Listen. You have a husband and a lover someplace else. Not everyone is as blessed as you are. Some of us must grin a bare the pain just to get some. And I didn't just let it go like that. The next day he had someone come over and fixed my door. He also apologised and he meant it. Plus he also made it up to me in many ways."

"You're crazy. You allowed some crazy ass woman to come in here and kicked your door off and then you had your kids sleeping in the house with the door off the hinges in the night. You're crazy. Even if it was just a night; his ass would've sat there and guard my house."

"You don't get it. He showed me his love in so many different ways. For instance, last Christmas he's with his family but he found time to text me to tell me how much he loves me. He was with his wife but he had me on his mind. And there were many other times he was at home and sneaked in a call just to tell me he loves me, while his wife was in another room. Why wouldn't I believe that he loved me as much as he said?"

"Well that's just bad for his wife. I guess she doesn't know all of that cause no woman would stay with a man who treats her like that, whether she's the wife or girlfriend. Damn. That's disrespecting her for sure."

"That's just it. He didn't care enough not to. There was so much more to our relationship than sex. There were times when we'd talk on the phone for hours in the daytime. He'd forget that he's working and we found things to talk about. We called each other several times a day and still found things to talk about."

"I bet after doing that all day with you he goes home to his wife and act like he's piss tired from it all. Acting like all day he's been working for his family, and having nothing else to do out there."

"That's just it, after talking to me all day he came to see me before he goes home to her. I found out later that she gets everything else she wants though. Anything she asks for she gets. I only wish I'd found that out before it was too late. I really thought he was separated."

Monica understands from both sides. "If it's one thing the three of us know, it's that financial support isn't emotional support. While he's helping you with your troubles he's causing trouble at home. Who's helping his wife with her problems? Remember that I'm also married and I could've been in her position."

Sharon feels the need to remind Monica about her life. "Yaw, and remember you also have a lover on the side."

"Any problems in my marriage will be caused by me. I can't be any trouble for anyone in theirs since I'm not looking to take anyone's husband away and I don't make demands. I'm the only one here who can talk as a wife and as someone's lover. You believe because you see a man with a good life that he did it all by himself. The wife has a part in making that life you want to takeover. If you want that same life you'd have to take that wife with it because she's half of who made the life style you see."

"You have a good man so why'd you get involved with someone else?"

"That has nothing to do with other things that I'm not getting, it's just a sex thing."

"Yes, meaning you're not getting good sex."

"I have a good man for stability among other things. Now the bad man is for the excitement I need to help me make the good man feel good at home. I'd be miserable and making my home environment miserable without that. With that said, I wouldn't sit and let someone take my husband without a fight. And I mean any kind of fight, even if it needs to be physical."

"Well people will look at me and think that a man like that can't love a woman like me with my kids. I can't hide the fact that I've a few fathers for my kids so he knows that also. But he still gave me love. He even put me first sometimes. How can I stop loving him after all that? I said I don't but I do." The pain is showing again on Sharon's face.

I can only hope she faces the reality sooner rather than later about what's going on now. "Well you need to learn to take care of you because it sounds like he's not coming back this time."

We talked and talked and for a while it turned into Monica scowling Sharon. She understands why Luke decided to do the break-up using the message but I don't agree. He said he wouldn't see her again in any way, so that must be one of his promises to his wife; must have given him an ultimatum.

I can only imagine her telling him that the first time he speaks to Sharon after those messages, he'll be heading back to the road he's now leaving. That might mean the first time she gets any indication suggesting he might be sleeping with her again, it will end.

From what I read in their conversation, I try to understand why she's losing sleep over him. I couldn't help but ask her why if she says she understands it all. That's when she actually told the truth and said she isn't fine with any of it. She only told him that in her messages because she didn't want to seem desperate. She didn't want to give him the upper hand along with the breakup.

She said he told her once that he never stopped loving his wife and he knows that she still loves him even though they were separated. That even makes her angrier since he suggested again his marriage was over.

Monica looks disgusted. "When I look around me all I see are these men leaving their wives and going to other women's bed for comfort. So many of them go back home and not think about the pain they leave behind while their lives go on. Assholes. Yes even mine."

Monica thinks that some men give their wife everything because they think she'll have no need for anyone else if they do that. They might actually think wives only need material things since other women out there wants them because they see what they can provide. They use the 'I'm not getting it from you so I went somewhere else' speech when they get caught.

She keeps getting more angry thinking about the men's actions. "Do they every think that they're the ones messing up? It never crossed their minds that they're the ones not giving their wife something that she's missing so that she can want her husband more; stay attracted to him. Whatever the wife is missing might be the reason she lost interest. Sex and money is the easiest thing that either of them can get, it can come from anywhere or anyone. But, it's what nobody else out there can give, that's what makes the difference in the marriage." We all kinda look at each other in quiet, with that thinking gaze.

We spent hours trying to help Sharon as much as we could. Monica was less vocal than our last time here but she still got her point across. She also realized that she must handle her business as well before her marriage falls to the waste side like so many others.

She loves her husband and couldn't handle if he finds out that she's cheating. But like she said, he's not giving her something at home. For all she knows he's being faithful to her. I personally wouldn't swear for any man when it comes to being faithful. Like they say, the quiet ones are the worst.

We talked about as many other things, trying to keep Sharon's mind from Luke. After sitting with her for a few hours we got her smiling, but how long her smiles will last after we leave isn't certain.

We left Sharon's and Monica drove me home. Now I sit thinking about Dwayne and some of the things Kimberly said to me before. My feelings are almost damaged with all she said. I think I did a lot with my life as a single woman and mother. I worked hard while going to school to have a career. Even though

Sharon took longer, she also worked hard and took her children out of public housing and can now take care of herself. Her main problem is finding a way to protect her heart and not falling for the wrong man.

I'm confident that she'll be fine after a little while. She always seems to land on her feet and I'm just glad that she didn't get pregnant again and add another baby father. I know that I'd be okay, eventually, if Dwayne and I were to really break up.

With all my thinking, it does bother me that Dwayne never mentioned that Jenny is planning to move back soon. I knew eventually she'd come back but I had no idea how soon that would be. Why does he feel the need to keep it from me? Like I said, I do expect them to have a relationship since they do have kids together. Even though I don't have a good one with my kid's fathers I know that he's different, which is why I've these feelings for him.

I told Monica about the party and what happened with Kimberly. She just thinks I shouldn't waste time thinking about anything she said. That she was only trying to upset me and nothing else. She also thinks that Dwayne might be uncomfortable talking to me about Jenny and that's why. I want to agree with her even though I can't understand why he'd think I'd have an issue after what we talked about. I told him I can live with her and him so I'm still not sure of his motives.

When I told Dwayne about my first run in with Kimberly and the joy she seems to get from telling me about Jenny having the right to do anything with her husband, he looked right through me. When I told him exactly how she took pleasure in telling me about Jenny's plans and her moving back, he didn't even have any comment. He didn't feel the need to confirm or deny anything, as if I wasn't even talking to him.

To me it was as if she was getting off on seeing my pain, which of course I had no intention of showing to anyone. Even though I just played it off to Kimberly like I already knew, I expected sympathy for my feelings when Dwayne heard but he didn't show any interest in hearing any of it.

I still can't help wondering what's going on in his mind. Why haven't I heard from him about it before? After all I've said to him about our relationship and keeping it a secret, why is he still hiding things from me that I'll eventually find out about? (Could he be testing me?)

Evelyn Once Said:

"Never forget what they did so you won't end up back there and never waste time by not forgiving cause anger will keep you from leaving there."

Chapter Twenty Three

We're at the 'if he has the time' place right now. I guess I've been around for so long that he thinks he can give me the nonchalant treatment; the way he did Jenny in the beginning when he and I started. He and I have gone through the brake up talk more than once so now it's a waste of time to worry about it anymore. He would've left already if he wanted to.

Kimberly is the one that bothers me the most right now. I really don't need to hear from her about Jenny and what's going on between her and Dwayne. I don't even know how Dwayne became friends with her and her husband anyways.

It's sounding desperate when I hear myself now but in this case I am. My feelings have been so strong for such a long time and I never had to let go of a man like him before. I really don't want to go on like this anymore.

Sharon said to me once that sometimes she doesn't recognize herself because of all she was putting up with. Sometimes I don't want to recognize myself either and I've been living with high hopes for so long when an unsure future is more my reality.

All the words I wanted to hear, he used in the beginning and I can only go by those words now. The fact that he breaks up then comes back to me over and over always confirms in my mind that it's love when it's really just disgusting. But I'm fighting with my feelings. Still every time I hear the word 'over', my body drains some.

The times I told myself I can go on without him, I meant it then but being able to do it is another story. I've no confirmed future and yet every thought of not being with him again hurts me. The most terrifying is me not knowing if each moment we're together will be the last; brings me fear. I put on a facade sometimes to convince myself I'm good.

I remember that night when we actually had sex for the first time I felt my body singing when he entered me. I don't know how else to explain the feeling that travelled through. I've had many feelings from him but that night I was satisfying an itch coming from an invisible place.

Now, coming to that point where I felt tears falling off my nose travelling to my mouth, when he said the 'over' word, was scary. Then after going to where my many calls are ignored and even having fights with Jenny's friends because she decided to leave, it all stops here. It all comes down to me; my fault. If he had left when she found out about us I would've been better off. I'd be over him by now. Now how late is it for me?

If he felt nothing then he wouldn't have keep coming back but nobody else sees that. Sometimes I know what I say and what I do differs, especially when I say I must move on but I do want better. I just don't know how to do that yet and, yes, it does scare me the most; confusion.

I know sooner or later I must face myself but not yet. How many times I've said that, and how far have I come since then? Not very far. I travel daily without safety for my heart; no insurance for the future. (I want my life back.)

No one is perfect and he knows I'm not vindictive but if he hurts me anymore I won't say I won't be. I wouldn't make any unnecessary trouble to hurt him but I can't say I wouldn't cause hurt for his wife. I wouldn't hurt her physically but that mind of hers would hear more than she cares to. I've always asked him for more time and now he knows that I'll take whatever time I get but I sure as hell won't take nothing at all. I need some more time before I can handle this.

It was so much easier before Jenny moved away and he was running from her and coming to me. Now he has nobody to run from and I'm still alone. Maybe it'll be good when she does come back. I think I might have to switch up and try another tactic.

    My parents were never ashamed of their kids but always wanted better for us, like all parents do. It was never in their vision to have two single parent daughters where none have ever been married but have kids. Both Sharon and I know it disappoints them somewhat but they've always been a big support for us.

The last thing I'd want to tell them now is that Dwayne and I didn't make it, even with the love he and I feel for each other. I may've planned too far ahead when I told them he and I were together but I was sure this was it. I was excited and not thinking.

He said he'll stop by later so I want to make him a home cooked meal. I do all I can to help him when his kids are away, whether just out or away at school. Sometimes I feel like an unmarried wife even though it's not as often lately. It still doesn't stop me from doing any of it though. What others should realize is that it doesn't matter what anyone says since it's my needs that are being met.

 After Dwayne got here I didn't bother to give him any food or take time to relax. I couldn't waste any time to get undressed. I've been waiting for him for days and have no intention of waiting another minute. I figure we can eat after.

He could tell I had something planned as soon as he came through the door and saw me wearing heels inside. I also saw the hidden smile on his face when he figured out what's coming. I sense his curiosity is getting the best of him so I know he's not leaving without having some of me tonight.

I watch him easing back in the couch getting ready to enjoy my strip show. I'm a lady dressed in a way to bring out the bitch in me; to perform. I already had on the outfit I picked up from the party and isn't going to let him leave without seeing it.

He sits there watching. My right leg raise to allow him a better view then it land beside him on the couch, still in my heels. His smile burst again looking to control his face but he stares at me and I see the front of his pant rising. Watching my dance hastens his arousal as he cups his crotch with his hand; making my body react even more-hungry than it already is.

My legs spread apart with one still on the couch, and slowly, my hands travels down between my legs. My split sitting on air, up in his face, slowly easing back then forward again; away from his touch but not away from my own.

He can barely contain himself; leaning closer almost touching his body with mine. Easing down, leaning in while he leans forward and kisses my stomach. His touch going there, between my legs, feels really good. My thinly laced panties sits between my lips making way for his hand to ease it out of his way; coaxing my panties to comply.

These sensations trying to force their way through my underwear is too much. His slight hold is very taunting. The soothing breeze is seeping close from the fan I left going. His kisses, calls moistness to wet everything while leaving a trail for his slowly sliding tongue to go down; easing up slowly, looking to do more.

The intensity of the moment is almost uncontrollable and the flickering candle light is not helping my calm. Much like it was our first time together. (How can I leave this behind? This feeling.) Eagerly, patiently, I watch his pants rise.

I mock his cravens a little too long causing his patience to quit and give in. My body forces him into surrendering to me, as my built up frustrations speedily runs to freedom. My mind insisting it's planning to get all it can while trying to enjoy it all at a snail's pace. His pants falling to the floor gives my senses the boost it needs as he stands and allow his legs out. He eased me over and down after going closer to the couch, allowing me to sit on his lap.

The feeling of ecstasy hugs me while my body goes down and his eases up, repeating over and over. Lingering for seconds, pausing as my inside try to overcome the grab and release game going on inside. I feel my inner muscles cleave to his, making sure he's really in there; in the right place, right position, and ready to be enjoyed.

His arm holding around my waist, while the other hand lifts my nipple to his lips; my senses are running into another realm. My toes are curling, fighting my shoes for space. Sitting intertwine in each other's bodies pleasuring the other, I know we're the only ones left on earth as my heels hits the couch with each pump. The power of his hold won't allow even the breeze to pass between us.

With every motion and with every moan, I feel more reasons for holding on tighter and not let go. Feeling him pulsating between my legs sends a reminder, letting me know how good we're together.

Two anxious bodies that won't allow each other to move to the bedroom, then I ease off and lay on the floor, and he follows.

Without hesitating he turns me to my stomach. His warmth covers my back while his aim is to re-enter. He pries my legs slightly wider from behind, giving him a cushion of comfort. The too-wet opening creates a challenge, causing a slippery slide with each try. And my body continues to work towards the ultimate goal; our orgasms.

The massage he gives my legs feels so good, opening them more to permit a better approach. They obey his command without hesitation. His rigidness piercing through going up inside, touching my pleasurable walls deep, sends me in a world wind of confusion flowing through.

(Holy fuck!) His body's going rigid. His hands are holding to my waist, easing my hips up enough for him to hit as far in as my path allows, using my senses to search for that special place. That place where accomplishment means I've achieved my goal, "Holy fuck, I'm there. I'm th . . .". My orgasm with every convulsion sends another volt of sensation from one body to the other; my body reacting beyond intense.

His hold from behind, allows me to squeeze every ounce of my relief. My contractions are playing the squeeze-and-let-go game again. He pulls my hips tighter into his, pressing it to the last drop.

Again, my walls give him that place to relief himself while strapping tightly, pulling as if milking it dry. (How can he want to leave this behind?) With both bodies relieved, we stay lying on the floor too long, relaxing.

Every minute passing I wanted to ask, but don't, about Jenny and why he hasn't said anything to me about her coming back. The last thing I want is for him to start thinking about her after he just made love to me. Tonight's not a threesome night. But I figure I can talk to him in the morning and clear up my confusion.

Before it got too late, Dwayne got dressed and left to go home. He never gets the urge to spend the full night and each time we're together I hope that night will be the night. I'm used to it now so I stayed lying on the floor and didn't get up to let him out. He slightly touched me and told me he'll talk to me later. I respond with a slight movement with my head and after a while, I came upstairs to get in my bed and go back to sleep.

* * *

Since Dwayne was here several nights ago I haven't really talked to him. Each time I called, he's busy doing something and tells me he'll call me back later. Today I'll ask him for answers to all the questions I've been waiting to get, so I called him again.

While his phone is ringing, I'm organizing the questions I want to ask in my mind. At the top of the list is what made him keep Jenny moving back here from me? The next one is where do we stand with her coming back? I've more coming at me with every thought but his phone stop ringing and someone answers.

"Hi. Dwayne's phone."

"Hello. Who is this?"

"Dwayne cannot come to the phone right now. Who should I tell him called?" I had no idea that she was here visiting.

"I'm sure you know who is calling. And yes you can tell him I called. I'm supposed to get some information from him. That's all."

"Oh. Is this you Sandy? Should I tell him that you need him right now or after I'm finish with him? He has some work he needs to do around the house so it might be a little while."

"I thought you lived in New York and moved on with your life. I'm sure he's happy to have you back home."

"I'm sure you didn't call for me. He's in the shower right now but I'll let him know you called."

I've no intention getting in a long conversation with Jenny on Dwayne's phone. I can only sarcastically say, he forgot to tell me again that she's in town. I was upset enough before and now I find out again that he didn't tell me she's in town. I figured she's at their house since she's answering his phone. Wonder if she answered because she knew it was me calling.

Several hours later he decides to call me back. He and I got into a disagreement when I ask why he didn't mention Jenny's visiting and he thinks it's none of my business. He told me he's not obligated to explain to me what his family does. I told him I couldn't believe he said that to me after we decided it was alright if nobody knows about us. I told him I need to know what's going on so I can handle surprises.

Although we couldn't get into any long conversation, I let him know that I must know certain things. His family is nothing like it was and I think he forgets that. Yes I'm partially responsible for that but he's to blame since it's his family. What I've been doing is living my life, with him controlling every parts of it.

In one of our arguments he went as far as saying his family is more disappointed about the type of woman he used to damage his family than they're about the damage. Telling me he'll have an easier time putting his family back together without me. Saying it'll be good for me to move on with someone else and I should start looking for that someone.

He wants me to forget about any future with him and just pretend we never happened. Now how the hell does he think that makes me feel? We've argued too many times in the past little while but then we usually give us some time to calm down and move on like nothing happened.

Now because Jenny's there he's talking to me like I'm intruding. I've bent over backwards for him in more ways than one. We'd have too many years to wipe out like it never happened and that's impossible. I can't pretend that years of my live didn't exist, so many good years.

* * *

Jenny left two weeks ago to go back to New York and I got a call from Dwayne. Now he tells me he wants us to clear up the confusions between us. I already knew that eventually he'd have needs for me and we'd move on like all the other times.

There's no time left for me to be bickering since I've wasted far too much. I know how this works since I've seen my parents lived their lives through all the problems they had. My father had women on the side all through their marriage and my mother lived with it as if it wasn't important. As long as he came home to her she didn't make it a problem. He worked hard to make sure we had everything we needed and that was enough for her. But I know it's not her wish for us. She always said she lived with certain things so that we can have better.

Now everyone make it seem like having an affair is like death and it doesn't have to be. As long as Dwayne is able to take care of my needs I won't mind anymore. Every time I think I can go on without him he proves me wrong and even though I wouldn't admit that to him it's true. It's too late for me.

Everywhere I look around me, there's a man having an affair; whether it's in my family or friend's family. Now it's normal in my adult surrounding. As it was in my childhood so it is in my adult life.

Now I wonder if my kids will understand what's going on and think it's alright to live like this. That's why I make sure they don't see much of anything that's going on in my love life. To me it was normal but with all I'm going through, it would hurt me knowing my child had to manage through the same kind of situations as me.

In the past I've told friends in bad relationships to move on and not let their man have control over them. Now look at me. I'd like to find the strength to let go but I'm finding that I'm lost. It's so hard.

     Dwayne decides to call me instead of coming to my house, after I sat waiting on him. He says he doesn't want to hurt me but he must call it quits for good this time. Saying he must move on and he wants me to do the same with my life.

He also wants me to know that he'll not blame me for anything that happened between us but wants to forget as much of it as possible. He wants to try to erase me from his mind if possible. He knows that might be impossible but he needs to forget all the turmoil he and I brought into his life.

He said he's feeling bad for hurting me, and all the pain he brought to Jenny is unbearable and it's a lot for him to handle. I listened to him talk and not say much to respond. By now I'm so use to the break ups that I'm not responding the way I thought I would. That's mainly because I know when his guilt is talking. He gets guilty and then comes for forgiveness when his feelings call for me. It's just taking longer each time before he comes. I'm only a tiny bit worried because I need a little more time.

* * *

I'm still waiting for his call since we talked a few weeks ago; I expected him to call me by now. The other times the sex was usually unbelievable for both of us and that's what made it work. Right now I'm at a loss and I don't even know what make-up sex is anymore, since that's the only times we do it. It's like normal sex now.

* * *

A month since I've talked to Dwayne and still not a word. Now I heard that Jenny moved back home. It hurts like hell but there's nothing I can do about any of it. I've spent many hours trying to come up with ideas for him to see that I'm still good for him while I figure out me. I've no idea how I'll do it but I thought why not tell Jenny how sorry I am for everything that happened. Apologise for all the turmoil she said I caused in her life and tell her that Dwayne and I have been over for a long time now.

I can tell her I'm apologising to ease my conscience. Let her know that I'm doing it because I don't want to create an uncomfortable situation if we should ever run into each other again. Tell her I know it wouldn't be comfortable but I'm trying to make as little discomfort as possible. Use the night we both ended up at the party as an example.

I still have Jenny's old number and dialling it got me nervous. As soon as I hear her voice I'm acting like I wasn't expecting her to answer. I start to tremble so bad that I almost drop the phone.

"Hi Jenny."

"Whom am I speaking to?"

"Jenny this is Sandy. Please don't hang up the phone. I just want to welcome you back and to apologize for everything that happened."

I won't give her a chance to talk because I just need her to listen to what I have to say. I tell her I feel remorse for everything that I've done and needs to apologize. I said I wouldn't want anything like what I've done happening to my daughter and that's why I need to tell her that.

"Isn't it a bit too late to be thinking about your kids? Do you think because you say sorry now it will prevent karma? Maybe you should've given more thought before you invited my husband inside you."

"Jenny that's why I'm calling you now to tell you I'm sorry. I can't tell you how really sorry I am but I truly am."

"If you really are, then that's your feelings and it has nothing to do with me. If you're waiting to hear me say that it's fine, then you'll have a long wait. I've no intention to forgive or forget. Nothing that I've gone through because of your affair with Dwayne can be erased."

"I'm not asking you to forgive or forget. I just want you to know that I'm sorry and have no other problems with you."

"Since you're saying you and Dwayne are finished and that you have no problems, then take your problem free self and go wait on my husband; you know, the one you keep calling. If you and he are really finished, then go seek the next married man you're waiting on to come. If you find that new man and he don't come when you want him to, remember you can keep calling his number a dozen times a day. You might even tell whoever comes along that you'll belong to him forever the way you used to tell my husband. Yes I see clearly that you have no problems."

"Jenny I called to apologise. I could say a lot more but I don't want any more trouble with you."

"Listen, that's just talk. You never could say anything to upset me because if you did, it would've jeopardized Dwayne coming to your bed. All three of us knew it then so we both know that it's all bullshit coming from you. You're full of it. Full of shit." Now she's getting on my nerves. I know what I want to say but she's right. I don't want to get Dwayne upset and defeat the whole purpose of this call. I'll just let her get all the anger out. "You claim you're an intelligent woman so show it. Would a smart woman take a married man words to heart, even though he's still with his wife? Would she still believe him after years of hearing his shit? Listen to yourself and you'll see that you're worse off than you sound."

"You shouldn't judge me since you've being dealing with him and that same shit even longer that I have, and you stayed. I thought you were smart also but your words and action shows you're no different."

"I'm a married woman with children, but you're acting like a teenage girl who's giving it up because she doesn't know her crotch's value. Have your crush. If you want to teach your kids then teach them to accept responsibility. Let your daughter learn not to give it up carelessly. Teach her because she isn't capable of understanding the repercussions of her actions as you should've. You're a grown woman. The next time you decide to be with a married man, whom you might be lining up now, make sure he comes differently. Make sure you don't show your desperation and not have you believing he'll leave his family for you. Maybe the outcome will be different if you learn. Do you think everything has to do with sex? Your crotch won't always work. As for the ones who fall between your legs, just remember sex won't keep them forever. You're wearing it out."

"For some reason you keep thinking that what Dwayne and I had was all about sex but you're so wrong. I won't tell you anything about that right now. You can keep wondering what goes on between us as you have no control over what happens." That mouth of hers makes me forget why I called her in the first place. She just reminds me of how much of a bitch she is.

"Whatever he tells you is of no importance to me. And whatever it was, he still didn't leave me for anyone. With all that I did, whether it was tracking him or other things, did you think I was worried that he'd leave me if I didn't stop? You think I did it all because I was afraid. All I did, only strengthen his love for me since he knows I wouldn't have done any of it if I didn't care. If you want to tell me what he has done with you, it has no consequences here. In his eyes he was only doing what men do and doing it didn't affecting his love for me. And all it proved to me is that he's just a man taking what was given away for free. Child, please!"

"I could say that you're the only idiot here but I won't."

"When you picked up the phone to call me, did you think you'd say sorry and I'd say that's okay so don't worry about it. You must be an even bigger idiot than I think."

"I expected you to act like a woman and say something different. I don't really know what but move on."

"You're the one with a married man or maybe men crawling through you for years with only your hopes. Over the years he and I mould each other into whatever we turned out to be. I should've done something about his actions long before I did but I chose not to. You on the other hand sat soundless in the background listening to his and my conversation right before or after he's in you and you don't feel used. You see his sneaking around as his love for you instead of it being that he's hiding you. That's not love. You enjoyed being the thing on the side with little self respect. You think about that and tell yourself you have no problems. In my opinion, you're sick. And you can proudly tell your daughter all you did."

"I called you with the idea of making peace but I see you're not mature enough to do that."

"Please. If you want me to believe you called to apologise, it'll never happen. I can't say I know a lot about women like you, but you taught me enough to know you have an ulterior motive. It matters nothing to me what it might be, but if you want to keep opening your legs for my husband, then it's yours. Your problem is that you can't find a man of your own and after Dwayne used up your good years, what do you have to offer. But then again, I'm sure you'll have no problem getting sex since there're so many married men out there like him. Just doing what men do and taking what is given away like from a bowl of free candy in a store."

"Ha. You're sounding like you're not getting any." I think the fact that she wasn't good enough to keep him happy is what's bothering her still.

"Since you sound like a child let me talk to you as one. Listen child, what you do with him is good for you. Whether or not I'm getting any as you put it, is of no importance in this conversation. But to put your mind at ease, every time the subject comes up I talk about you and he gets turned off quickly. I've no intention of craving him after he entered something like you. I guess that answers your question after all. This is the last thing I'll say to you today Sandy. In the past I did many things because of you. I play fool to catch wise, but be assured that you're not the wise I caught."

Talking to Jenny is a waste of time and she only want to piss me off, and it's working. Now I realize that it was a bad idea but it's too late to change it. I managed to hold my tongue as much as I can and I want to be nasty to her but I won't make it any worse.

"Good. Believe that if you want.

"You told me many times in the past that I couldn't survive without Dwayne but you could. Who needs who? You're a waste even to yourself. You're only good for one thing and that's as a release place for men; like a urinal. Let me put this clear to you so you might understand. There's only one wife. You're now on the string with all the other women who gave and got nothing. The kind of woman who gives it up for a few desperately needed nice words from his lips. You think you're the first he might have told those words to. You should've wondered what happens after he gets what he wants and where you'd be after. I was never worried about him leaving me as you believed. I can do or say anything to you and there's nothing he can or will do about it. You on the other hand need him in your bed since that's the only way you can feel needed. You'll forgive, and all while keeping your thoughts to yourself since you can't take the chance of upsetting him. Please. Please child. Grow up."

The bitch just hung up on me!!

Verona J. Knight

Evelyn Once Said:

"It's amazing how many times we hear 'that which doesn't kill you makes you stronger'. So many of us already have the strength hiding and only brings it out to fight a problem but can't use it to walk away before it become a hurting problem."

Evelyn Once Said:

Why do some ask questions they might not like the answer to, then get angry when they hear honest answers? Would they rather hear the 'save your feelings' version. If so, isn't it same as not knowing the answer before the question was asked.

Chapter Twenty Four

Talking to Jenny yesterday was stupid. I called Dwayne this morning but my calls when to his machine. I left messages telling him to call back but I guess he hasn't checked his machine yet. I needed some company so I came over to Monica's house just to spend some time and relax for awhile. Whenever I need cheering up she usually knows how to do it. I don't want to think anything negative right now but I still find myself drifting in and out of that bad space. I've tried calling him again since I've been here but still no answer.

Monica and I talked about some of my problems then we move on to talking about her. I thought we'd have to deal with her problem but she's okay. She said she's been giving her life some serious thoughts and now she thinks it's time to move on. She wants to put all the attention she's been giving away, into her marriage.

She actually talked to Dave about some of her sexual fantasies. Even though she already performed some of those fantasies with Luke, it doesn't feel the same doing them with Dave. She said it's like a man taking a woman's crotch and putting it on another; it'll feel different. She even wants to go as far as talking to him about having a threesome and other kinky shit. She believes it's too soon to talk about that but she believes he'll be up for it when she does.

She said she can't overwhelm him with everything all at once so she'll wait. I don't think she'll have any problems getting him to bring another woman in bed with them, but I know like most men he won't say yes if she wants another man in there.

We spend all afternoon together passing the time talking about small things. She figures I'm here to keep my mind off troubles and also for some support. I told her about my call to Jenny and she was pissed at me but I can't reverse that now. She thinks Dwayne isn't taking my calls because he might be pissed also.

That I didn't think about. I figure if he's pissed he might be heading to my house after seeing all my calls so I'm leaving to go back home.

    I came home last night and still didn't hear anything from Dwayne. I left Monica's house yesterday with so much to think about. Sharon is more alone now after she spent all her better years giving herself to a married man who then got up and left her. Without warning he got up and left, now she's more single than even before she met him. And that was the last thing she thought would happen.

Monica getting her life back on track is good to hear. I watched her live another life without her husband and in the long run she ends up happy with what she has at home. I've no idea how her married man felt when she told him it was over between them but I know that they both had deep feelings for each other too. She did say one of the reasons she broke it off is because of her feelings. She didn't want it going any further.

I've to wonder if he'll find another woman to fill her place or will he go through withdrawal symptoms without her? They had some out-of-this-world sex together and I doubt if they can ever forget each other easily. How long will she be able to do without him? Will the sex between her and Dave be as good as it was with her and Luke? I personally think she made a good decision coming out to Dave about what excites her. It'll be new for them together.

    The past few days I've spent a lot of my time thinking about my family's lives. This morning I got up thinking more about my own so I called Dwayne again and I still got his machine. I know he's been staying at Mark's again so I know he and Jenny haven't been together. I'm assuming he's still confused about his feelings with her back here again.

I've called him too many times and left too many messages on his machine so I'll wait without putting pressure on him. I even let him know that I understand what he's going through and we should talk about it when he gets my message.

I confess that sometimes I wonder if it's worth it, but hey. Walking away is hard and fighting to stay is just as hard. I'm just not emotionally ready to do it yet. I gave myself in every way to this man and didn't use any of that time to meet anyone else. With everything going on and my confused feelings, I don't get the urge to be with anyone else. How can I move on when I'm not ready?

* * *

Two weeks now and still I haven't gotten a returned call from Dwayne. Now I'm really pissed since he should have the decency to return my calls. I came over to the bar to see if he's here so I might talk to him. It's time we talk so we can fix it.

I got here and he's here with his friends so I walk over to let him know we need to talk and he followed me outside. A few minutes later Anthony comes out to check up on him and went back inside. I tell him to explain why he hasn't returned my calls since I know he got my messages. I ask him if I hadn't come to see him how long would it have been before he started returning them.

He said he hadn't been checking his messages since he didn't really want to talk to anyone. Telling me he can't deal with us right now because of everything else that's going on in his life. He wants me to take some time and find someone who can offer me a better future. He tells me he doesn't want to hurt me but it might be unpreventable and if I start looking now, my pain would go away faster.

He said even if he had checked his messages, he wouldn't have returned my calls. Saying he's trying to do this the best way he knows how and that means leaving each other alone; no contact between us. He said I must get rid of the idea that we can go on living the way we have. Pressing the issue that he needs me to know he does have feeling for me but not enough to continue on like this.

I listened to his every word but not concentrating on any after he told me to find someone else. All I kept hearing over and over in my mind is him saying, we can't keep going on like this. After his voice stopped all I could say is that we can manage.

"If you had listened to my messages you would've heard me telling you that it's fine if Jenny comes back in the picture. I also told you before that I can be there for you and nobody needs to know. I've no intention of moving on without you. You need to understand that I'm not ready so you can't just come telling me to find someone else. I'm not ready so you live with that."

"Listen Sandy. Every time I think of us I feel sick because of what I've put Jenny through. You remind me of pain. I don't want to hurt your feelings but there's no way to say it any better. For years now you've been pain for Jenny but I didn't take heed to her warnings and almost lost her. When I look at you now I don't see you, I only see Jenny's pain. You've turned into what's not good for me now. Your face is fading and I only see pain. I wasn't thinking about it before but now I'm putting an end to it."

"Do you hear what you're saying to me Dwayne?"

"Yes I do. While we're talking, let me tell you that everything I've said before and why we should break up I meant. You're forcing me to hurt your feelings but it's all true. Every time I look at you I feel pain and I see my mistake. Right now I just want you to leave and don't keep calling me. It's done whether you want to believe it or not and I'll never answer your calls again."

Before I can say anything else he walks away to go back in the bar. And before I can take a step one of the guys come out to check on him again. I've been through all the draining feelings now and have nothing left. My body is numb.

* * *

I tried to make sure Dwayne heard everything I had to say so he'll understand that it wasn't going to end the way he thinks. But, after he left me standing in the parking lot that night to think, my mind went blank. I didn't even get the last word, he just left me there. That was two weeks ago and I haven't heard or seen him since.

Every time I called him he answered and tells me to stop. He keeps doing it and now it's getting hard. He wants me to walk away from years of my life and turn it into a bad memory. I'm finding it the hardest thing I'll have to do. My mind and good sense tells me that it's over but my body and heart won't let it happen.

The pain of my loss will not go away. How long will I have to go on like this? Help me Lord. I'm so sorry but I've never loved like this before. The best love I've gotten in my life, he took from his wife and gave to me. The same love that brought me a reason to feel, to hope, to succeed, is now the same one putting my heart in prison. I'm paying hard for stealing and I don't know how to survive losing.

I need help through this now. I think of all the times I've given advice saying what they should and shouldn't do. Now I feel like I'll be heading nowhere, and I need someone to help prevent me from reaching there. The teacher has now turned into the student. The same hard lessons I tried to prevent them from are the same lessons I've packaged for myself to feel. How they learned to prevent their pain is what they can use to help me through mine. And who I've taught are the same ones that will now have to teach me how to manage.

The pains I was worried and try to help my sister to prevent are the same ones I didn't help myself to prevent. How do I take care of this pain that cradles my heart? It's almost frozen and for the first time I pray for numb. I don't want to feel anything right now. He holds my peace of mind in his hands and it's not protected from him. Why?

For years my friend from work being telling me that things have a way of catching up to us. Now I understand. Evelyn I understand what you said to me. *"Love is: when you find your dreams in each other's reality."* Now I know that can never happen since I'm the one that was seeing my dreams in Dwayne's reality and he wasn't seeing me in his dreams. Have mercy on me. I'm gonna need help through this. I need to call someone who knows how this feels.

"Hello."

My body's so drained. I'm crying so hard but too numb to bring any tears. "Sharon. Please, help me! I need you. I need your help. It's over. Dwayne left me."

"Are you at home?"

"Yah."

"Stay there. I'll get Monica and we'll come to you."

Five years of my life washing away. I don't know how I want to feel, how I should feel or what I'm feeling. I just know I don't want to feel anything right now. "All this pain!" I'm going crazy screaming at myself. "Why! Why! Why!" My world is falling.

My head is resting on my knees and it feels heavy. I can't lift it up. My body is shaking and I can't stop from rocking forward and back. (Please let me stop feel. Please let me stop feel. Please let me stop . . . .).

Evelyn Once Said:

Be careful where you place your trust since that's where the greatest pain can come from.

Verona J. Knight

Evelyn Once Said:

Emotional baggage didn't come cheap but don't make them a collectable. That's not fashionable.

*My tears form a pillow for my sanity to think
while recouping to take action*

About the Book

    In our world, so many are falling in that space; causing hurt, but never thinking of their pending pain. To those who are already trapped in that place, just keep trying and praying to find the strength to exit there. Reading THE CHEATERS THE WIFE THE REVENGE lets you understand Jenny's pain and her choices that caused others pain. THE CHEATERS THE MISTRESS HER STORY, showed Sandy's world that resulted from her part in their relationships. When you read THE CHEATERS THE HUSBAND THE PAYBACK, it will bring you into Dwayne's world for his whole story.

One might be better off staying on their own until someone comes along for them, and only them. Whatever is decided should give comfort and some form of safety. If you are not able to show respect for your body, why would you think another will. Strength is not given it is possessed, so make sure you find it for you.

Many should not have the right to judge but it won't stop them. One cannot teach what they haven't already learned elsewhere. If you've walked that path then we shouldn't judge. We are not the ones who will suffer the consequences of whether or not they stay or go. Dwayne and Jenny's past can never be repeated or duplicated with anyone else. Trying to change that is a waste of Sandy's time. The hurt from Sandy and Dwayne's affairs might go away then they will help each other heal. Who will be there to comfort and help Sandy?

Never try to change a person into what you want him or her to be. Whatever Dwayne has that caught Sandy's attention she should look for it in someone who can be her partner in every way. The steamy love making, which is explicit, and the heightened romance can bring temporary satisfaction, but what happens after that wears off.

The sneaking around and everything that goes with it can be exciting but for how long. These three books, *The Cheaters The Mistress Her Story*, will take you along with each character and pull you into their story so you can have the experience along with them as did the *The Cheaters The Wife The Revenge*. All that is experienced by the characters in this book, with or as their lovers, will resonate in your mind and you will judge their actions.

Now we have to see what else Sandy has in mind for Dwayne. Is she finally willing to move on without him or try other tactics to get him back? What will happen when Jenny moves back? *The Cheaters The Husband The Payback* will tell it all.

Evelyn Once Said:

Strong: using your strength to walk away from him/her who holds your heart carelessly; especially if you deeply love him/her."

About The Trilogy

There are three sides to every story and *THE CHEATERS THE MISTRESS HER STORY* is the second instalment of THE CHEATERS TRILOGY. This is Sandy's, the mistress, time to tell her side of this threesome. *THE CHEATERS THE WIFE THE REVENGE* told the wife's, Jenny, side and Dwayne, the husband, will tell his side later in *THE CHEATERS THE HUSBAND THE PAYBACK*.

You've already walked along with Jenny in *The Cheaters The Wife The Revenge* and heard her side of the story. Finding out about Dwayne's cheating changed her in many ways while doing everything she could to stop him from ruining their marriage. After, meeting William, things changed for her and the cheating took her places she thought she would never go.

As shown in *The Cheaters The Wife The Revenge*, her attempts to get Dwayne to fix his marriage was not successful and caused her to find a lover that took her mind and body where Dwayne couldn't hurt her. She turned pity into anger, passing the blame stage into revenge, and laying her guilt away because of where William's heart took hers.

Now that you're here its Sandy's time to tell you what she has to say. You can't know the full story until you hear all three sides of THE CHEATERS TRILOGY. You'll meet Sandy's sister Sharon with her drama and seven kids and a few baby fathers. Her cousin Monica is sneaking around on her husband. While Sandy tries to play councillor and critique her sister's life she's not thinking that she's doing anything wrong; walking a dangerous line.

Even though Jenny is the wife Sandy think it gives her no right to believe she can take Dwayne away from her. She also believes that she doesn't hold a gun to his head when he decides to come into her bed, but she wants to blame 'the wife' for everything.

She also believes he loves her and even though he's not ready to leave Jenny, she's the one who's keeping him happy. She thinks it's not her fault that he finds what he needs in her and is not happy at home. Sandy is good at getting whomever she wants and she plans to show Dwayne how good; every time they're together he'll know that she's worth it. Sandy convinced herself that if Jenny didn't have Dwayne's two kids, even though they're somewhat grown, he definitely would've left and come to her.

While Jenny does whatever she can to find out exactly what is going on Sandy knows it's not enough to scare Dwayne into stop loving her. And while Jenny's unexpected visits does create problems it's usually temporary, and Dwayne constantly retuning gives her confidence.

Sandy thinking that the messages she sends him saying 'I want to feel the base of your voice vibrating my body to make my pussy jump', was a private message and Jenny had no right reading it because it was on her husband's phone. She wants Jenny to know if Dwayne wasn't as important as he is, then she would definitely show her bad side. Thinking if Jenny finds out about her and Dwayne she must deal with it as the rejected wife and stop turning herself into a nuisance in their lives.

"Jenny needs to find a man that can love her the way her husband loves me. Even though she thinks that he belongs to her he really belongs to me, and she should do the right thing and leave him so he can be mine in every way. I'm the one going out of my way to make him happy. I can only say that when she does the things she does to invade our privacy, it makes her look like a scorned woman. That alone should tell her how much he loves me, since even though he won't leave her, he also won't leave me. The sex between us is out of this world. I make sure that when he goes home he needs nothing from her. Every time I think about him with her at home, I call him to let him know how much I miss him. That's what loving a man is all about, good sex and as much attention as he needs."

Naturally, not all relationships are bad but walk along with Sandy and see if you recognize anyone there. Couples stay or leave each other every day and that is a reality. The mistress might not think about her lover's family stability, but instead will see what is there for her to take. Many times the cheater is not thinking about the hurt they create but just about the free sex. The mistress decides her role whether or not to become a mistress but the cheater's spouse has no say, since their mate already made the decision for them.

If you've read *The Cheaters The Wife The Revenge*, you'll see if Jenny was right and whether or not her actions were warranted. If you haven't then take a glimpse into the mind of the other woman after you know Sandy's story then go see what Jenny had to say. Whichever, it's most important for all to think about the possibility of loneliness in a relationship.

Why would Sandy want to take on a mistress position recognizing that there might be pain ahead for her? Is she that confident in her vagina? Can it hold and keep Dwayne happy for the rest of his life? Sex might take his attention from his wife but is it a guarantee that it'll keep him satisfied. If it's possible to love two at the same time, then why would she think he would take her as a wife knowing how she came, and while he already has one he loves? If she gives her all, why wouldn't he enjoy it the way she gives it and find others? Why would she be the last mistress? Why live waiting for karma? Will he stop loving his wife for the mistress?

Those are questions Sandy asked herself while she still tells him she belongs to him. Along with dealing with her sister she gets the surprise of her life when she meets the side of Jenny she never heard about.

With that said, Sandy will do anything to keep Dwayne so whether it's with friends or foe, she thinks she's prepared. Her love making will make your body react while understanding the lengths a woman will go to 'thief a man'. Yes she's that good so come listen to her.

After this, Dwayne will tell his side in *THE CHEATERS THE HUSBAND THE PAYBACK.* Then you'll find out how the wife handles a cheat and his mistress, how a mistress thinks and how the cheating husband eludes himself; expecting to have a happy life.

Other Publications By Author

A MIND NOT LOST—Book of Poetry Book 1 and Book 2 (Now on sale)

Books One, Two and Three, each presents a collection of more than 100 pages of poems and thoughts that helped kept me strong and maybe can do the same for you; as others said helped them through. It's my thoughts on paper where I can re-read, to keep boosting my good thoughts and remind me of my strength on a daily basis. My thoughts of the day are included as they are ones that came to mind while observing and thinking about different situations and experiences in mine or friends lives; they have helped me through turmoil times. These thoughts also remind me daily of the strength of my faith, the balance required to soothe each other's mind in a relationship, and of my sexuality.

A Mind Not Lost

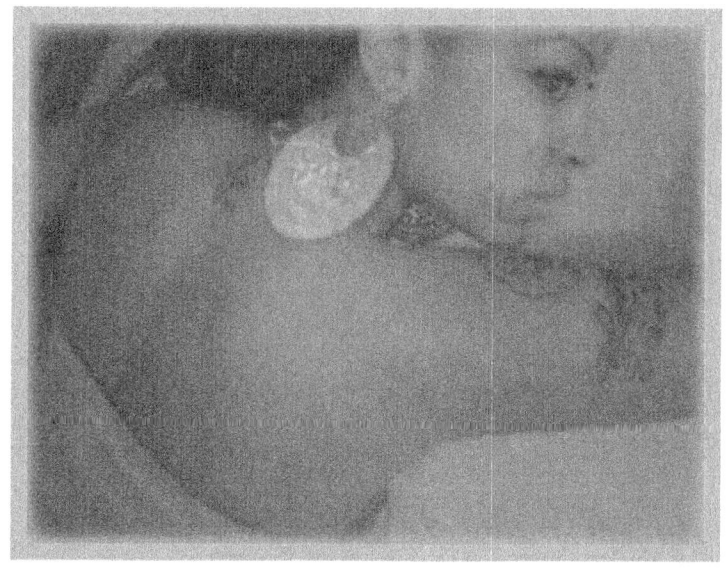

Book 1

Verona J. Knight

Verona J. Knight

A MIND NOT LOST
BOOK 2

"The Cheaters Trilogy"

The first of the Trilogy THE CHEATERS THE WIFE THE REVENGE tells the wife's side of the story, the second THE CHEATERS THE MISTRESS HER STORY tells the mistress's side of the story, and the third THE CHEATERS THE HUSBAND THE PAYBACK tells the husband's side. As it is said, there are three sides to every story. THE CHEATERS TRILOGY tells all three from the Wife the Mistress and the Husband's view of this threesome. Available in E-book and Paperback

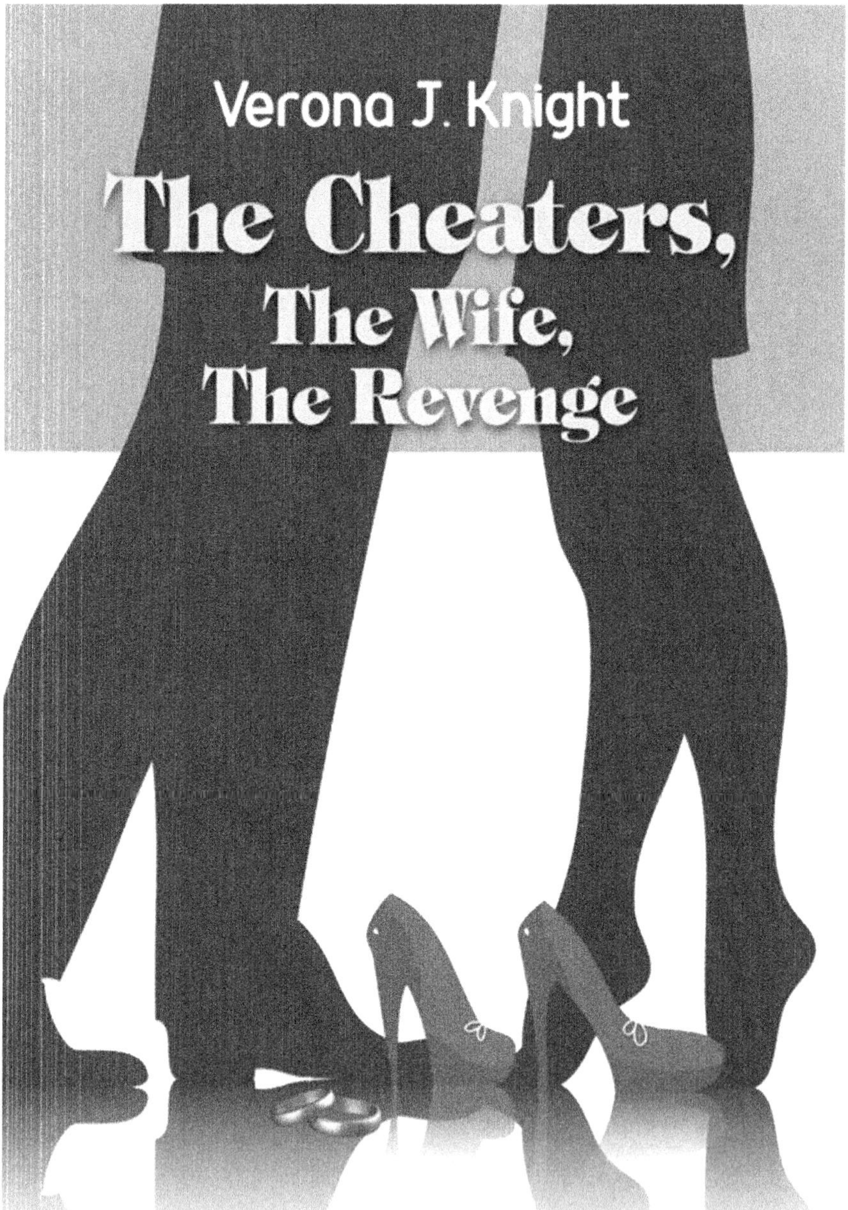

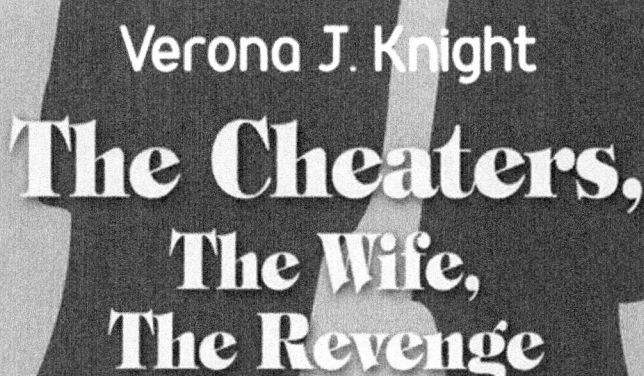

'The Cheaters the Wife the Revenge'

This is the first of THE CHEATERS TRILOGY. Tells the story of Jenny, Dwayne's loyal wife and mother of his kids, who finds her marriage in trouble as her husband strays into Sandy's life. Follow Jenny as she uses her detective instincts to uncover the truth while deciding how to face it, then finding ways to deal with her husband and his mistress Sandy. Unhappy with her findings, she tries to put her marriage back together but ends instead finding herself a lover, William, who she wasn't looking for. William now brings her more than she expected or is unsure she wants, starting her on a whole new path.

'The Cheaters The Husband The Payback'

The third book of THE CHEATERS TRILOGY. Dwayne must now deal with Jenny after she finds evidence of his cheating and keep his relationship with Sandy without putting himself in deeper trouble. Thinking he's man enough to manage them both, he's unable to cope at times and makes mistakes to put him further in but believes he'll be fine since Jenny is too in-love with him to leave him. While denying all of Jenny's accusations and finding ways to prevent the end of his marriage, he knows in his heart that Jenny wouldn't betray him the way he has her. Then one day it all came tumbling down. By the time he finds out about the other man, William, he's already a problem and Dwayne now feels the shoe on the other foot, watching his world falling apart.

CPSIA information can be obtained at www.ICGtesting.com
Printed in the USA
LVOW04*0620050515

437172LV00017B/1031/P

9 781496 914194